ing inner-city college, but is now a part-time lecturer for the University of Birmingham's Continuing Studies Department. A trustee of the City of Birmingham Symphony Orchestra's Benevolent Fund, she is on the committee of the Birmingham Chamber Music Society. She is also the Secretary of the Crime Writers' Association.

Judith has enjoyed considerable critical and popular success with her first six novels featuring Sophie Rivers, all of which are set in Birmingham. She has also written a number of short stories, most notably for the BBC Short Story slot.

'From PD James onwards, British detective writing is crammed with feisty young female sleuths. But in Cutler's Sophie Rivers we are undoubtedly dealing with the *crème de la crème*' *The Times*

'A winner . . . Sophie's a likeable heroine and it's a good tale, full of West Midlands atmosphere'
  Coventry Evening Telegraph

'The narrative is, as always, witty and erudite, moving with assurance' *Nottingham Evening Post*

'Its appeal to Birmingham readers is obvious, but it must also appeal to any crime-fiction addict' F.E. Pardoe

Dying by the Book

Judith Cutler

HEADLINE

First Published in 2001
by HEADLINE BOOK PUBLISHING

First published in paperback in 2001
by HEADLINE BOOK PUBLISHING

10 9 8 7 6 5 4 3 2 1

British Library Cataloguing in Publication Data

ISBN 0 7472 6212 8

Printed and bound in Great Britain by
Clays Ltd, St Ives plc

HEADLINE BOOK PUBLISHING
A division of Hodder Headline
338 Euston Road
LONDON NW1 3BH

www.headline.co.uk
www.hodderheadline.com

For Sara Menguc, with love and gratitude

Acknowledgements

Thanks to Jonathon Davidson, Mike Baird and John Philips for their generous assistance and expert advice.

Chapter One

I could have killed Andy Rivers, there and then, in my kitchen.

'You're never going to marry *Mike Lowden*. All brawn, no brain. For God's sake, Sophie, what's got into you?' He slammed down his glass on the work surface and whirled to face me.

But I would keep my cool, even if my favourite cousin had lost his. 'He's one of the best England cricketers of his generation—'

'That's not saying much, is it?' he sneered.

I suppose I'd asked for that. Nothing daunted, I took up the cudgels again. 'He's a good, kind man, socially aware – highly intelligent—' His degree was considerably better than mine.

'"And I recommend him for the position he's now seeking." Come off it, Sophie. You sound as if you're writing a reference for him.'

I flushed. What if I added, 'And he's beyond my imaginings in bed'? Which he was, but which was none of Andy's business. Or anyone else's, for that matter. 'I don't need to. I love him. That's all you need to know. Like you love Ruth.'

Ruth was Andy's wife. When they'd met she was the headmistress of a particularly good comprehensive school in a part of London which guaranteed an exceptional number of

MPs' children on its roll. Now she was actively involved in running the trust which Andy had set up to divert wads of his enormous wealth to welfare work in central Africa. Andy, meanwhile, was swanning around the world as a roving ambassador for UNICEF, blissfully ignoring a past which had made him one of the pop stars the media most loved to hate. A past which included a night of which all too soon I would have to remind him: it concerned me and my newly discovered son, Steph.

'Ruth – Ruth's different. She's a quite exceptional woman.' His hackles had risen visibly.

'Exactly. Which is how I find Mike.' My hackles were pretty vertical too. But we needed to talk, so I decided I'd better slip into peacemaker mode. I took a deep breath. 'So – are we going to have that curry or are we going to stand here argufying all night?'

He gave a sudden smile, the sort that had melted the hearts of mothers even when they were condemning their daughters for lusting after him. 'Harborne Tandoori?'

It was a lovely spring evening, so we set off on foot towards what the denizens of Harborne like to call the village, a shopping area a couple of miles from my house in Balden Road. Harborne, a couth suburb of Birmingham, was in turn a very few miles from the Black Country town of Oldbury where we'd both grown up. I wondered how much of it would feature in *Raging Rivers*, the autobiography Andy was about to launch at the Big Brum Bookfest – a new literary festival which the organiser pledged would cast Hay and Cheltenham into the shade. I also wondered how much of the text Andy had produced himself, given his distaste for the sort of prolonged commitment that I presumed writing a book must take. It sounded to me more like a job for Ruth, or a professional ghost. But since I'd seen not a word of it, not even to comment on any appearances I might make, I couldn't judge. To be honest, I hadn't even known it was in train until I'd seen his name in the Bookfest schedules. But that was Andy for you. He'd no doubt planned to mention it next time he stayed with me. He regarded my house as a second home, which I suppose it always had been, and the sight of one of the world's pop icons slipping into the local shops occasioned no more comment from the natives than my own visits.

One thing I could guarantee: if the press got hold of my part of Andy's story, the thing would sell faster than it would roll off the press. So, much as I hated it, I'd have to wait till all the hype had simmered down before I introduced Stephan to his father.

Or would I? One of my faults, as Mike had gently but firmly pointed out, was my habit of making decisions for people, not so much without consulting them as without even telling them a decision had to be made. True, Stephan had shown rather less interest in who his father might be than in introducing me to his parents. But Andy ought to know. It was only my absence from the country – I'd joined Mike for the second half of the England cricket tour of Australia – and a reluctance to do anything other than tell him face to face about his son that had kept him in ignorance. The trouble was, the longer I waited, the more difficult it became.

And I did have other, major problems to worry about.

We walked along Court Oak Road, and then cut along Crosbie and Wentworth Roads. Perhaps it was a trifle further than sticking to the main route, but the gardens of the big Regency and Victorian houses were a pleasure at this time of year, all sleeked up ready for the summer. And maybe I could find a moment to speak to him. *The* moment. Or would that spoil the curry? The trouble was, Andy didn't give a hoot about other people's reactions. If he wanted to have an emotional scene in a restaurant, he would, and damn the ambience.

'Chris, now,' he was saying, as if we hadn't walked nearly a mile since the last moment my love life had been under the spotlight, 'Chris – I always thought you'd get it together with him eventually. A decent man. Plays a good game of chess.'

'Chris is the dearest friend I could imagine,' I said firmly. 'But being lovers didn't work. He's – he's so hidebound by convention,' I added lamely, suppressing more graphic expressions. 'For a Catholic, he's remarkably puritan.'

'A lot to be said for self-control,' Andy said sagely.

'As if you've ever exercised it,' I said more sharply than I meant. If I weren't careful, I would fling the news about Steph at him as an accusation. 'Sorry. I know you're a reformed character—'

'Thanks to Ruth,' he said fervently.

To my certain knowledge, his love for Ruth hadn't stopped him getting involved in some highly questionable dealings, from which, in fact, I'd had to extricate him.

'But you were a wild lad at times,' I pursued. Any moment now I could—

'Too wild for my own good,' he agreed. 'Hey – isn't that Ken Foreman over there? Ken!' He waved and crossed the road. 'Isn't it time you stopped worrying that garden to death?'

Andy bounded up the stairs to the restaurant as if running on to a stage. Was that what drove him, his need to be wanted and welcomed? If it was, the maître d' didn't let him down, abandoning to a minion the party whose orders he was taking, and rushing over, beaming, for a double handshake.

'I shall be here for a couple of weeks,' Andy told him. 'For this Bookfest. Sophie's running it, you know.'

I demurred. The policy and financial decisions were taken by a board, who'd appointed a director responsible for everything from booking the authors to booking the venues, not to mention ferrying one to the other. There were also such delights as stuffing envelopes with publicity material and briefing the media. So although the director, an enterprising ex-librarian called Brian Fairbrother, had done a magnificent single-handed job in the early stages, now the Bookfest was about to hit the West Midlands, there was no way he could manage everything himself. No one could have. Which is where I'd come in. As a volunteer. Even if I was staying as something else.

The maître d' smiled disbelievingly. 'But you have a job. You're always so busy.'

I smiled vaguely. I didn't want to go into all the ins and outs of my situation. 'Just a favour for a friend,' I said.

The truth was that the previous autumn I'd started a year's sabbatical leave from my job at William Murdock College to study for a Master's degree in education at the University of the West Midlands. It was meant to give me a break from a job which had become steadily more stressful and less fulfilling. More positively, it would give me a qualification to enable me either to hang on to the William Murdock job – mass redundancies were in the offing – or to get another one elsewhere. What the University had discreetly referred to as staffing problems had, however, prevented me from making much progress with the course, and it had been agreed that I should start again, *tabula rasa*, as it were, next academic year. *Gratis*, more to the point. Oh, and with some compensation for the mess they'd landed me in. William Murdock, whom

I'd like to have made some token protest at being deprived of a star lecturer for another year, were simply grateful to be saving my salary.

None of which Rezah, the maître d', needed to know. He smiled us to our favourite table – tabula Rezah, as it were – and left us to attend to more guests.

'I still don't see why you should have got involved,' Andy said. 'Not your sort of scene at all, I'd have thought.'

'Afzal asked me,' I said.

'That solicitor friend of yours? But how did *he* get involved?'

'A bit of up-market *pro bono publico* work,' I said. 'Most of his practice involves people with appalling social problems. He joined the board to offer legal advice and rub shoulders with people he saw as influential.'

'Ah, the idealist always becomes the pragmatist in the end!'

I forbore to comment on that gem. 'When he realised Brian couldn't possibly do everything single-handed, he asked me if I could spare a few hours. And since Mike was up to his ears in pre-season training, I agreed. And I've just roped in a couple of my ex-students for a bit of work experience.'

Andy rolled his eyes. 'A student is for life, not just for Christmas!'

OK, he exaggerated. But there was enough truth about my attitude to my protégés to put me on the defensive. 'Well, these two have had major personal problems, and this will look good on their CVs.'

'As it will on yours.'

A waiter – a new face – brought us a couple of Indian beers to go with poppadams light enough to fly and some wonderful dips.

Andy drank deeply and then stared at me. 'I know you,' he

said. 'You're holding something back, aren't you?'

So which bits should I confess to? The personal or the public? No, I'd have to put off the personal to a less public place, really would. The public it would be.

I shifted slightly in my chair. 'There can't be many literary festivals,' I admitted, dropping my voice to the barely audible, 'that open with not one, but two death threats.' And one or two other problems.

Andy must have been getting older; he asked, just failing to maintain the insouciance to which he no doubt aspired, 'Do they involve anyone – I might know?' I couldn't blame him. After all, he'd been on the business end of such threats himself in the past. And now he was not only going to be centre stage himself a couple of times, he'd agreed to help host other people's events.

I shook my head. 'Not unless you're intimately acquainted with a violence-preaching woman rap singer who wants to do to men what men promise women in their violent raps? Or a Russian who seems to attract enemies like my hostas attract slugs.'

His shrug revealed more relief than he might have liked, but he produced a cynical smile to be proud of. 'Darling, if you want international celebrities, you must expect international problems to come with them.'

'It'd be nice if we had an international police force to deal with them,' I said. Suddenly the truth started to emerge. 'Honestly, Andy, I thought this job would be money for old rope—'

'I thought you were a volunteer!'

'I'm getting an honorarium. All I was supposed to be doing is everyday clerical stuff. Oh, and ferrying you celebs around. And then I found I was fielding sinister phone calls and hate mail. Not at all what I had planned.'

'Oh,' he said, without needing to add, *is that all?*

A waiter arrived; it was time to choose our meal. A vegetarian *thali* for Andy, a meat *thali* for me, a feast of lots of individual dishes. What was the betting, however, that when the time came, Andy would suddenly forget his vegetarianism, and start picking my chicken? But until the food came, we had acres of conversation to fill.

Talking has never been a problem between us. There was always family gossip, political chitchat (if you're a UNICEF ambassador, you tend to snap up trifles that don't reach the *Guardian* till a week or so later) or just plain conversation, the sort you have with someone you've known and loved for ever.

But over the last couple of years, things had changed between Andy and me, hadn't they? For a start, I'd realised what had stopped me falling in love with a variety of eligible men – the fact I'd been in love with Andy since my teens. And once I'd realised I was in love with him, and discovered that his feet were solid clay, then I could, with my usual brisk efficiency, set about falling out of love with him.

Which I did to such effect that when Mike strolled into my life, he strolled into a heart best described as receptive. Not to mention a body, ditto.

So this was the first time I'd met Andy since I'd realised that there was more to life than hanging round for crumbs of his affection. And my announcement to him to this effect hadn't, of course, gone down especially well.

If only Mike were with me. We never had a moment's unwanted silence. If only he hadn't felt those *Andy's-family-don't-want-to spoil-family-meal* reservations and had agreed to join us, rather than go out with the lads on the beer.

The silence deepened. Andy studied the prints on the wall: women with impossibly large hips or breasts in states of less than dress. They managed to combine artistic panache with a decadence I found uncomfortable.

'I wish they'd change them,' I blurted at last.

'Not like you to be prudish,' Andy said.

'But they're so bloody coy,' I expostulated. 'Stockings and corsets and big hats.'

'A lot to be said for stockings,' Andy said.

'But not on the wall of a family restaurant,' I said. 'Come on, Andy, whatever happened to your political correctness?'

'I just don't see a problem,' he said. Then he changed gear, almost visibly. 'If you're worried about women being exploited, believe me, sister, I can show you exploitation.'

'And if you decide to patronise, believe me, Andy, you can patronise.'

He had the grace to flush. And the food had the sense to arrive.

'So what are you doing about the death threats?' he asked, nodding at the waiter for more Kingfisher beer. 'Assuming, as you implied, you've not brought in Interpol.'

'I'm sure they'll swoop in fast enough if anything actually happens. In the meantime, we're doing our best with what Brum has to offer.'

'Don't tell me, Chris Groom looks in on his evenings off!'

'Chris isn't much of a man for evenings off. Not now he's in charge in Smethwick.'

'Smethwick! What on earth's he doing out there?'

'Operational Commander. Smethwick's part of an operational command unit. So he's what used to be a superintendent in charge of the area.'

'Quite a promotion. Thanks,' he smiled to the waiter, who topped up the glasses carefully and withdrew.

'Quite a promotion. I was afraid he wouldn't hack it at first, but he seems to have everything running smoothly now. I rather think he's enjoying it, actually.'

'So we can expect the powers that be to transfer him to a new job any moment now.'

We exchanged an ironic grin.

'So what are you doing about security?' he pursued.

'We've brought in another volunteer.'

'A retired park keeper with one leg?'

'Are you suggesting that I'm the female equivalent! Thank you, Andy.'

He blushed. 'Well, you're not exactly trained for the job.'

'I have what are called transferable skills, thank you very much. You can't run the work-experience programme at a place the size of William Murdock College without learning how to organise yourself and other people. Since the college could never afford secretarial support for us, my filing and word-processing skills—'

'Have you ever thought of becoming a PA?'

'Pain in the arse?'

'You don't need any training for that! Personal assistant was what I was thinking.' He scooped up some food with his naan. 'To me, as a matter of fact. Ruth's too busy with her work for the foundation, and I have awful difficulty with matching time zones and things.'

'You couldn't afford me,' I said, as if it were a joke. Did he really want me to spell it out that as long as Mike was based in Birmingham, that was where you'd find me? That half the time I was tempted to throw up any idea of paid employment simply to follow him round the country and spend my days watching his every game? And my nights sharing every joy of his bed?

'The offer's there, Sophie,' he said, looking me straight in the eye. 'If you should ever need to take it up. Ever.'

So he was offering me far more than a job: he was offering a bolt hole. I squeezed his hand across the table. 'Thanks. I'll remember that.'

Anyone else, and there'd have been a moment of embarrassed silence, to deal with the fact we were both moved. As it was, we smiled at each other with the love we'd shared for the last thirtysomething years, and returned to our food.

And to the park keeper with one leg. 'So who *is* keeping an eye on the Bookfest?'

'I told you, a volunteer. But a volunteer with contacts, not the least of whom is the man who turned my home into Fort Knox.'

'Ah! The bloke who plays a mean game of golf. Gavin Whatshisname.'

'Spot on. So you won't die of shock to learn that it's Ian Dale in charge of security.'

'Good God! Old Eeyore!' Andy slapped his thigh in what seemed a mixture of amusement and exasperation. 'Ian dealing with not one but two death threats! My God!'

'You know how conscientious he is,' I said, sounding more defensive than I liked. 'And – as I said – he's got all the right contacts.' And now the backing of Chris himself, though his involvement was still so secret I would keep quiet about it.

'But he's so . . .'

In the past, I could have supplied him with a number of adjectives, most of them more or less derogatory: staid, tight-arsed, old-fashioned. Since the explosion of Mike into my life, however, Ian and his wife, Val, had been consistently kind and supportive. No matter how much they'd have liked me and Chris to get it together, they'd warmed to Mike, and done everything they could to make bearable our separation during the first weeks of last winter's tour. They'd even invited me to stay overnight so I could watch their satellite system as long as Mike was on screen.

Val had taken me on one side soon after we'd got back from Australia. 'You know,' she'd said, dropping her voice even though the men were out in the garden sorting out a problem with Ian's new solar fountain pump, 'we know you and your dad don't get on. So if ever you wanted a man to give you away, Ian would die of pride. Though he'd never admit it.'

I hesitated: we hadn't planned the sort of wedding that would involve anyone being given away. Rather more to the point, we didn't want anyone to know we were going to get married.

'After all,' she'd pursued, 'you could hardly ask Chris.'

Tearing his naan, Andy was still groping for *le mot juste*. '. . . so – so—'

'Decent and reliable,' I said firmly. 'Ian's the sort of man I'd trust with my life.'

'Ah,' said Andy, 'but would you trust him with anyone else's?'

Chapter Two

The first threat had arrived in the morning's mail at nine
o'clock on Monday morning a week before my conversation
with Andy. Brian Fairbrother, who'd probably been at work
since soon after seven, was sipping a gloomy cup of coffee
and staring dismally at the meagre view afforded by his Central
Library office window. I made myself a cup and joined him.

'The trouble with civic architects,' he said sadly, 'is that
they can never get it completely right. I mean, notwithstanding
what Prince Charles said about the place—'

'You mean that crack he made about it looking more like a
place for burning books than for keeping them?'

He nodded, pushing back short blond hair, cropped not quite
short enough to be a fashion statement. 'I'd have thought that
for borrowers there can be few more user-friendly libraries.
But for the staff . . . Imagine having to work here all the time!'

Birmingham had been so keen on the Bookfest's
development that it had provided venues at very much reduced
booking fees and a free office suite to run the whole caboodle
from. Except the term 'office suite' seemed a bit grandiose to
describe two rooms eight feet by eight and a tiny lobby with a
collapsed armchair and an electric kettle. The main problem
was not size, however, but the fact the neither room ever saw

natural light. The lobby had one window, but it was only two feet square and was angled into the wall at about six feet from the ground. The offices had bigger, more accessible windows, but they overlooked the inside of Paradise Forum, one of my less favourite shopping malls. As originally conceived, the Forum's centrepiece was a stall selling nothing but Lottery tickets. The function might have changed with the times, but there were still enough clues to the original conception. Misconception. There were also a giant McDonald's, a pub, and the skeleton of a former American fast-food restaurant the chief claim to fame of which had been that the waitresses had all worn vests and running shorts and little else apart from cheery smiles.

But it wasn't these delights at which Brian was staring so dismally. He was looking at the less distant view. A balcony of sorts ran round the roof of the Forum. It was supposed, I think, to allow easy access for maintenance men. Certainly assorted cables and pipes were in evidence. But so were all manner of other things. It had become a general dumping ground. Christmas decorations jostled giant fibreglass statues intended – but not by nature – to remind pedestrians of the vaguely Roman nature of the Forum. Since, however, most of the customers were far too sensible to be taken in by spurious statuary (and indeed by shorts-clad women), as the statues got damaged, they were simply abandoned, limbless. (What happened to the waitresses no one knew.) So were cardboard boxes, maintenance manuals, and endless nub-ends.

'At least the punters don't have to come up here for the readings,' I said. 'There are the Library Theatre, the Door at the Rep, Waterstone's, the Midlands Arts Centre. And all the branch libraries, some of which are very nice. One or two are listed buildings,' I added, determined to be cheerful. 'Acocks Green, for instance.'

When he didn't respond, I added, still brightly, 'So what's on your agenda for today?'

'I talk to Sheffield some more,' he said, 'about Vladimir Myakovsky and his visa.'

I nodded. Vladimir Myakovsky had become Brian's albatross. Not the novelist's fault. Brian's actually. When Myakovsky – currently living in New York – had been asked to open Bookfest he'd duly applied to the British Consulate for a visa. Brian's letter of invitation – the one the Russian had to show the Consulate – had foolishly included the fact that he was paying him a fee. Brian had only meant to show that Myakovsky was going to support himself during his UK sojourn. But, as a result, Myakovsky now had to have a Green Card to enable him to work.

'If only I'd said he was to be our honoured guest!' Brian castigated himself for the umpteenth time. 'If only Immigration didn't take so long to issue visas. I mean, three months!'

Three months – when the initial application was made only two months before Myakovsky was due to open the Bookfest with a high-profile series of readings. So it wasn't surprising Brian was stressed. I wondered how much good his repeated nagging at Officialdom in Sheffield did; if it had been me on the far end of that phone it would have been distinctly counterproductive. However, he was the boss, and I just a volunteer.

'So will you carry on with your usual excellent work?' He turned to face me. 'Those PR people really need chasing. And you said you'd schmooze with the sponsors for the poet in residence – is that still OK?'

I pointed at today's outfit – the suit I wore for interviews and funerals. 'Lunch at the Mondiale all booked up,' I said. 'And while I'm there I'll confirm the menu and drinks for the launch. And be terribly nice to them too.'

'Terribly, *terribly* nice,' Brian said. 'The discounts the hotel's offering our performers are breathtaking.'

I nodded. 'But first things first,' I said, going back to my own office. 'The post.'

I'd developed a neat system, a slightly more sophisticated variant of the one I used at home. The most important part of it was the recycling bin. Then there was a big envelope for stamps, which would go to Oxfam. Then there were the Do Now pile, and the Do Soon and Do Eventually piles.

In this office, however, they weren't piles, but part of a plastic vertical stacking system which I took apart to make the process quicker and then reassembled when the relevant plastic baskets had been filled.

As usual, the recycling bin was filling the most briskly. It was amazing how much junk mail the Bookfest was attracting. The stamp envelope was not doing well, since most envelopes were office-franked, but there was a handful of interesting – and, I always hoped, valuable – overseas stamps. This particular envelope, a white A4 one with a computer-generated label, had an ordinary British stamp on it, but I opened it carefully none the less. What was everyday over here might be valuable somewhere . . . well, foreign, I concluded woollily. On automatic pilot, I fished out the folded A4 sheet inside. Laser printer, by the look of it, and good-quality paper too. But no address. Indeed, no preliminaries.

If Stonkin Mama comes to Birmingham she will *die*.

No valediction, either. But by then, I didn't expect one.

I retrieved the envelope. The police would want to see that. And the postmark could be useful.

I placed it in another envelope, and tucked it into my desk. The letter had better go to Brian. Now.

He was just putting the phone down. 'Oh, this jobsworth attitude!' he moaned. He must have seen from my face I didn't want yet another rehearsal of his woes. 'What on earth's the matter?'

'This,' I said, holding out the letter.

He said pettishly, 'Oh, can't you deal with it?'

'I could. But you ought to see it first.'

Shrugging, he took it. I expected a bit of a reaction along the lines of a howl of *Why-haven't-you-called-the-police-yet?* I certainly didn't expect a repeat shrug, and to see the paper compressed into a ball.

I caught it as he slung it towards a bin. 'You can't throw away something like that!'

'You're not taking it seriously?'

'Seriously enough to show it to you,' I said, 'and to ask you how you want me to deal with it.'

'It's some hoax,' he said. 'Probably one of my mates winding me up. They know I'm a bit on edge. Just the sort of thing they'd do.'

'Nice friends.' I passed him the phone. 'Better get on to them.'

He hedged. 'Might even be another festival trying to cut us down to their size.'

Personally I didn't quite see it as the act of someone running Hay, Cheltenham or Edinburgh. My expression no doubt told him as much. He grimaced.

I waited. Holding the paper by the extreme edges to unfurl it, I put it on his phone book, and plopped Yellow Pages on top. Action worth a thousand words, and all that.

He squirmed again. I waited implacably.

'Look,' he said at last, 'perhaps I should talk to the chair of the board. Off the record.'

I nodded. What little I'd seen of Martin Acheson had convinced me he had at least his fair share of common sense.

'Could you get on to it? Make an appointment?'

As if I were his personal assistant. But I didn't argue. I rather thought I'd put more effort into talking my way into today's diary than he would. After all, I had the power of conviction on my side. And years of dealing with potential employers for my work-experience students had taught me a little secretary-speak.

'Leave it to me,' I said. 'I take it there's nothing on your schedule for today that can't be postponed.' It was more of a statement than a question.

It was one thing to chat up solicitors such as Afzal to persuade them to take on one of my protégés. It was quite another to persuade the PA of the Managing Director of one of the Midlands' most flourishing medium-sized companies that her boss could spare time to discuss a problem with what she clearly considered merely one of his hobbies. And not a particularly useful hobby either. What possible reason, her tone if not her words demanded, was there for Mr Acheson's interest in a literary festival? Books had nothing to do with water filters. For that was what made Acheson his latest pots of money. He'd realised that Middle England's obsession with pure drinking water, the excellent quality of Severn-Trent H_2O notwithstanding, could be turned into profit. So he made and fitted in-kitchen systems. No lugging bottles of wicked French water back from the supermarket, no fiddling with filter jugs.

He would take mains water, run it through a system under your sink, and bring it through a tap beside the others. Easy. He had fingers in other lucrative pies too, I was sure of that, but the most important thing in Acheson's life was literature.

I knew he had subscriber tickets to Birmingham Rep. And whoever came to read at Waterstone's or wherever, he'd be there, buying up what I'd now learnt to call backlists and getting everything autographed. There weren't too many writers of national status in Brum, and not all went to other authors' signings, but he'd be there, talking familiarly to any who turned up. And they did more than tolerate him as a literary groupie. I'd seen them waving to him to join them. When the Bookfest had first been mooted, it wasn't surprising that he gathered together a board and had more or less driven the whole project through.

Not, presumably, with his secretary's approval.

No, she simply couldn't find a single diary window. Not today, definitely. No. Probably not this week. There was a very good chance that Mr Acheson was flying to the States on Thursday.

'In that case,' I said, pouncing, 'he'll consider it imperative to deal with this matter before he goes. It's essential you give it the highest priority. I can't,' I added darkly, 'vouch for the consequences otherwise.'

'If you could just indicate the nature of the problem—'

'Absolutely confidential,' I said. 'I'm not permitted to discuss it with anyone except Mr Acheson. In fact,' I said brightly, 'if you could put me through to him it might obviate the need for a meeting.' It was worth a try. 'It's of the utmost urgency.' I pressed her.

In the end I had to settle for an appointment for four that afternoon. Not the speed of response I'd have preferred, but better than nothing. Particularly as it was at a time when I was free myself.

'I'll brief you about all that as we walk to the car park,' I said, hustling Brian into his coat. It would be my car. Brian shared a car with his wife, who, since she had to ferry their three children wherever their full social lives took them, had priority.

He wanted to know about my meetings with our sponsor and with the Mondiale. I wanted to stop him giving any impression that the death threat was trivial. I'd photocopied the letter – sightly recovered after being pressed between the two directories – and locked the original in the office safe. Perhaps this did more than anything else to convince Brian that I was deadly serious – as serious, in other words, as I thought the letter itself was.

Acheson's factory was in what they probably call an urban regeneration area. It was very near Junction 2 of the M5, in an industrial estate on the outskirts of Oldbury. Everything about the place spoke of profitability. There was a Queen's Award in the foyer, numerous photographs of the great and the good of industry, and – one that fascinated me – one of Acheson himself addressing a TUC Conference to the apparent approval of those on the platform. Big frames contained passport-sized photos of all the workforce, arranged in alphabetical order of surname. Under each photo were a couple of lines about the person in question – when they joined the firm and as what, and their current role. Directors jostled cleaners – all very democratic. Whose job was it to rearrange the frames whenever a new body was hired or fired?

Probably his secretary's. A woman for whom the fashion of those small-rimmed glasses you can peer over disapprovingly might have been invented, she peered in spades when Acheson saw us immediately. He was one of those men whom middle age more than suits – it enhances. His smile insisted he was genuinely pleased by our arrival. The chairs were comfortable, the décor restrained good taste. In deep frames around the walls were nuts and bolts and various other bits of gubbins. He smiled when he saw me looking at them.

'My water filters,' he said. 'All the constituent parts. I like to remind myself what the business depends on.'

'Like the staff photos in your foyer.'

'Exactly! Do you like the idea?' His smile shouted that it was his own brainchild, but even if it hadn't, I'd have expressed the enthusiasm I did.

The door opened. The tea – it must have broken his secretary's heart to make it – was as good as the biscuits that came with it. Only when he had provided all the courtesies did he sit down, put his hands together and his head on one side, and start listening.

'You are sure that it isn't some dreadful malicious joke?' he asked Brian, minutely rearranging an item on his desk-set as he did so.

'Sophie saved the envelope.'

'"Saved the envelope"?' He looked at me quizzically.

'Evidence. Should it ever be needed,' I conceded. 'And to check with Brian he didn't have any friends who might have found it amusing to wind him up.'

Acheson's smile showed both amusement and approval.

Brian put in quickly. 'The postmark was indistinguishable. I don't have any friends – good or bad – in indistinguishable.'

His smile thinner, Acheson turned to him. 'We really can't simply ignore this, much as I would like to. We'd be entirely culpable should the young woman come to Birmingham and experience any trouble.'

Full marks for knowing that Stonkin Mama was a young woman. But then, he was, according to Afzal, a very hands-on chair.

'I'd like to take absolute responsibility for this myself. But – well, you know the delicacy of the whole situation. Local politics; equal opportunities – race and gender; sponsorship; not to mention the poet herself.' He spread his hands. 'At least we have a couple of weeks. I shall call an emergency meeting of the board – tomorrow night. And although I shall have a very strong view, I never allow myself to be more than *primus inter pares*. Whatever decision is taken will be a corporate one.' He nodded to Brian, then to me.

I had a very strong sense that whatever his opinions on other things, he approved wholeheartedly of my suit's rather short skirt. But that he'd be far too courteous to say anything sexist.

Chapter Three

The next morning was improved, for Brian at least, by the decorative – entirely decorative – presence of Alexandrina Melford, our PR person. Her agency had landed the job by dint of her mother being on the festival board. The general idea had been that she'd do it at discount for us. I'd have been happy for her to do it at all.

There were, I gathered from various new contacts in the world of publishing, PR agencies that specialised in the world of books. Alexandrina's was not one of them. Her chief area of expertise, she confided to me as we shared a mirror in the ladies' loo, was sport. At last! Something in common! I could talk about the fortunes of Warwickshire and West Bromwich Albion. But it wasn't that sort of sport, it seemed. It was point-to-point, that kind of thing, she said, consigning me with a gesture of her lipstick to beyond the social pale. Yah.

I waited till we were in the office we were to share until I raised the matter of her day's work. What was her schedule?

'I'm so flexible,' she said. 'You just tell me who you want me to phone and I'll go ahead. No probs.'

I shook my head. 'You're the expert. I just need to know when I shall be able to use the phone. Morning? Afternoon?'

She blenched. 'I'm only here this morning, Sophie.'

'OK,' I said. I was fuming. Since I'd typed the contract I knew exactly how much she would be getting for her Bookfest work. Perhaps she did most of the graft back at her agency office, however, or perhaps from home. And as I tried to remind myself, it was none of my business. I was only the hired help. Not even hired, come to think of it. 'Be my guest,' I said, pushing the phone towards her.

I sauntered in to disturb Brian a bit. He'd no doubt just completed his verbal assault on some innocent denizen of Sheffield; his hands were white-knuckling the phone as he appeared to hold it forcibly to the desk.

'This meeting tonight,' I said, 'what line are you going to take?'

'Meeting?' He looked blanker than Alexandrina.

'The festival board.'

Blank transmogrified to pure round-eyed horror, as if Stonkin Mama's corpse lay expiring at his feet.

'But I've got to take Adam to Daventry. There's a big Scouts' do. Ohmygod, ohmygod. What shall I do? God, it completely slipped my mind – I should have said something yesterday, shouldn't I?' I couldn't quite read the expression sliding across his face, but I was certain he wouldn't want me to. 'Oh, Sophie, you couldn't do me the most enormous favour. My wife's taking the other two to their drama workshop at MAC. Just down the road from us, thank goodness. And the funny thing is, they'll be in the room we'll be using for our readings.'

I waited, not laughing.

'I suppose,' he continued, 'you couldn't take my car and—'

I shook my head firmly. 'I don't do Scouts. But I could hold the fort at the board meeting provided you gave me your 'authority.' For some reason the prospect gave me more pleasure than I cared to admit. A meeting. Perhaps my time at William Murdock had addicted me to them and I needed another fix.

Quite at peace with the world I headed back to my office to check the e-mail.

Alexandrina was holding the phone as if it were a week-old kipper. 'Well, really. How rude!'

I raised an eyebrow.

'This man,' she said. 'Dreadful little oik.'

'What did he say?' I expected her to report the odd f- or c-word, I suppose. But then, surely a young woman like her would take such expletives in her stride.

'Just slammed the phone down.'

'What had you asked him to do?'

She stared. 'Nothing.'

'So why should he get so ratty? What had you said?'

'Nothing. It was what he said to me. I couldn't quite hear – dreadful line – and I asked him to say it slowly so I could write it down. And he just slammed the phone down,' she repeated.

This was like extracting teeth. Less lucrative, perhaps. 'So you've no idea what he was saying?'

'Oh, something about someone with a funny name.'

Had I been a dog, my ears would have pricked. 'What sort of name?'

'Something foreign.'

'Not Stonkin Mama?'

She shook her head blankly. 'No. Foreign. Something like Tchaikovsky.'

My huge sigh of relief stopped on a sharp intake of breath. In for another molar. 'How like Tchaikovsky?'

'Well, sort of. But the guy had this thick accent, you know?'

'Russian?'

'That's what I was saying. And he said something about this Tchaikovsky guy being dead meat.'

'Dead meat.' I hesitated. 'I suppose the name couldn't have been Myakovsky?'

'Oh, yes! That's right!'

'So something's going to turn this Myakovsky guy into dead meat.'

'That's what I said. So I asked him to repeat the message so I could write it down and he slammed down the phone on me.'

I nodded with great sympathy. 'That must have been very upsetting for you. Now why don't you write down everything you've said to me while I make you a cup of coffee?'

Because I needed one. A very strong one.

Knowing it was a waste of time, I dialled 1471, to be told, surprise, surprise, that the caller had withheld their number.

'His or her number,' I muttered, replacing the handset.

So how would Brian react? It would be wonderful if he'd parody the Wilde line about two parents and carelessness, but I rather doubted that he would. Perhaps I could do it myself, at a judicious opportunity.

It took me a couple of minutes to realise that I was trembling. Yes, this anonymous message business was upsetting me. I'd better go and tell Brian, at least, knowing that he'd probably be as underwhelmed as before, and strongly suspecting that I would have to agree simply to raise the issue tonight.

'So why don't you simply pull out?' Mike demanded, not unreasonably.

We'd been in the middle of getting an early supper at his house when our hands and mouths had reminded us that we had far more urgent appetites to satisfy than those involving pasta and salad. So now, naked in bed, our bodies cooled by the spring breeze blowing through the open window, we were enjoying a post-coital glass of wine and a discussion of each other's days.

'You know me,' I said.

'I do. But there's bits of you I don't understand. Like why you should have to put yourself out for prats who are prepared to put people at risk for the sake of some poxy book festival.'

'Thus speaks a man who reads far more books per week than I do.' Not just popular paperbacks, either. Mike was a man who absorbed history and biography and Booker-type novels as easily as some of his colleagues absorbed the *Sun*.

'Only when rain stops play,' he conceded mildly. 'But you're evading the issue. I can – just – understand why you should put up with shit from your colleagues, even from the staff at the University of the West Midlands. But you're not some highly paid lecturer— Hey! Stop! I'm not ticklish, remember—'

We discussed this assertion to my satisfaction – highly paid was not a description appropriate to my William Murdock job – before I let him continue.

'Nor are you dependent on him for good grades. You're purely and simply a volunteer.'

'A volunteer who knows more than anyone else, Brian excepted, perhaps. If I pull out now, who'll keep things together while Brian's busy being nice to the great and the good? Besides which,' I added, 'the board will no doubt sort out everything at this evening's meeting. Which I shall be late for if I don't rush.'

* * *

The Bookfest board had been allowed to meet in the Shakespeare Room, one of the most impressive locations in the city. The panelling and contents had been rescued from the original Central Reference Library before it had been knocked down, and reinstalled as part of a complex involving the Library Theatre and Birmingham Conservatoire. Seated round the enormous table on heavy leather-seated chairs, the directors would make their deliberations surrounded by Shakespeareana, under the blind gaze of Shakespeare himself.

And the open-eyed gaze of Sophie Rivers.

I was to present my information, that was all. I wasn't to participate in the discussion, not unless questioned by the directors. Well, I'd been in that sort of situation before – and not enjoyed it. At least I could comfort myself with the knowledge that I was very well prepared, and not ferrying small boys about the countryside.

Martin Acheson's eyes widened when I came in, not because of my skirt, which epitomised sober reliability, but because, it transpired in the half-minute's conversation we had, Brian had forgotten to notify him of the change of personnel. I didn't like the way things were going with Brian. He'd been working such extraordinarily long hours and under so much solitary pressure, this absent-mindedness could presage the sort of problems I'd seen in so many overworked lecturers. And he clearly couldn't rest when he finally did get home. The joys of parenthood.

I was about to tell him about the morning's phone call – I never liked to hide things from chairs – when he was seized by a voluminous woman who introduced herself as an adviser from West Midlands Arts. Knowing my place   which was suddenly behind her left elbow – I retreated in order to attack better later.

The directors eventually straggled in, Martin looking more and more ostentatiously at his watch. They were an interesting mix. My solicitor friend, Afzal, who'd arrived early, managed to corner me.

'Any idea what this is all about, Sophie?'

They hadn't been told?

I smiled the sort of noncommittal smile that tells a friend volumes. 'I've not seen the agenda,' I said. 'I'm only the substitute for Brian.'

He nodded, and, turning further from the room, asked, 'How is he? Coping?'

'Do you have any doubts?'

'Not now he's got you there to help, Sophie. As soon as this is over you must come over for a meal, you and Mike. Meet the new one.'

'*Au contraire*,' I said, 'you must find a baby-sitter, and bring Najma to us. We're longing to see the baby, but you don't have a Caesarean and find yourself cooking for visitors six weeks later.'

'She'll be going back to work in another six,' he said, 'if she has her way.'

'You have your way with this meal, and absolutely forbid her to cook,' I said. I touched his arm. 'More arrivals.'

He turned to smile at two of them. 'Sophie – do you know Wendy Thane? She's the City Librarian? And this is Alan Jones, Literature Officer for West Midlands Arts. He's the one holding the biggest set of purse strings.' Two representatives from West Midlands Arts? But before I could sort things out, Martin was starting to herd people to the table. His courtesy was tinged with asperity. I sat by Afzal, and was joined by a young white man who had to be a poet. Maybe not the sort of poet who actually wrote anything, but one who liked to be clearly visible as one. Wild hair, wild teeth, wild eyes – that sort of thing. Then another poet, an Afro-Caribbean man whom Afzal had described as a hard worker. He had shoulder-length dreadlocks, topped by a crocheted hat, and the sort of eyes that missed little. Marcus Downing. Next to him sat a white-haired white woman with wonderful Greek jewellery. At last the only gaps at the table were marked by name cards. Councillor Perkins; Councillor Roberts; Councillor Burton. Since no one else had a name card, I gathered Martin Acheson was making a point.

He might also have been making a point when he circulated the agenda, though I wasn't sure which one.

1. Apologies
2. Minutes of last meeting
3. Up-date on Bookfest
4. Death Threat
5. Any other business

Well, sooner or later I would have to ask for an amendment to Item Four. For death threat, read death threats.

Chapter Four

So why did we – correction they – have to plough through all that bumf before they got on to the matter of life and death? OK, *possible* life and death.

They haggled over the minutes till the young man who'd taken them was nearly in tears. He was really an accountant so my sympathy was limited. Then they quizzed me over hotel rates and reservations until I could have pulled the Mondiale down on top of them. It seemed I shouldn't have accepted the services of such a big company. Well, politically, I couldn't have agreed more, but until Oxfam or whoever ventured into the hospitality business, there was little I could do. And what had once been acres of small family-run hotels two or three miles from the city centre were now acres of Social Security bed-and-breakfasts. In any case, the writers wanted city-centre accommodation, possibly, though I wouldn't float the idea here, not if I wanted to get out alive, because they wished to make good their escape as quickly as possible.

There was a debate about the sponsorship of the storyteller booked to go round local schools. The subtext was less concerned with the sponsorship, I thought, which was provided, appropriately enough, by a company making industrial gases, than with the fact that the poetry side of the table wanted Brian to have booked a poet, rather than a storyteller. It became clear that there was a poetry pressure group. There was no doubting the disparaging sniffs every time I mentioned novelists, whatever their genre. Despite Acheson's obvious irritation, all the poets declined to come to the launch of Marietta Coe's latest book. OK, bestsellers like doorstops weren't my favourite reading, but hers weren't badly written, and the woman had come up the hard way, writing as she continued with a full-time job. Not just the odd forty-line poem, but great wodges of prose – over 150,000 words a time.

Somewhere in *Northanger Abbey* Jane Austen fires off an angry page attacking people who read 'only a novel'. I'd have loved to quote it at these people. But apart from not wishing to damage Brian's position, I was all too aware of the passage of time. There was still the matter of Item Four to chew over. At, I strongly suspected, great length. Perhaps I would have been better off ferrying little boys about the Midlands. At least little boys had bedtimes.

No sooner had I got the last of the increasingly petty interrogations over than I had to expose myself once more. I had a feeling that they would perceive the doubling of death threats since the printing of the minutes as yet another administrative failure, but I could hardly pretend this morning's call had not happened. I cleared my throat, surprised to be anxious for the first time in fifteen years – teaching gets you used to such things – about speaking in public.

The door opened. A cadaverous man inserted himself into the place marked Councillor Roberts. I glanced at Acheson. He nodded: I was to go ahead. The councillor accompanied my opening sentence with such a clattering as he assembled pens, spectacles, mobile phone and water from the choice of bottles that no one could have heard my announcement. Except, it was clear, for a feminist poet, who declared her calling by dressing from a down-market charity shop, dying her hair puce and leaving it unwashed and uncut.

'And you're more concerned,' she declared, 'at the fate of this over-publicised, over-published, overweight political turncoat! Christ, he was in the KGB once—'

'Would you repeat that?' Martin demanded at the same moment. Yes, I should have made sure I'd up-dated him first.

'And you're more concerned at the fate of this over-publicised, over-published, overweight ex-KGB—' Puce Poet repeated.

'I have to inform the board—' I projected my voice as if trying to quell a recalcitrant class.

'Would someone be kind enough to pass me the *fizzy* water—' which then exploded as Councillor Roberts opened it, showering half a dozen of us. Even Martin joined in the general production of tissues and clean handkerchiefs – excusable, in his case: his shirt front was soaked.

I sat in complete silence. Not a quiet silence, however. The set of my shoulders, neck and jaw declared that I was keeping my temper with the most extreme difficulty. I probably allowed my nostrils a millimetre of flare.

All around the table the ashes of the previous conversations were fanned back to life. The councillor was demanding a complete reprise of the items he'd missed, totally oblivious of his role in the chaos.

Eventually my stillness penetrated, just as it would have penetrated (in a far shorter time, incidentally) a noisy class. One by one the conversations petered out. At last I allowed Martin to catch my eye.

This time there'd been no interruptions. I laid out the facts –

just the two – very quietly, and mentioned the options before us. The rest was up to them.

'You have established to the best of your ability that neither of these is a joke – in particularly bad taste?' Acheson asked.

'Neither Brian Fairbrother nor I can think of anyone who would do such a thing, so we *have* to take the letter at face value. As for the telephone threat, the accent certainly convinced the young woman who took the call.' I would not admit what in my heart of hearts I really feared – that someone in Sheffield, irritated beyond endurance by Brian's harassment, had had some not-so-subtle revenge.

'When you've had this sort of situation before, Miss Rivers,' the councillor began, 'how have you dealt with it?'

I looked him straight – and mendaciously – in the eye. I wasn't about to admit I was simply a volunteer, and that Brian had chosen to put family responsibility before his job. Of course he was entitled to free time – goodness knew he put in far more hours than he should have done. And of course his family had needs. But while in my heart of hearts, and knowing the background, I didn't really approve of what he'd done, if I showed that then surely a head on a platter was the least some of these people would demand. A grim smile was called for. 'Could you imagine the media and legal implications of not taking such threats to the police? If their advice is to ignore them, then that absolves us.'

Acheson nodded. Not to approve, I thought, but to acknowledge that my part in the proceedings was over, except when it came to implementing the board's decision.

Acheson was a strong chair, but Samson himself couldn't have held that meeting together. He'd no sooner brought one speaker to order, than another would release more red herrings, until there were veritable shoals of the things swimming round the notes I was trying to take. The arguments – no, that's far too rational a term – the utterances were along the following lines. The Councillor didn't want the matter to go beyond the Shakespeare Room's walls; if it did, it would be a terrible slur on Birmingham's ability to run a festival. Puce Poet seemed to want Stonkin Mama preserved, Myakovsky thrown to the lions, but then conceded that such a proposition might violate equal opportunities guidelines. I wished quite desperately that someone would come up with the information that he was a blind bi-transsexual, prolific writer of passionate poetry (to both genders) and the possessor of at least one wooden leg. But no one did. They came up with practically everything else, from public liability insurance to a firm of private detectives. No one seemed to have registered that two human lives might be at risk.

At this point the door swung open to admit a tall woman in strong tweeds, with a distinct resemblance to Alexandrina. Although she swept into Councillor Burton's seat, she flicked over the name label as if it were some importunate insect. Not Councillor Burton, then, but Mrs Melford.

I settled back for a dramatic rendition of her daughter's shock this morning. I was not disappointed. The bonus was that she shut everyone else up.

Acheson leapt in the instant she paused for breath. 'So, ladies and gentlemen, we clearly have to take both these threats seriously. Having listened to you all, I am minded to suggest the following.'

Minded! Still the verb seemed to weigh heavily with the board, who sat nodding while he spoke.

'As your chair, I will approach the publishers of the authors concerned and discuss with them – in the strictest confidence – the current situation. The Bookfest staff will maintain vigilance at all times, and meticulously record any further threats, concerning whomsoever.'

Whomsoever: I'd never heard that used in conversation before, not even by Superintendent Christopher Ramsay Groom at his most pedantic. Which reminded me – at what point would the police be notified? If at all? But I didn't need to raise the point. That was done with terrific force by Alexandrina's mother.

'My own feeling,' Acheson said, 'is that any such action would be premature. But if further communications are received – and, as I said, I expect the Bookfest staff to be in a state of constant alertness – then we should reconsider. In the meantime, I'm not averse to the idea of seeking expert advice. I know this board has access to an amazing range of expertise in a variety of fields. Has anyone . . .?'

There was what he would no doubt have called a negative response from the members. On the other hand, thinking of Chris had made me think of Ian Dale, Ian having been Chris's favourite sergeant for years, until they'd been separated by Chris's promotion and Ian's retirement. In fact, there was a rumour, which Chris refused to confirm or deny, that Chris had refused to take up his new post until Ian had left the force, knowing that Ian wouldn't have taken kindly to new ways for such a short time. Personally I felt this did Ian an injustice just as much as it did Chris credit.

Ian Dale, then. My hand went up.

By now it was ten thirty. I was quite convinced that had not the pubs been calling loudly, my suggestion would have been chewed over and spat into the dust. But it wasn't. Which was how, in response to my late-night phone call, Ian came to join our team.

* * *

The next morning later there was a tap at the office door.

'Ian!' I called. 'Come on in!'

He stepped inside, smiling as if not quite sure of his welcome. Usually he wasn't happy with routine hugs or social kisses, so I was surprised when I got both. I introduced him and Brian to each other.

As they shook hands, it was clear each was appraising the other. They were much of a height, and each carried himself well. Ian would note Brian's sensible jumper over a shirt with both collar and tie, he'd suspect, rightly, that there'd be a smart jacket on a hanger behind the door for more formal circumstances. He'd also note, with approval, the tidiness of Brian's desk.

Brian might be disconcerted by the aura of policeman that still hung inexplicably around Ian, though his hair was longer these days than Brian's own – quite a fashionable cut, no longer the short back and sides he'd favoured for so long. A touch of Val's influence, no doubt. He wore a jumper closely related to Brian's, slacks and shoes which, while comfortable, were nothing like regulation beetle-crushers.

Brian gestured him to a chair. 'I'm very grateful to you for coming along at such short notice. And for agreeing to give us some advice. Fancy a coffee, such as it is, while I brief you? OK, Sophie?'

If only he'd get it into his head that I wasn't his secretary!

But Ian patted his briefcase. 'I can do better than that.'

Before Brian's fascinated eyes, he produced a china mug, a clean spoon, a lemon in a polythene bag, and a Tupperware box containing aromatic tea bags and a sharp knife. 'I've worked in offices before,' he said simply.

I held out a hand. I'd been a friend of his long enough to know how he liked his tea. And making tea for a friend wasn't quite the same as doing it because the Bookfest director expected it. Was it?

A mug of delicately pale Earl Grey – with the thinnest slice of lemon, not milk – in his hand, Ian listened attentively to Brian. I sensed he'd have loved to interrupt a couple of times, but he stayed shtoom, making an occasional note in a new reporter's notepad.

At last he looked over his reading glasses and asked, 'You're sure you've had no more letters, no more calls, about either Myakovsky or – er – Stonkin Mama?'

'No,' Brian said quickly.

Too quickly for my liking. Had he received anything he hadn't told me about during those early or late stints of his? Maybe I'd have to forget all my promises to myself not to be dragged into the silly-hours syndrome, ridiculous though it might be for a volunteer to be tottering into the office before seven thirty and not leaving it till at least twelve hours later – Scout trips apart, that is.

Ian gave him the sort of look I reserved for students with less than credible excuses for not handing in assignments.

'Well, there was one a couple of days back. I – well, you know, I thought it was a joke and I binned it. A joke. Same as I thought this was.'

'What did it say?' Ian asked with above average forbearance.

'Same as the one Sophie opened.' He looked on the verge of tears.

Maybe Ian noticed. Certainly all he did was make a note. 'Pity. But if it casts no new light . . . Right. Venues. We're all right on the major ones, I'd say. The Library Theatre has its own security staff, as has the Rep.'

'But the libraries are run on shoestrings,' I chimed in. 'They hardly have money to buy books, let alone install any sort of security system.'

'One elementary precaution, then,' Ian said reasonably, 'is to make sure these two people speak at venues with at least a modicum of security.'

Brian gaped. 'But the venues were decided months ago. The brochures with all the details are everywhere. Imagine what chaos changing them now would cause.'

'Imagine,' Ian grinned sardonically, 'what chaos a couple of murders would cause.'

Chapter Five

When I'd phoned Ian I'd carefully avoided asking him to promise not to talk about the death threats, if such they were, to his old police contacts. There was nothing like a good gossip to disseminate and indeed acquire useful information. So I was rather hoping he'd dash straight out and start talking. Ian wasn't like that, of course. He'd want to establish everything he could before saying or doing anything precipitate. He even gave his last comment plenty of time to penetrate before asking his next question.

'What about the writers' accommodation? If they're staying overnight, that is.'

'Most have declined the offer of overnight accommodation,' Brian said rather stiffly. 'But some have to stay overnight – or in some cases, like Myakovsky, a whole week.'

'Where?'

'The Mondiale, just along Broad Street,' Brian said.

He didn't mention the wonderful discounts I'd wangled out of them, even when Ian pulled a face. 'Didn't know writers were so extravagant. Or that the Bookfest can be on their behalf.'

'The Mondiale is one of our best sponsors,' I said. 'But the management might not be happy to have someone wasted in its best suite.'

'Quite. Now,' Ian said, shaking his head, 'the more I think about it the more I think we should persuade the artists in question to pull out. The way I see it is that they're only here for the publicity. What better publicity for Stonkin Mama than to go on TV and say she's scared out of her wits and is going back to Harlem or wherever?'

'Harlesden,' Brian corrected absently.

'If you don't put it to them as an option, you could be in deep trouble. I'm surprised they haven't thought of it themselves. They or their agents.'

'I suppose a death could sell a lot of posthumous books,' I joked. 'Maybe the whole thing's a publicity stunt anyway.'

Brian looked at me balefully. 'These are Artists,' he said. 'Look at the programme,' he urged Ian. 'Top-class artists. Here' – he opened the brochure, not quite at random – 'Jose Martinez del Core is probably the greatest writer of magic realism the world has ever known—'

'Better,' Ian asked quickly, 'than Isabelle Allende? Though some prefer Gabriel García Márquez. And I've even heard it argued that Isaac Bashevis Singer might be called a magic realist.'

Brian swallowed the dregs of his coffee. The act seemed to cause him some pain.

'Police officers can read,' Ian said mildly. 'Not just those with degrees. One of the best SOCOs I ever met was an expert on Byzantine history. Which is possibly more than can be said for Stonkin Mama, or whatever the rap lady calls herself.'

'Helen Casper-Brook, in real life,' I said. 'Degree in History from Cambridge. So she may not be a total idiot.'

'Stonkin Mama,' Ian repeated, more in sorrow than in anger.

'So,' he said, closing his notebook, 'I'd like to talk to the artists or their publishers and put the situation to them. I'd have thought some sort of indemnity form would be useful – saying we'll do our best, but that ultimately we can't be called upon to guarantee their safety.'

Brian shuffled a couple of files.

Ian looked at him – hard. He said, very slowly, 'You haven't told them yet, have you? Two writers threatened with death and you haven't even told them? And may I make another informed guess? That you haven't told my old friends in the police?'

The word bluster might have been designed to describe Brian's next few minutes of utterance. But whatever he said, it came to one thing: the matter wasn't in his hands. It was in the hands of the board, and in particular those of Martin Acheson.

The look on Ian's face should have been framed. But he said nothing. Not until he'd swallowed a couple of times. Then he said, very quietly, 'Looks as if I've got my first assignment then, doesn't it?' He put his mug carefully by the kettle and the tea bags, picked up his jacket and left.

At this point Brian's phone started to ring. I don't think it stopped for the rest of the day. I'd have helped, but I was too busy doing Alexandrina's PR work for her. By the time I left – and he showed no sign of quitting – we were both pale and frazzled. And hungry. Neither of us had been able to take a lunch break.

Mike was playing in Glamorgan, and had been invited to stay with an old friend for the duration of the match. So I was preparing a solitary supper – why did I always cook twice as much as I needed? – and was wondering whether I should put it on hold so I could mow the lawn before the threatening rain set in. I was almost glad when the phone rang. Chris Groom!

'I've got this case you might just be interested in,' he said.

'Why don't you come and have a bite of supper and tell me about it?' I asked.

'It isn't the how so much as the why and the whom that interests me, Sophie,' Chris said. 'Though I must confess the how taxes me at the moment.'

I poured him the half-glass of Rioja he'd asked for and sat down on the sofa opposite his chair. 'Let me get this straight,' I said. 'You've got this lock-up shop. No access except through the front and back doors, to which only the owner has a key.'

'No sign of forced entry,' Chris confirmed. 'And the owner has an absolutely watertight alibi.'

I raised my eyebrows as I raised my glass. 'Are alibis usually watertight?'

'This one is. The lady in question—'

'Woman,' I corrected automatically. As a senior police officer, Chris should know better than to use such an old-fashioned term.

He pulled the face I'd expected. '—is a Samaritan. She spent the night at Samaritan headquarters answering the phone. And, as you know, all calls are monitored by a second counsellor. She was there, all right.'

'She might have given someone the key; retrieved it later.' I stopped. Something about the expression on his face told me that he wasn't talking about a simple attack of arson.

Chris smiled grimly. 'Maybe,' he said, as if I'd come straight

out and asked, 'you should come along and see for yourself.'
He looked at his watch. 'The scene of crime team should have
finished by now.'

The shop, in an unexpectedly good part of Oldbury, was, as
Chris had said, one of a modern block: florist, interior design,
designer pets, and a couple of other boutiques, all covered by
thick grilles. So was the one currently swathed in police tape
– overkill, I'd have thought, for a simple act of vandalism.
Chris nodded at the constable standing stoically in what was
now the cold evening drizzle, and unlocked the door, pushing
it open so I could go in first. He leant past me to flick on the
light.

Bridal wear. One side of the shop was lined with dresses,
virginal in heavy polythene wraps. A table, tasteful with
flowers. Comfortable chairs. All the other accoutrements of
bridal fashion were no doubt concealed in those cupboards to
my right and at the rear of the shop. And, in the middle of all
this order, all this elegant promise, a circle of black, topped
by a grotesque modern sculpture. A blackened caricature of a
woman's head and torso.

I looked up. Yes, smoke on the ceiling. And the sweet smell
of burnt fabric everywhere.

'Electrical fault?' I asked, as much for something to say as
anything. My voice certainly wasn't functioning very well. I
answered myself. 'But why should just this item be affected?'

Chris shrugged. 'Quite.'

'So whatever it was was singled out? Targeted?'

'I'd have thought so.'

I looked at the sad circle of charred fabric, and
unconsciously repeated Chris's speculations. 'So how did
they do it? And who? And why on earth should they want

to destroy a wedding dress? Or rather, just one wedding dress?'

'So why,' I asked, as he started his car, 'are you taking all this trouble over a simple attack of arson? One dress, for goodness' sake. In a little Black Country suburb. What's all this policeman on guard and SOCO business? And why should someone of your exalted level be involved?'

He fastened his seat belt and, checking as carefully as if he were on his driving test, he pulled out into the traffic before he spoke. He should have been a film director, should Chris. He wasn't so hot on making them laugh and making them cry, but he certainly made up for it on making them wait.

At last he said, 'I can't tell you.'

'You bastard! You've got me all worked up and – you don't really mean to tell me you're not going to spill a single bean?'

'I do. Sorry. Not the best couple of words in the circumstances.' He said it with a finality I simply had to accept.

For the time being at least.

I tried a different approach. 'Tell me about the dress. Was it gorgeous?'

He sighed. 'How would I know? The owner said it was eye-catching, that's why she had it on the mannequin. But not necessarily the height of sophistication. Tight in the chest, very frothy skirt. Available in creamish or whitish.'

'I like the technical descriptions,' I said.

'All these silly names for colours,' he said. 'You know, I was trying to match the emulsion in my hall the other day. The shade they said was nearest was Adorable Peach!'

No, Chris was not the man for an Adorable Peach hall.

I sighed. I was busy trying to suppress a nasty little niggle in the back of my head. And finding a horrible wet burning in my eyes. All the cool discussions I'd had with Mike, all our agreements that the wedding should be totally simple, totally private. Just going off to the register office with a couple of witnesses. Now I had this terrible feeling that that wasn't what I wanted at all. I swallowed hard, hoping he wouldn't notice.

'Have you got to get home to Mike or do you fancy seeing what the SOCOs have come up with?' he asked, as if he hadn't.

I didn't like the implication that I 'had to do' anything in my relationship with Mike. It was true, we both tried to get home to the other at a reasonable hour, and when Mike was away he'd always phone and we'd talk for as long as we could. But neither was tied to the other. Though I did hate it when he had to stay over. Nonsense. He had a job to do. He was part of a team. A team who quite desperately needed him if they were to succeed this season.

'He's in Cardiff,' I said as lightly as I could. 'Where are we off to?'

'Piddock Road nick, of course.'

What I'd hoped for, back at Smethwick Police Station, was, despite what he'd said about secrecy, a goggle at the gory evidence. What I got, from a straight-faced Chris and a vaguely amused SOCO, a middle-aged man called Philip Johnson, was a set of photographs.

'The items themselves are all in a secure room,' Johnson said, 'ready to go either to the Forensic Service or to a detained property store.'

'Forensic Service?' I asked innocently.

'Just look at the photos,' Chris suggested, his voice as dry as Tio Pepe.

I looked. As you'd expect, they were high-quality 35mm. A very good record. But also an attempt to recreate an atmosphere, perhaps: the damaged mannequin dominated everything.

At its feet was what looked like a cylindrical piece of wood, six inches long and perhaps a third of an inch in diameter, according to the scale. That was it. No, not quite. Johnson produced three close-up photos. The wood was ridged and hollow. What was almost certainly string trailed from one end. Johnson pointed to the blocked end. 'Most of the rest of it burnt. That bit didn't, for some reason.'

'So what did it smell of?' I asked. 'Ah,' I said, responding to the gleam in his eye, 'something with a distinctive smell. Like petrol of paraffin?'

'Like petrol or paraffin.'

'Did you know how paraffin got its name?' Chris asked, ultra-casually.

As a matter of fact, I did. Part of my long-ago degree had naturally involved a study of the history of the English language, and for some reason that bit had stuck. Johnson knew too, I guessed, but we both gaped eagerly at Chris.

'Because,' he said, 'it had *parum affinitas* – "little affinity" – with any other chemical substance known at the time.'

'It's a clever sort of invented word, isn't it?' Johnson observed, rather kindly.

'Anything else of interest you might be able to tell me about?' I asked, less kind. Well, I wasn't even sure about the accuracy of his Latin.

'Not yet. But I'll tell you what—' He stopped short; he'd nearly revealed something he shouldn't. 'The sooner the team can sort it, the better. If I'm not careful I'm going to lean over their shoulders and start to point. Like helping people on the train to solve a crossword or something,' he added. 'Or slotting pieces in someone else's jigsaw.'

Johnson laughed. 'There you are, Gaffer,' he said. 'You may have all those fancy pips on your uniform and be swanning round being a manager, but you mark my words: once a detective, always a detective.'

Chapter Six

Brian was already harassing Sheffield when I got in the next morning. I made myself tea, some of Ian's Earl Grey, and started on the post. Using the same system as before, I systematically sorted as I went. Nothing untoward, thank goodness. Perhaps the whole business had been a prank. OK, a pretty gross prank, but a prank all the same.

I certainly hoped so. The Bookfest needed only good publicity. Everything looked so promising. The advance bookings were higher than Brian had forecast in his initial business plan; the venues reported plenty of additional interest; the media were favourable. Oh, not the South-orientated broadsheets, which a couple of years back had contrived to ignore Brum's triumphant hosting of the G8 Economic Summit. But there was a distinct feeling that Birmingham was inching on to the literary map.

Today's job was to finalise the people who would introduce the speakers – the great and good of Birmingham who could speak with charm and authority about the writer in question. We'd got some university teachers – Birmingham is blessed with three universities, plus several within striking distance. We'd also brought in local councillors. So most presenters were in place already, but there were one or two gigs in awkward places or at awkward times which still needed someone.

When you've checked all the possible candidates, it's time to check the impossible ones. And to pull in favours. Now, if ever anyone owed me anything, it was my cousin Andy. He never admitted it but he was very bright, and, though his formal schooling was negligible, he'd contrived to turn himself into something of a polymath. He could read and speak fluently three European languages, and get by in a couple of African ones. He had a working knowledge of European history. His marriage to Ruth hadn't been as crazy as it might have seemed to outsiders at the time; in fact, she always pointed out that he was in many ways far better educated than she. But it had been a very romantic marriage. Perhaps I could, using devious arguments like that, persuade him to come to the launch of Marietta Coe's latest romantic novel and give it the buzz it was lacking at the moment. If I put the word round unofficially that Andy would be there, I was damned sure half the people who'd sneered at the poor woman at the board meeting would be panting for tickets. I might also use him to chair the discussion between two eminent scholars who'd produced rival books on the Arthurian legends. The ticket sales for that were scarcely in double figures. And yes, Andy did have enough expertise in that area to nudge the discussion along and invent questions if the floor failed to produce them. Would he be a box-office draw – or had I better keep quiet about the whole thing?

He responded to my e-mail almost as soon as I sent it. Yes, he said, he'd love to do both. But hadn't I better check with the writers that he was acceptable?

I would have done without his advice. Especially the Arthurian academics. To them I simply proposed the name

Andrew Rivers, a keen amateur. Neither demurred.

Marietta Coe picked up her phone first ring, but said nothing until I prompted her.

'I'm sorry. I was miles away.' She sounded as if she'd rather be.

Had I known her better, I'd have asked what the trouble was. For there clearly was trouble. Unless she was suffering from acute hay fever.

While she calmed down, I nattered about the Bookfest in general. She was not just having a formal drinkies launch, she was also giving readings in a number of branch libraries, so she would have a busy week.

'Is there any chance of a lift to these places?' she asked abruptly.

Shit! Not the sort of question you wanted from someone living within spitting distance of Brum. Nor from anyone, to be fair. Not with me as the chauffeuse, when I needed to do seventeen other things every day. And the budget wouldn't run to all those taxi fares – we couldn't get a cab firm to sponsor us! There was always Andy himself, of course. He knew Brum and the Black Country like the back of his hand, and he'd blithely announced his intention for staying for the whole Bookfest. At my house, of course.

'I can't guarantee to ferry you to them all,' I said, after too long a pause, while I found the right screen on my computer. 'But I'll do my best.' I thought so: her database entry clearly said she had her own transport. 'Certainly your launch,' I added more positively. 'You wouldn't want to sink champagne and then have to drive back to Sandwell.' Andy, on the other hand, often had non-drinking periods – he'd better make this one of them, hadn't he?

'Oh,' she said. 'Thank you.'

What I itched to ask was why she wasn't driving, but though I am – as Mike and Chris have both pointed out with varying degrees of kindness – incorrigibly nosy, even I couldn't ask point-blank what had happened to her car. Or to her, of course.

Perhaps now was the time to break to her who would be hosting her event.

She gave a little gasp. 'Andy Rivers! But I was in love with him when I was a kid. For years and years.'

Funny of course she came from the same part of the world as we did, but I'd never known a Marietta, in his circle or in mine – and, of course, the two tended to overlap.

'Really?' I giggled, in a neutral sort of way.

'Oh, not him really. Just pictures on my wall. I lived in Knowle then,' she added, as if that explained everything.

Maybe it did in a way.

We talked a while about copies of her novels being available for signing, and how she was getting on with her latest book. Not well, from what I gathered. Then she asked me about my role in the Bookfest. It almost seemed that she was prolonging the conversation.

'A volunteer!' she repeated. 'That means unpaid. Hell's bells – we should get you unionised.'

Warming to her immediately, I explained that my own trades union, NATFHE, was hardly involved in clerical work.

'NATFHE! So you teach at a college. So does my fiancé . . .'

And we were soon chatting like long-lost cousins. Yes, I was beginning to be pleased I'd waved a magic wand over her launch. Except I did rather wonder why the fiancé couldn't drive her once or twice, at least.

Ian looked very much as if he wanted a wand waved over

him. He'd never been asked, never offered to work regular hours; he was simply a consultant. But here he was, at nine fifty-nine, slinging his raincoat on to a hook and switching on the kettle as if he were a regular. He made his tea, and came and plonked himself in the spare chair in my office.

'Never get much tidier, do you, Sophie?' he observed sadly, looking at the piles.

'These will stack,' I said, irritated to be on the defensive, but suiting the deed to the word. 'And we don't have much filing space.'

He verified this with a steady look round the room. 'So long as those wall charts stay up you should be all right. I suppose all those colours mean something?'

They did. But this wasn't necessarily the moment to explain the system.

'How long will Brian be on the phone?'

I shrugged. 'Sheffield's always been a nuclear-free zone. I should think it'd like to be a phone-free one.' I explained about Myakovsky's visa problems.

'I've got to talk to him. Well, both of you,' he amended, with a grin. 'Anything useful I can do while I wait?'

I narrowed my eyes: 'How good is your handwriting? We've got all these envelopes to address to the Great and the Good.'

'Whatever happened to computer labels?'

'When the database should have been set up, they didn't give Brian any support to do it. In any case,' I added, 'some people prefer a hand-written invitation anyway. That,' I added, 'is presumably why Brian had them printed with spaces for their names.'

'Like wedding invitations,' Ian observed, looking at me over the reading glasses he'd fished out in readiness.

'Exactly so,' I said, passing him a pile of invitation cards, a list of addresses and a ballpoint. At last I relented. 'You'll be the first to know, as and when.'

'Strikes me,' he said, writing on the topmost card, 'that Mike'd like to do it properly, and you'd like to do it properly, but you're both too damned stubborn to admit it.'

'Has he said anything to you?'

'No. Nor have you. But I know you, young Sophie, and I certainly know you'd look nice in a pretty white dress carrying a bunch of roses.'

Brian's head, appearing round the door, spared me the necessity of a reply. I was grateful. A couple of days ago I could have managed an authentic denial. Today I wasn't so sure.

Ian opened his notebook in a way I'd seen many times before, though it had always been Chris the far side of the desk, nodding as he absorbed information and made judgements. Brian's nods didn't, I have to admit, carry the authority of Chris's, perhaps because he felt Ian had rather exceeded his authority.

'I told you,' he said a mite pettishly, 'that the Bookfest chair had it in mind to—'

'To contact publishers and authors? I've left that to him. When will he be reporting back, incidentally?'

I didn't quite see Martin Acheson 'reporting back'.

'All I've been doing is checking out your venues and having a quiet drink with one or two of my old mates.'

'Let me have a list of your expenses,' Brian said. He hadn't got the measure of Ian if he expected that to divert him.

'Now, they've come up with nothing on Helen Casper-Brook to suggest she's any specific enemies in the Midlands. Of course, all that stuff she – er – sings about isn't going to make her friends amongst men. Castration and what she'd like to do with the bits cut off,' Ian said, radiating disapproval. 'But I'd have thought the sort of bloke who saw her as – as a challenge to his manhood, shall we say? – would just simply go in there and rough her up. Not send a well-presented written warning.'

I nodded. 'So who would send it and why?'

Ian shrugged. 'Everyone's keeping their eyes and ears open. And I've been on the blower to a friend in the Met – see what he can dig up. Nothing yet, but give him time.'

'Time! We don't have time!'

Ian looked at Brian. 'He does have a day job, after all.'

'But this . . . The Bookfest—'

'As far as Vladimir Myakovsky's concerned, well, tap and his enemies hurl themselves out of the woodwork.' Ian counted on his fingers, still showing signs of all his hard work in his garden. 'He didn't endear himself to the Communist Old Guard when he got asylum and spilt some very well-informed beans about the system. He's not pleased the present regime with his refusals to return – he says it was better under Communism. The Russian Mafia don't like him for the same reason. Mossad wish him up a gumtree—'

'Mossad? What have the Israelis got against him?'

'Not Israelis so much as Zionists,' Ian said. 'You know, those who say there's only ever been one lot of people to suffer in history in general and the last war in particular. You tell that to my dad,' he said in parentheses. 'He was an ARP warden in Coventry. Anyway, this Myakovsky was supposed to be emigrating there, if you remember, only his mum wasn't Jewish so they turned him down. And then he started banging on about twenty million Russians dying in the war, and no one caring a toss for them. Which didn't endear him to people in the country across the Atlantic known to have won the war. So the CIA were a bit anti at one time.' He looked hard at Brian. 'Why on earth did you invite such a liability?'

'He's one of the world's greatest writers! That's why!'

'Fair enough. Anyway, one of my mates happened to have this little device about him.' He held up something his fingers dwarfed. 'We'll attach it to your phone – oh, don't worry, I've got one for yours, Sophie – and it'll activate this when you take a call.' He produced a tiny tape recorder. 'You'll have to wipe it every so often, but not if you get a call about Myakovsky,' he said, heavily ironic. He wiped the phone with his handkerchief and slipped the electronic – and presumably magnetic – whatnot into place. 'What we need now, of course, is a call to test it.'

As if on cue the phone rang.

Chapter Seven

The bathos of it! We were poised for dark threats in guttural voices. We got a swingeing rebuke in a cut-glass English one.

Brian covered the handset and mouthed, 'Councillor Burton.' It was quite unnecessary. We'd heard her announce herself at the start of her onslaught. The gist of it was that she had not been asked to introduce any of our speakers. Catching Ian's eye, I slipped out. At least Councillor Burton would be top of our pile of invitations. Ian followed.

I was head down, producing what passes in my case for calligraphy, when Brian filled the doorway.

'Well?' he shouted. 'What the fucking, cunting hell do you think you've been playing at?'

I'd never known him angry before, except with his own folly in mentioning money to the British authorities in America. But he wasn't going to lose his temper with me. I raised a warning finger to Ian, who hated that sort of language, especially in front of a woman, and most especially to a woman. But I didn't want him to leap to my defence. I'd had thirty-odd years of dealing with potential bullies my own way.

'I see: Councillor Burton is throwing a tantrum.' I leant back in my chair. 'Any reason why?'

'Plenty of reason why. She made it abundantly clear she wanted to chair some of our events. And no one has involved her in any of them. Since the person organising the chairing of events was you, I'm sure you'd like to explain why you've snubbed her.'

'Snubbed her?' I repeated coolly. 'I was desperate for her to chair some. Did she tell you about the seventeen messages I've left on her machine? Or the times I've tried to reach her mobile? Or about the e-mails clogging her system?'

Brian deflated, as quickly as he'd blown up. 'Or,' he nodded, 'the times she's failed to come to the board meeting without sending apologies. Not that it's the meetings that count, I suppose. After all, if you're a busy councillor you've probably got loads of other meetings to go to. It's what the members do between meetings.'

'Which in her case . . .?' I prompted.

'Is nil.'

Ian looked up. 'What's her gripe, then?'

'Councillors don't need reasons to gripe. Not when they're on all the committees that count. So we may have to reschedule some of the chairs.'

'For "we" read "me"? No way, Brian. I've persuaded and cajoled till I'm blue in the face and our phone bill is astronomical. I'm not unpicking all that just because some local politician wants to play the prima donna.'

'There's something else, isn't there, Brian?' Ian asked. His shrewd eyes missed very little.

'She wants us to cancel Myakovsky's suite at the Mondiale. Myakovsky is to stay with her. Well,' he flannelled, 'it would save us hundreds. And she does have a very nice place in Edgbaston.'

Ian raised an eyebrow.

'Champagne socialist,' I said tartly.

'As a matter of interest,' Ian asked quietly, 'did you agree that Myakovsky should stay with her?'

If I expected bluster, I got a simple caving in.

'Yes.'

Ian shook his head. 'Well, I hope she's got public liability insurance and a top-class security system. Otherwise this could be the most unwise decision you've ever made. I know it's no business of mine, Brian, but I really think you should reconsider.'

I'd promised Mike that however great the pressure, I'd always take a break for lunch, a promise I'd broken once already. It had taken nine months' absence from William Murdock for the gastritis to go away; there was no point in inviting it back again. So I emerged from the gloom of the office, via the Central Library itself, to the sunny amphitheatre of Chamberlain Square. I'd meant to buy something in the Edwardian Tea Room in the Art Gallery, but the sun called, however frail the ozone layer. Time to dig out my sun hat and SPF15. I strolled gently down New Street, remembering without affection the traffic-clogged days before pedestrianisation. I'd pick up a well-filled sandwich from Prêt-à-Manger or Costa Coffee – and then? Well, it might have been mad to go into Waterstone's, to be surrounded by books when I was involved in a whole festival of books. But after my life at William Murdock it was such a luxury to be able to read non-syllabus material I couldn't help exposing myself to temptation.

I don't know how long I stood and stared at the crime section. There must be dozens of books on those shelves devoted to locked room mysteries like Chris's. Their spines gave no clues, however. So I copped out. Buying a copy of an early Marietta Coe, I returned to the sun. There were no empty benches in New Street, nor in the nearby Cathedral Close. So I dawdled back to eat my sandwich at, as so many times in the past, my desk.

When Brian looked in, however, he found me not writing invitations, but staring into space. Or rather, at my memory of a charred circle occupied by a grotesquely twisted mannequin. How? Who? Why? And, of course, why did it interest me when it was nothing to do with me?

Brian was quiet all afternoon – seething, I rather thought, even if I wasn't quite sure at whom. His seethe could be felt even through the office wall. It occurred to me that on an afternoon like this I wasn't paid to be seethed at. There was a school on City Road that was hosting the storyteller. It wouldn't hurt to find out what they'd placed at her disposal. I blade him a blithe farewell and headed for the car park.

OK, who was I kidding? Him, maybe, but not myself. I might be looking at a school, but I was certainly heading in the direction of Smethwick, and Chris's police station. The visit took little more than ten minutes, in which I established that the woman needed parking space, space to work, space to rest and space to eat. And food to eat. Water. All the appurtenances of civilisation beyond the means of most state schools, including, probably, this.

Before I left what they optimistically referred to as their campus, I phoned Chris to invite myself to share his afternoon cup of tea. He didn't sound surprised to hear from me. 'But what's this, Sophie? Using your mobile phone! I thought you counted how many brain cells each call cost you!'

That was rich, considering it was his colleagues who had given it to me.

'And how much money each call costs me. Trouble is, I really need one for the Bookfest,' I said. 'See you soon.' And I switched him off.

In truth, of course, the case was nothing to do with him. Operational commanders are too concerned with budgeting, staffing, resourcing, liaising with other units and generally managing the whole caboodle to be dealing with the minutiae of everyday crime. It was his job merely to see that the people he'd delegated to were coping with whatever was on their desk.

But Chris was a detective. Once a detective, as his SOCO colleague had observed, always a detective.

Because of security, I could never just breeze in. Not these days. But I was still a privileged visitor, Chris and his colleagues escorting me to places in theory I shouldn't have gone to. Not that I was ever left alone anywhere, except for very rare occasions like today, when Chris waved at me a hand indicating three minutes' absence and dashed out, leaving me in his room. My own sense of honour always forbade me to look at anything except the photos on the walls.

And, today, at an inviting afternoon tea – scones, cakes and sausage rolls – left on the meetings table he was so proud of. Bridget had been doing what she saw as her job. To hell with the fact that her word-processing showed a knowledge of the computer the envy of a woman half her age, that her filing was exemplary: the woman could cook. For cakes and scones she could cook me out of the kitchen. Chris would miss her when she retired. Yes, the paragon of culinary and office virtue was to retire back to Dublin, to make, as she declared, her fortune in a guest house. The question vexing everyone was who would replace her.

Everyone except me. At least, at the moment.

I was too busy pondering the hollow tube, the string smelling of paraffin, and the burnt dress. Pulling Chris's blotter towards me, I'd drawn a little picture of a sealed room with a model on a plinth when I noticed there was one there already. Oh, yes, Chris was as fascinated as I was. His perspective was slightly different from mine – more from above. I'd decided to try from lower down, as if I were squinting through something. Something like a letter box.

Of course. How stupid of me. And I wouldn't mind betting I was three steps behind the police and fire services.

But how would you get the tube and the string through the letter box?

A little experimentation was called for. The materials were within reach, on the top of the desk.

Fortunately the pencil landed harmlessly at Chris's feet.

'What on earth . . .?' he demanded, closing the door and staring.

'Seeing how far I can blow a pencil through a paper tube,' I said, twirling the tube.

He picked up the pencil, a grin lighting the whole of his face. Yes, we were on the same wavelength.

'It depends on the diameter of the tube, of course,' I said. 'Too tight and it sticks, too loose and it stays put.'

'So if you strike a happy medium—'

'And nearly a superintendent!'

'—it'll fly – what, two yards? Not far enough, I'm afraid.

Letter box to plinth is nearer four yards. And you've got to get the direction right. Not easy with rolled paper.'

'A blow pipe?' I suggested.

'Possibly. One thing Philip's found is a tiny notch in the end of the Rawlplug.'

'Rawlplug!'

'Yes. They identified it this morning.'

I mimed cutting a notch in the end of the pencil. We smiled at each other. I mimed fitting the notch into taut string. He mimed shooting an arrow. We shared a high-five.

'It'd be even nicer if this bod from the fire investigation team hadn't come to the same conclusion half an hour ago,' Chris said. 'Cup of tea? You can see I've at last managed to train Bridget to give me hot water and separate tea bags. I'd had enough of that tooth enamel-stripping brew of hers. Too many plants were dying from the dregs.'

I pricked my ears, ignoring his digression. 'There's another expert involved? You're throwing an awful lot of resources at a simple case of vandalism.'

He wasn't to be drawn, and poured me a cup anyway. 'It's intriguing, isn't it? It engages the part of the mind engaged by crossword puzzles. Actually, we got a few more letters in the grid this morning. Philip Johnson had another look round then: there's a tiny triangle of smoke on the letter box.'

'I suppose – thanks! – that it isn't possible to ID paraffin?' The tea was indeed a vast improvement.

'Funnily enough, it isn't. Any more than you can tell what octane petrol a sample is.' He gave a self-deprecating grin. 'I hope I sound authoritative; it's what I picked up from the FIT guy. What you can pick up is any contaminants. So if the paraffin's been stored in a contaminated can, you can prove a relationship between them. But only if.'

I nodded. 'So what you're looking for is a man with a tiny bow and arrow and a contaminated paraffin can. Easy.'

His face was serious again.

'And?' I prompted. 'Or is the "and" something you can't tell me about?'

'Not yet. Not yet. I'm sure it'll come out into the open all too soon. But until it does . . .'

'No problems.' I helped myself to a sinful sausage roll. The pastry was so light it exploded everywhere. I sat down at the table to minimise damage.

'And the Bookfest?' He joined me, sitting at a slight angle to reduce the formality.

With a sympathetic audience, I could lose my temper good and proper over the irritations of the wretched Councillor Burton.

He was roaring with laughter by the time I'd finished. 'They're all the bloody same, aren't they? I mean, the strife I get from elected representatives. But,' he said, his face serious, 'what I can't understand is why you should be taking all this shit.'

'CV-building and nonconformist work ethic, in almost equal measures. Plus my grandfather's dictum that if a job's worth doing it's worth doing well. And anything's a bit of a rest after William Murdock.'

He nodded, almost as if I'd convinced him. 'But what if you walked out when this Brian character yells?'

'He's only ever yelled once, and that was on the principle of the office boy coming home and kicking the cat. He didn't yell long. And I was in yell-repellent mode, so it couldn't have been very satisfying.'

'Yell-repellent?' he asked, grinning.

The phone rang. He sprang to answer it. His face became

serious, then concerned. 'Act, and we'll worry about budgets later,' he said. Replacing the handset, he looked at me. 'Missing child,' he said, already ushering me to the door.

Chapter Eight

In other circumstances I might have watched the local news programmes to discover the details of the child's disappearance, but Mike had come home, and had his first century of the season to celebrate, which we did in a highly satisfactory if essentially private way. It was too late to go out for a celebratory meal – we'd postpone that till the following evening. I did manage a quick scan of Ceefax, but apart from a house fire in Wednesbury there were no tragic or dramatic news items. Maybe if Mike hadn't been home I'd have phoned Chris at this point. But though the two men got on reasonably well in public, there was a constraint between them. Mike was uneasy about the big part Chris had played in my past; Chris unwilling to relinquish me to a new love. It was better to push neither down the other's throat. It might seem duplicitous to phone Chris from work the following morning: I preferred to see it as tactful.

By the time I'd left a message with Bridget, Brian was once more haranguing someone, presumably in Sheffield. Time for the post. I opened it carefully these days, saving no stamps, destroying no envelopes till I'd read the letter inside. If the threat against Stonkin Mama had been genuine, I reckoned there'd be one more at least: whoever it was would surely want to make sure his or her message got home. Like Brian and his mission to persuade Sheffield to speed up Myakovsky's visa.

When the phone rang, I answered it almost absently. 'Big Brum Bookfest office.' Then I remembered I was supposed to be charming the punters in. 'Sophie Rivers here. Can I help you?'

'Ah, Ms Rivers,' said the voice at the other end, 'Martin Acheson here. I wonder if you could check Brian's diary and let me know if he'll be free today. We need to talk about the death threats.'

Hmph. So where had he got the idea I was Brian's PA? He knew I was a volunteer, didn't he? But perhaps he thought I'd volunteered as a handmaiden.

'Why don't I put you through to Brian?' I asked, but not unpleasantly. 'I think his line's free now.'

Within seconds Brian appeared at my door, clutching his Psion thingy. 'Look,' he said in a stage whisper, 'I can't be in two places at once, and now I'm supposed to be in three!'

'You should have worked at William Murdock,' I said. 'It was *de rigueur* there. OK, what's the problem?'

'There's this interview at Pebble Mill – Radio WM. And there's a chance of a last-minute sponsor. And now Acheson wants a meeting.'

'I can do the sponsor while you do the BBC. Acheson isn't God. He'll have to wait his turn.'

'But it's about the death threats.'

'Fine. But he'll still have to work round the BBC. If we don't get publicity we don't get punters. Are you supposed to be going to him or is he supposed to be coming here?'

He spread his hands.

'If he's coming here, then divert him to the Midland Arts

Centre. It's only two minutes from Pebble Mill. It's a lovely day. You can have your nice confidential chat with only the geese to overhear.' No Sophie, either, bother it, to strengthen Brian's resolve.

'What about you?'

Ah-ha. That was better. 'Why me? I'm talking to this new sponsor, aren't I?'

'Acheson wants you there as well.'

Did he, by God.

'Where's the sponsor based?'

He flourished a scrap of paper. A solicitor with a couth address in Edgbaston.

'I might just make it,' I said. 'But you can't hurry sponsors, especially ones volunteering to come in at this late stage. Why not simply tell him we'll just have to meet later? We could close the office at four thirty and beetle over to him then.'

Brian looked as if he was trying not to wet himself.

'Problems?' I asked.

He grimaced. 'More ferrying.'

I suppressed a sigh. This was a new man, with the right attitude. Women had been under pressure like this for years.

'Your car's here, is it?'

'Elly can't manage without it.'

'For Christ's sake, Brian, couldn't she take a mini-cab? Or pull in a favour from a neighbour? And – hell! You haven't still got Acheson hanging on the phone? Go and tell him five and we'll sort the kids and their transport later.'

So how would the kids feel about being ferried round Brum by a man in a car declaring he was a Warwickshire cricketer? It was either him or Ian, and I wasn't sure quite how keen Ian would be to do that sort of favour for Brian.

I was just about to ring Mike to cajole him into offering

when there was a noise in the outer office. A woman and child had arrived. Brian would still be talking to Acheson so I popped out.

'Where's Brian?' the woman demanded. This must be Elly, his wife. She was in her mid-thirties, sharply dressed. Her skin was so dry that if she wasn't careful those anxious lines would soon be etched permanently and deeply round her eyes and mouth.

'In his office. Hang on – he's taking an important call.'

'Oh, he won't mind me. Come on, Tabs.'

Hell, if I was treated like a PA, I could act like one. 'No, let him finish the call, please. It's terribly important we don't upset the caller.' I stood between her and Brian's door.

The child – a girl of about four, dressed in blue dungarees and pink sparkling plastic sandals – set up a wail for her daddy. Her mother glared at me.

'Don't be ridiculous. What's your name?'

'Sophie Rivers. And you're—'

'Ah, the woman who's supposed to be helping. That's what you'd better do then, isn't it? Help.'

I put on my useful and obliging face, but steeled myself to be neither. 'How?'

She seemed taken aback by the monosyllable. She looked at her watch. Tabs, released from her mother's grip, bounced experimentally on the sagging chair. I tapped on Brian's door and shoved my head round it. He'd just finished his call. What I'd have liked to say, in the best tradition of secretaries I'd seen on film, was 'Your wife, Mr Fairbrother'. But was she wife or was she partner?

Whatever, she was fuming and she was in the room. I left them to it.

Tabs was nowhere to be seen. Hell! My post!

It could have been worse. She hadn't drawn on anything vital, and she hadn't stabbed herself on the paperknife. So what had she been doing that had kept her so quiet? It seemed to me that the best place for her was with her parents. I took her through, and returned to the post.

Despite my efforts to ignore them, the sounds of her parents' colloquy were unmistakable. The general tenor was that Brian was to take charge of the apparently ailing Tabs for the day. He, quite rightly, said he couldn't. She, quite rightly, said she couldn't take her into court with her. I played dumb. This was one job I wasn't about to volunteer for.

My phone rang; it was for Brian. I thought of putting it through, just to make a point and to help him make one to his wife. But it was quicker to deal with the problem myself, so I did just that.

So what did parents do when they had a sick child? One of them ought to be able to take time off. But what if there was no one else they could ask to do their job? Presumably magistrates got ratty if the defence solicitor announced an outbreak of toothache and asked for an adjournment. And today the Bookfest simply couldn't manage without both Brian and me. Could it? If I got on the phone and talked hard, I might be able to reschedule stuff. Which would mean Brian doing his job and me coping with Tabs. A consummation devoutly to be avoided.

My God how would I have coped as a single mother with Steph?

I stepped up my sympathy. Strapping a smile to my face I went into Brian's office. While the altercation took place around her ears, Tabs was quietly taking the phone apart. I removed it from her grasp. Before I could attempt some quick repair work, Tabs tried to bite me, howling when I restrained her. I had a feeling neither of us would enjoy it if I were her nanny for the day.

'It seems to me,' I said, when comparative order had been restored, 'that if I could reschedule some of Brian's important meetings, and go in his place to a couple of others, then Brian could take Tabs to the doctor, collect the antibiotics or whatever, and drop her back in school. She doesn't seem feverish, does she? But there are some things he simply has to do. Meanwhile,' I added, while that sank in, 'I'll get on the phone to a couple of my ex-students; offer them a little work experience – provided the budget runs to paying their expenses too. Which it may, of course, provided we get this sponsorship.' My voice became very meaningful.

They were still undecided. I passed Brian the phone. 'Why don't you call the surgery and talk your way in?'

The phone rang in my office. I scuttled back. A guttural voice warned me that if Myakovsky came to Birmingham he and all who sheltered him would die. The message should have activated Ian's little tape recorder. But the microphone had been removed from the handset.

Ian dropped everything and shot into the city, still wearing, as it happened, his gardening shoes. Putting down his Earl Grey, he sucked his teeth thoughtfully.

'How authentic,' he asked me slowly, 'would you say the accent was?'

'It was so thick it sounded like some cut-price actor on a cheap ad for vodka,' I said.

'The accent may be fake but does that make the message fake too?' He balanced on one finger the phone gizmo I'd retrieved from Tabs' pocket. 'I thought the adhesive for these things was pretty effective. Proof against most things.'

Without speaking I passed him the one from Brian's phone too.

Before he could say anything, there was a cheerful call from the lobby. 'Sophie! Sophie?'

'Come on in, Tasleen,' I called.

Ian's gloomy features lit up as she came in. As well they might. As a devout Muslim, she covered her hair and wore long skirts. But her walk was so decisive and her eyes so alert, anyone could tell she meant business. She'd had glandular fever in the run-up to her A levels, so she was now working for resits to improve her grades. Provided she got them, she was promised a place at Warwick University to study Law.

'Tasleen's already had experience of working in an office,' I told Ian, as they shook hands. 'She spent some time with Afzal Mohammed.'

'That young solicitor guy? Decent bloke.'

'Absolutely. So she'll be looking after the office while I'm out. Could you tell her about the phone calls and about the gizmo? Because I'm expecting Una Davies.'

Tasleen's face lit up. 'Una? The Afro-Caribbean woman from William Murdock?'

'The same.'

'Great! But I thought she was up in Sheffield doing International Politics or something.'

'Her mother died in October. She had to come home to sort everything out.'

'That'd be Una. But what about uni?'

'Birmingham University are offering her a place next year. It'll be tough, holding the family together and studying, of course—'

'If anyone can do it, Una can.'

The lobby door opened. Una sauntered straight through into

the office. All six foot of her. Her beaded braids clacking, she bent to hug the much shorter Tasleen, and then me, the shortest. I smiled to myself. There'd been, according to Brian, a great deal of angst from the board members about equal opportunities. Well, I wouldn't argue about that. And if any of them were to turn up today they'd see how it had been taken to heart.

'Right,' Una said, 'point me at this work.'

'Tell you what, Sophie,' said Ian, clearly impressed, 'why don't I make a cup of tea for everyone while you explain what's what?'

Chapter Nine

So far, so good. I'd persuaded Brian to return his car to the family home for his wife's use only after his appearance on Radio WM. He'd sounded good: I'd listened on my car radio as I headed to Moseley myself to collect him. We'd then pick our way across various unpleasant roads to the Black Country, and if I was feeling especially generous I'd run him back to Moseley after the meeting. If I wasn't, he'd have to take the bus from my house in Harborne. And another bus. And maybe a third. His problem. This was Friday, and tomorrow was the weekend and I was going to have a wonderful indulgent time watching Mike play at Edgbaston. And bother the Big Brum Bookfest.

'So how did the sponsorship meeting go?' he enquired, in the breathy tones of one who has successfully broadcast to the nation – at least the part of it living in the Midlands.

Had I not been negotiating the Russell Road-Wake Green Road island – no fun when you want to go towards Edgbaston and all the traffic wants to go to Kings Heath right across your bows – my tones might have been breathy too. Our new sponsors, far from being red-braced professionals doing cocaine and not much else, had proved enthusiastic and generous.

'We now have a sponsored car,' I announced. 'It's a joint venture with a Mazda garage and these solicitors. They rent the car for the duration of the Bookfest, and loan it to us. They fix the insurance and everything. So long as we blazon their names and the Mazda people's all over it. If the Bookfest runs next year' – I must remember not to volunteer! – 'they want to be in right at the start.'

'A sponsored car,' he said doubtfully.

'It'll certainly solve you and your partner's problems,' I said. Why this lack of enthusiasm? 'With transporting the kids. How is Tabs, by the way?'

'The GP's useless,' Brian declared. 'Couldn't find anything wrong with her. But her temperature was very high this morning.'

I wondered where he'd taken it and with what. Andy had learnt the effect of a cup of breakfast tea on a thermometer very early in his life. And taught me.

'Anyway, she seemed a bit better, and she was very upset when I said I didn't think she'd be able to go to her swimming lesson tonight, so I took her into school. I've phoned a couple of times to make sure everything's OK.'

After a nightmare journey along the A4123 (loads of traffic backed up from lights with the bonus of extensive roadworks) I slotted my Clio in Acheson's water-filter factory car park into the slot reserved for the general manager, who, like most of the senior management, appeared to have knocked off in time to beat the motorway rush. Not that they'd necessarily succeed. The M5's junction with the M6 regularly makes the national travel news, it clogs up so thickly and so frequently – and, come to think of it, sometimes so inexplicably.

The security guard locked up behind us, keeping us in the

foyer while he phoned for permission to take us up to Acheson's office; no doubt the frosty secretary had left for the weekend too. Well, I suppose unsocial hours were part of Brian's contract. But I wouldn't have minded a bit of payment for my overtime. At least a bit of gratitude. I thought I'd done really well to swing that sponsored car, and Brian's response had made underwhelming look excessive.

The guard put the phone down and tried again. Then a third time. Just as he was walking across to us with the obvious intention of returning us to the maelstrom, Acheson walked through the front door. He nodded pleasantly at the guard.

'I'll take them up myself,' he said. 'Delayed in a meeting,' he said to us, over his shoulder.

Acheson was miffed, there was no doubt about that. Perhaps it was at Brian's cavalier attitude to the phone this morning, or perhaps at our – well, *my* – insistence that we honour our existing commitments. But he was courtesy itself, if cool courtesy, pressing us not to tea but to G&Ts and whisky. Perhaps Water-filter Man couldn't manage kettles. He could certainly manage spirits, even if he did have to slip from the room for a new bottle of whisky.

My interest in widgets and gromits exhausted last visit, I looked around for other things to occupy me: a hint whether he was married, for instance, or what sports he liked. No clues on his unnaturally tidy desk, however.

He breezed into the room, the amount in Brian's glass amazing me. I was glad I'd settled for the merest dash of gin in a long glass full of tonic.

'Have we had any further communications?' Acheson asked me as he fiddled with ice.

'A phone call this morning. From someone with a heavy accent, possibly genuine.'

'Now, you told me Brian, that this ex-policeman was going to fit up some listening device. Has he? Did it work?'

It was vital to stop Brian going into bluster mode. 'There was a small technical error,' I said, 'to do with adhesive. But it's now been rectified. The message was the same as before, with the possible addition of a threat against anyone giving him shelter. So the Mondiale—'

'Or Councillor Burton,' Brian interjected.

'—ought in all fairness to be told.'

'What's this about Councillor Burton?' Acheson demanded.

'She would prefer to offer Myakovsky accommodation at her home,' I said deadpan.

'It would save the Bookfest a great deal of money,' Brian put in, too eagerly.

'I doubt if that was in her mind when she suggested it,' Acheson said drily. He caught my eye and smiled with sudden warmth, surprising a giggle from me. 'Have you met this woman?' he asked.

I shook my head.

Brian said, 'She's terribly charming, terribly enthusiastic.'

'And terribly not there when you want her,' I added. Shit. I'd intended to be a model of discretion.

It was Acheson's turn to laugh. 'Like when there's any work to be done. Still, it must be hard trying to be a conscientious councillor – doesn't she represent quite a tough ward? – and to pull your weight in something like this.'

It was out before I could stop it. 'You manage to be very hands on. And,' I added less gushily, 'to work very long hours. And think of the time Brian puts in – he must be violating every European directive there is.'

'There's this thing called motivation, isn't there, Sophie? This festival is fulfilling my dream. Brian's too, probably. For other people – I'm all too aware of this – it's a means of bringing themselves to the notice of people they perceive as important. Half of the people on that board don't even read books. But they know it would make a good CV item.'

I blushed.

'Is that why you got involved? Well, it seems to me you're working every bit as hard as if you were on a proper contract. In fact, I'd like us to have a word about that sometime, Brian. When we've thrashed out this Russian business, perhaps. How would you like to proceed with it?'

The neatest way out, of course, was for Myakovsky not to get his visa and for his events simply to be cancelled. Except Brian had invested far too much energy and phone time for me even to say that.

I batted back the question. 'How do he and his publishers want to deal with it? I'm sure they have a view. And Stonkin Mama's, of course.'

He snorted with laughter. 'They've put it back to us, of course. Local advice about the local situation. But they have intimated they'd rather have a live novelist than a dead one. Apart from anything else, he's got what they call a three-book deal, and he's only delivered the first. As for Stonkin Mama, the lady seems . . . I don't know, abstracted. I'd have thought, in her circumstances—' He broke off, shaking his head. 'What does your ex-policeman say?'

'He's talking off the record to colleagues up here and down in the Met,' Brian said in a rush, as if conscious he'd not played much part in the conversation for a while. He'd gone terribly pale, come to think of it. 'Until we get something positive, I still think we should treat everything cautiously – assume they're hoax calls, but make . . . arrangements.'

'What sort of arrangements?' Acheson asked.

The instant glaze over Brian's eyes made me jump in. 'The police are as good at preventing crime as they are at detecting it. I'm sure an official approach to the police for a discussion with a crime prevention officer—'

'Surely not. When I was burgled, I had a crime prevention officer round – some dumpy middle-aged woman with ads for window catches,' Acheson said.

'There are CPOs and CPOs,' I said darkly, hoping to goodness I was right. 'Ian Dale will point us in the right direction. And if he can't, I've got another contact.' Chris of course. He'd certainly come up with the goods.

'Why on earth should he drag us all the way over here just for that?' I demanded, as I let us into a surprisingly hot, stuffy car. 'He could have done that on the phone with you in five minutes flat.'

'God knows,' Brian collapsed on the front seat. 'Jesus Christ. Why did I ever take on this job?'

I shot a look at him: he was grey. 'Why did you?' I asked, pulling into the traffic.

'Well, it's a job, of course. And there aren't all that many around, if you prefer to work freelance. I'd done that stuff for Coventry, and then I set up those big events for the National Trust. But Elly said all that working away from home wasn't on, and I can quite see why.'

So could I.

'I've worked my bloody socks off, you know. Six- and seven-day weeks. Ten- and twelve-hour days. And now this. Now this.' His voice broke.

It dawned on me, rather belatedly, that his behaviour over the last few days might have been sloppy not because he wasn't working hard enough but because he'd been working too hard, too long, with too little support. Afzal had hinted as much, come to think of it. Certainly the too little support. I felt a surge of guilt. I'd better drive him all the way back home.

'You're not going in tomorrow, are you?' I asked.

He was sweating badly. 'Can't not, really.'

'Come on, why are you going in? Really?'

There was a long silence.

I broke it. 'Brian, you're on your knees, aren't you? You've got to recoup some energy for the Bookfest itself. Come on. This time next week you'll be straightening your tie ready for the reception.'

'Could you stop the car a minute?'

I found a bus lay-by and stopped. Just in time. He opened the car door and threw up.

I should have been round there, holding his head! I got out, got as far as putting my hand on his arm. But he pushed me away and leant against someone's front wall to finish the job. At this point my mobile phone rang. Not ungrateful, I took the call.

'Sophie! I never expected you to answer straight away.'

Chris: an opportunity to make a virtuous point. 'I happened to be off the road when you rang.'

'Good. Now, this Bookfest thing – how deeply are you involved?'

I looked at Brian's bent back.

'Deeply.'

'OK. I'd like to talk to you, soon as you can make it. OK, not me, but Harvinder and Peter.'

Brian seemed to be returning to the vertical.

'I've actually got the Bookfest director with me at the moment,' I said, 'but he's not very well.'

'I think – if he's up to it – he should come too. When?'

I looked at my watch and at Brian, who was leaning on the car door. 'Say fifteen-twenty minutes if the traffic's not bad. Is that OK, Brian?' I added. He managed to nod.

'I knew I could rely on you,' Chris said.

That was the trouble: he did rely on me, didn't he? That was why, instead of leaving Harvinder or Peter to call me he'd done it himself.

Sad – for Chris was a dear friend, after all – I waited till Brian had hauled himself into the car and set off for Smethwick.

'It's just something I do when I'm stressed,' Brian said irritably. 'You've heard the expression, "It makes me sick". That's what it does. Literally. The day of the interview I threw up in the gents. Just missed Acheson's shoes.'

'And you still got the job! What do you take for it?'

'Oh, it's not worth bothering the doctor.'

'Oh?' I had to say it. 'So it's worth taking a skiving tot to the doctor when she's probably used the thermometer to stir your tea, but it's not worth taking yourself, though you have very real symptoms?'

'What do you mean, "skiving tot"?'

'Forget it.'

'No. I won't forget it. You're implying my daughter was lying!' He was getting redder and redder in the face, a muscle twitching below one eye.

'I don't think children of that age lie,' I said evasively. He was clearly near an edge and I didn't want to push him over it. 'But I can see that you're ill. And I can also see that all the hospitality associated with the Bookfest could cause you problems.' Not to mention the rest of us, if he threw up with as little warning as that.

'I shall be all right.'

I drove a little further. 'What are you afraid of, Brian? That's often the reason people don't see their GP. Because they're afraid they'll hear bad news. I wouldn't go even when I was passing out with the pain of my gastritis because I was convinced I had cancer.' It had never entered my head, to be honest, but the big C always got people going.

'There's no time—'

'If you like, I'll pop in tomorrow, just to make sure everything's OK, while you go to the doctor. And if there's anything to do, you can always come in later. How about that?'

I pulled up outside Piddock Road police station. The flush of his anger had subsided, leaving him very pale indeed.

Chapter Ten

Detective Sergeant Harvinder Singh Mann collected us from reception, greeting me with the friendly kiss we'd got into the habit of exchanging, and shaking hands with Brian, whom he looked at with some concern.

'How's Suky?' I asked, as he ushered us into Peter Kirby's office. I'd missed their wedding back in the spring when I was with Mike in Oz, but Mike and I had since shared a couple of evenings out with them. Suky – short for Sukhvinder – was a physio specialising in sports injuries, who clearly adored Harvinder almost as much as he adored her. I'd been very apprehensive for them – two very Westernised people agreeing to an arranged marriage – but they'd done what Mike and I had done: fallen in love at first sight.

'Fine. And Mike?'

I clapped a hand to my mouth: we were supposed to be going out, weren't we? For that wonderful meal! 'I'd better make a phone call, if you don't mind.'

Mike wasn't pleased, but was understanding. He'd phone the restaurant to put back the booking. And he'd nip round to my house to meet me there, to save time. As we disconnected, I knew I was in a relationship with a prince among men.

Harvinder and Brian had been chatting quietly. As I finished my call, in walked Peter Kirby, once my least favourite detective inspector, but now much mellowed. Or perhaps it was I who had mellowed. Whichever, he took one look at Brian, sat him down and suggested some tea. 'Maybe even some of that vile herbal brew of yours, Harv.'

Brian agreed quietly that herbal tea would be fine. I settled for water from the chiller.

As we sat down round Peter's desk, I looked at my watch. 'We've all got homes to go to, remember,' I said, catching his eye.

He grinned: his marriage had teetered horribly on the brink but was somehow surviving. 'I'll be brief. Have either of you had any threats, either to you personally or, more likely, to any of the writers you've invited to your festival?'

Why on earth was he asking us that? The Bookfest was a Birmingham festival, not on his patch at all. And of course, he'd never worked with Ian. They were based at quite different stations and would have no reason to know each other. So he wouldn't be on Ian's list of useful contacts to talk to.

'We've had what I took to be hoax calls,' Brian said, sipping something loosely connected with hedgerows.

'But took them seriously enough to refer them to the artists' publishers and to Ian Dale. He used to be one of Chris's sergeants before Chris got promoted here,' I added.

'May I ask who was threatened?'

'A woman called Helen Casper-Brook, known to the music world as Stonkin Mama. And Vladimir Myakovsky.'

Peter whistled. 'Very big name. Very big name indeed for Brum.'

'Peter's a southerner,' I said parenthetically to Brian, 'who believes civilisation stops at Watford.'

To my surprise, Brian managed a pale grin. 'It stops before there: have you never seen Watford Junction?'

'So you've pulled in one of the world's leading poets and novelists and someone doesn't like it?'

'Someone with a very heavy Russian accent, so heavy I'd say it might even be faked,' I said, suddenly positive. 'Unfortunately the tape we tried to make of the second call – thanks to Ian and some surveillance equipment – didn't work. The fault has been rectified,' I added.

'Knowing you, Sophie, I could guarantee it would be,' Peter said. 'Now, no threats to anyone else?'

I shook my head. So did Brian.

'Such as who?' I asked. If Peter had got us all the way over to Smethwick on a hot afternoon, he might at least give us the guff.

Peter shook his head. 'It's still under wraps.'

Still under wraps? It was the thing that was worrying Chris, wasn't it? So it was something to do with the wedding dress fire. How on earth could that be connected to our threats? To the Bookfest? With Brian there, however, I couldn't ask. When Chris had shown me the burnt wedding dress, he'd done so knowing he could trust me to mention it to no one else.

'What we want you to do is be extra vigilant,' Harvinder said. 'Who checks the post?'

'Me. And henceforth, two of my ex-students, very bright women.'

Peter shook his head. 'Henceforth, not ex-students but Sophie, I'm afraid. And we may send someone along to make sure your taping device doesn't let us down again.'

'It won't,' Brian said, face grim.

'All the same—'

'You're welcome to check,' I said. 'And what about the

security of the venues, and so on? It's one of the things that's worrying us.'

'I'd like a list of all your venues, please. And who's reading there. And when. We'll take responsibility for the venues for – for the writers we're interested in,' Peter concluded lamely.

'This *is* serious, isn't it?' I asked, trying to persuade my hot Friday afternoon brain to recall which writers lived in Smethwick and which might be eligible for a wedding dress. And failing.

He met my eye and nodded. 'Very.' He turned slightly, but not obviously, to Brian. 'So you will understand we want your absolute co-operation. Even if you feel it's impinging on –' he groped for a phrase – 'artistic integrity or whatever. Absolute co-operation. OK?'

I shouldn't imagine many people would have failed to nod seriously. Brian nodded seriously. And clutched his mouth.

'Get him to the loo, quick,' I yelled, leaping to open the door. The problem was, when people threw up, I always wanted to come out in sympathy.

While Harvinder was acting as ministering angel, I had a quick word with Peter.

'I wasn't joking about getting home early. Mike isn't as committed to the Bookfest as I am, and in the cricket season we see little enough of each other. And I did promise I'd take Brian back to Moseley and that'll make me even later.'

He nodded. 'That's shorthand for not wanting to fuck up like I nearly fucked up?'

'Right.'

'Why don't you shoot off now? I'll get Harv to run Brian home. He lives out Hall Green way. It'll mean he gets to see his missus tonight too. You know she's . . .' He gestured a curved belly.

'Bloody hell! That was quick.'

'Biological clock, I gather. But it's a hell of a thing – a kid and a bride you hardly know. Ah!' There were voices in the corridor. He touched his lips.

'Exactly how long do you intend to stay in the office tomorrow?' Mike demanded, thumping a pillow into submission.

'About ten minutes,' I said truthfully. 'Just to check if there are any vital messages or anything – suspicious – in the post.'

He put his hand on my cheek. 'Suspicious doesn't mean unidentified parcels that have to be blown up? God, I was so scared when you got that one and I was so far away.' He pulled me on to his chest, stroking my hair.

'I promise it doesn't. And I promise that if I find anything bulky and suspicious, I'll do what I did when you were in Oz – be exceedingly careful. Anyway, I can't be long because I want to see you play.'

'You promise you won't be long?'

'Promise.'

'In that case, Ms Rivers, why don't I run you into town? And wait for you? And then escort you to the ground?'

I pulled back to look at him. 'Mike, there's only one thing I'd like more.'

He looked anxious. 'What?'

'This,' I said, showing him.

The Bristol Road – we might have started the evening from my house but we'd ended at Mike's – was almost empty when we set out for the city centre at twenty to nine. It was pouring with rain, but the forecast promised sunny intervals later in the day. They weren't likely to get a full day's play, were they?

The post had arrived just as we left the house, so I started leafing through the latest batch of estate agents' bumf. Both Mike and I had put so much effort into restoring our respective houses, we thought we should make equal sacrifices, and sell them both to pay for one new to us both. Till we found the elusive perfect place, we had a haphazard existence commuting between the two. At least I was still able to keep an eye on Aggie's house. My next-door neighbour had at last committed herself to moving into sheltered accommodation, down near her favourite granddaughter in Evesham. Her house was now empty, a For Sale board outside. I kept the garden tidy, if not as immaculate as Aggie would have liked.

'Anything promising?' Mike asked.

'Plenty suitable way out of the city; plenty unsuitable in the right locations.' I turned to him, watching his profile as he drove. Why couldn't I say what I wanted to say, that I'd like to snap my fingers at all our sensible decisions and simply move in with him? But that would lay me open to being rejected: he might not want to make room for my favourite furniture and pictures, since his house was complete in itself. And why couldn't I tell him too that I'd like a white wedding with every trimming going?

At the Bookfest offices I tapped our code into the security locks that guarded the place overnight and let us in. We were greeted by a good thick pile of post and several messages on the official answerphone. In Tasleen's rather curly handwriting was a list of queries they hadn't felt competent to deal with. While I sat in Brian's office and played the answerphone back, Mike made us coffee. Then he settled down in my room to check the post, using a variant of my system: a pot for stamps (yes, I'd trained him that far); rubbish; things for Sophie to check.

A low whistle told me there was something for me to check immediately.

He held out a sheet of paper to me. 'Your Stonkin Mama fan,' he said.

I read it without touching it. 'It's a bit more specific than the last one.'

'What did you say Peter Kirby's phone number was?'

Of course the police should be told. The clean white laser-printed note was what one might call sexually explicit, involving more words of Anglo-Saxon origin than occur in the average biological description. It was almost like hearing one of her anti-male raps turned round.

'I'll phone while you check the rest, shall I?' he asked.

'Hang on – have you torn the stamp off the envelope yet?'

Grinning, he passed me a white A4 envelope. The label was computer generated. 'This is my system, not yours,' he said, kissing me. 'Now, let's get moving.'

I passed him my diary, open at the K page.

I was checking the rest – nothing else to raise the blood pressure – when the phone rang in Brian's office. Should I let the answerphone take it? Curiosity always gets the better of me in these circumstances, so I popped back, in time to beat the machine to it.

It was the Myakovsky fan club again. On the grounds that the police would now officially be listening to the tape and that the more they heard, the more they had to go on, I engaged the man at the far end in a little conversation. Such as, 'What is your specific argument with Mr Myakovsky?'

I didn't expect any more luck than Alexandrina had had –

which reminded me, wasn't it about time she made another fleeting appearance on the Bookfest scene? – nor did I get it. So I pushed a little further. 'Look, if I cancel his appearances without explanation, our insurance company will go wild. Give me some reason, please.'

Perhaps it was my lack of logic that stopped the caller hanging up. I could almost hear the wheels of thought turning. I waited, and then found I was holding my breath, willing whoever it was not to put down the phone. Mike materialised beside me, tucking his arm round my waist and putting his ear to the phone. I hoisted it slightly.

I'd risk trying to prompt the caller again. 'You see, if you simply stop him coming, you're not achieving much, are you? If you say you don't want him to come for – for whatever reason – and he doesn't come, that really does your cause some good. Otherwise, it's simply negative,' I concluded lamely.

Yes! The gruff-voiced speaker cleared his throat. 'He is an enemy of the people,' he said. 'If he comes to Birmingham, he will die, and so will those who succour him. If he comes, lady, prepare to die.' He cut the connection.

'That makes it a little personal, doesn't it?' Mike asked grimly.

My pulse rate agreed with him. But I shook my head. 'I'm not sure. I'm not sure I believe any of it. "Enemy of the people"! If he's an old-style Communist who objects to the way Myakovsky attacked the Soviet penal system, then he'd have been more – more expansive. You know, used more of the clichés. If he's one of the new Russian Mafia, then the phraseology's all wrong anyway. His most recent set of enemies is in Israel.'

'So you'd have expected something along the "revisionist,

anti-Zionist" lines? Hmm.' Mike's face wore his *Guardian* crossword expression.

'What did you think of the accent?' I asked.

He shook his head. 'Not a lot of Russians play cricket, you know, so it's not one I'm really familiar with. Except on TV, or in movies.'

'And?'

'And I assume the police have people to call on who'll make electronic reductions of the sounds this guy produces and compare them with genuine Russian sounds.'

'That's not impossible, Mike,' Peter's voice came from behind us. Already! They must have left some rubber on the road. 'But I do think that while you wait to find out, Sophie, you should improve your security. We just walked in. Not like you to be as lackadaisical as that.'

I nodded. It wasn't. And the fact that leaving the place unlocked had been Brian's policy was no excuse, not now.

'No sign of Brian yet?' asked Harvinder, over Peter's shoulder. 'Not that there should be – he's a sick man, I'd have thought. He threw up again on the way home.'

'I suggested he go to his doctor before he came in. It'd be nice to get everything sorted out here and phone him to tell him not to bother.' I got into bustle mode. 'The Stonkin Mama letter's in the other office, the tape's here. I'd better fit the spare, hadn't I? And all our venues and speakers and times are, of course, listed in the Bookfest brochure.' I produced one with a flourish.

'What about transport between venues?' Peter asked.

Mike looked at his watch. 'I've got to be at the ground in half an hour.'

'You won't get much play today,' Harvinder said. 'Pissing it down when we came in.'

'Indoor net practice,' Mike said briefly.

'Why don't you push off?' I said. 'I can catch a bus. I'm in no hurry to go and sit watching the rain, after all. Team discipline doesn't apply to wives and girlfriends.'

'That threat – I don't like the idea of you tooling round the city as if nothing's happened.'

I stretched up to kiss him. 'Nothing has happened yet. Nor will it. Off you go. I'll meet you in the bar at – what? Twelve?' We kissed again.

Peter coughed. 'I'll drop her off, Mike.'

As Mike let himself out, Harvinder turned his attention to the kettle.

'How about transport?' Peter asked again.

I grimaced. 'Until yesterday, a real problem. I was actually going to ask my cousin Andy to turn his hand to a bit of chauffeuring since we can't afford taxis for everyone. Brian shares his car with his partner, so that can't be guaranteed, and sweet though my Clio is, it's not everyone's idea of a stretch limo. Actually only one writer has asked for transport so far. As she surprised me. Initially she'd said she'd find her own way around the city.' I stopped. The men were exchanging glances. I leant against a doorjamb and folded my arms. Why on earth hadn't I realised last night? Where had my brain been? 'So how,' I asked 'is Marietta Coe connected to the wedding dress arson?'

Chapter Eleven

Peter stepped past me to flick the door lock.

'The Gaffer told you, did he?'

I shook my head. 'He showed me the scene, just because he thought I'd enjoy the challenge. But he told me nothing about it. Nothing at all.'

'So what makes you . . . ?'

I enumerated on my fingers. 'I talk to a very upset Marietta Coe on the phone. She lives in the right area; no other Bookfest writers do. She's engaged – she mentioned a fiancé, and engagements usually lead to marriage. She changes her mind about getting to her venues herself. A wedding dress is set on fire. And now you're suddenly interested in venues and transport and threats. I just . . .' I waved a hand airily, as much to waft away last night's failure to make connections as anything.

Peter frowned. 'This is to go no further, Sophie. Not even to that Mike of yours. You're right, of course. We've got a stalker. And since she's quite a high-profile woman, and we've got the recent legislation to back us, we're taking things very seriously.'

'Especially when things involve somewhat symbolic arson to a wedding dress.' Why had the stalker only just got round to doing that? If he knew all about her, he must have known she had a fiancé. Perhaps he'd had to spend a little time working out just how to do it.

'Put it on top of the phone calls and the flowers and stuff – yes, I think we can assume the arson attack was part of the campaign.'

'"Phone calls and flowers and stuff"?' I looked, I hoped, alert and interested but not nosy – heaven forbid!

In vain. Harvinder passed mugs of coffee. 'You will keep quiet? The Gaffer'd skin us alive if he knew we'd told you.'

'Thanks. I doubt if he would. He knows my inveigling ways.'

'Police officers aren't supposed to be susceptible to – to inveiglisation,' Peter said.

He didn't laugh at his neologism, so I thought I'd better not either. To keep my face straight, I said, 'So if she were being stalked, she wouldn't want to use her own transport? Is that the picture? Because her venues are all public – and, indeed, publicised.' I patted the Bookfest brochure.

'We'd suggested something less obvious.'

Which no doubt accounted for her change of mind.

'I'm not sure a black cab or even a mini-cab's all that inconspicuous,' I countered. 'And no doubt you won't greet with overwhelming joy the news of our latest sponsorship. Which was supposed to overcome all our transport problems.'

'Don't tell me,' Peter groaned. 'A car with nice bright advertising deckles all over it.'

'Hole in one. The other problem, of course, is who would drive her. The person I'd earmarked for the job was my cousin Andy.'

Harvinder looked at me as if it was his turn to do mental arithmetic. 'We're not talking Andy Rivers here, are we, Sophie?'

'We are. Another scion of the Black Country.'

'But he's a perambulating kidnap target in his own right! God, the Bookfest should be spending all its security budget on him alone.'

'A. We don't have a security budget. B. He says he's over the hill and no one would bother with him.'

'And do you believe that?'

I looked him straight in the eye. 'John Lennon? George Harrison? But he says that if he gave way to all his fears he'd end up a gibbering recluse. So in his UNICEF work he's as high-profile as he can be, and he walks the streets of Harborne with me as calmly as if he worked at Safeway.' I paused to sip some coffee, but neither interrupted me. 'Anyway, he's doing not just his own gig for the Bookfest – and the Rep's main auditorium was sold out within an hour of booking opening – but he's chairing a couple of events. Including Marietta Coe's launch party.' I finished the coffee.

'Well, isn't that nice for the people over here?' Peter observed, his voice dripping with irony. 'One festival, and only four likely targets to protect. Not necessarily from the same person.'

'You mean different *modi operandi*? Only phone calls about one, only letters about another—'

'A ragbag for a third – and, as far as we know, nothing about Andy. Well, let's be grateful for tiny mercies,' he added, his voice now awash with irony. 'Four villains, not just one.'

Harvinder tugged his lip. 'Why didn't you discuss security with the police before you even started?'

I shrugged. 'I've only recently joined the team. And if Brian didn't, it probably wasn't because he thought it unnecessary, it was because he was trying to juggle too many jobs and couldn't do them all. Damn it, he's organised all this.' I flourished the brochure. 'He done good, the lad. And now,' I added grimly, 'it looks as if he's paying the price for working far too hard for far too long.'

'You know there was blood in his vomit, Sophie?'

He'd seen enough of it, by the sound of it.

'What does that mean?'

Harvinder shook his head. 'I don't know. I don't want to guess.'

'Three kids under fifteen,' I reflected. 'And I don't know what happens if you go sick if you're in a job like this.'

'He was saying that his wife works, of course.' Harvinder was suddenly bracing. 'And it's a nice little earner, being a solicitor. They'll be all right.'

'Have you got any more to do here?' Peter asked.

'No. And there's nothing Brian need come in to do either. I'll phone him and tell him to take it easy till Monday. But you don't need to wait for me. I'll catch a bus.'

'And break my word to Mike? No chance. It won't take you a minute to phone, anyway.'

It took less. The number rang and rang, but no one answered.

Watching the rain drench down from the warmth and comfort of the Tom Dollery Bar, I reflected bitterly on the injustice of it all. When there was fine weather, and Mike was scoring runs, I was stuck in an airless office. And now I could justifiably enjoy myself, the weather was like this. But there were worse injustices in the world, of course. From millions going to bed hungry to Brian's stomach problem. And I still hadn't been able to tell him he didn't need to go in. Of course, it would have made everyone's life easier if he'd had an answerphone. I retired to a corner where, with luck, I'd irritate no one and tapped his number into my mobile, wondering how many brain cells would fry this time.

This time someone did pick up the receiver. Tabs.

'Hello, Tabs, is your daddy there?'

'No.'

'Is your mummy there?'

'No.'

'Is there any other grown-up there?'

Silence from Tabs, but an explosion in my ear as she dropped the phone on something hard. After much padding of feet and opening and shutting of doors, I heard it being picked up again.

'Hello?' I prompted.

'Oh. Oh, hello. Thing is, you never know if she's having you on or not, do you?'

'I suppose neither of the Fairbrothers is there?'

'Gone to the hospital. That's why I'm here. Usually only do Tuesdays and Thursdays, like, but being as this was hospital, and they wouldn't want to have the children hanging around, I had to step in, like.'

'Hospital?'

'Ooh, ever so bad, he is. Doctor took one look and sent him off to casualty, she says. So then she had to take his clothes in and all that.'

'They're keeping him in?' I tried to keep my voice down.

'Oh, yes. Tests,' she added darkly. 'My gran started like this, you know. Bleeding from her stomach—'

'I'd better phone Mrs Fairbrother later,' I said. 'My battery's just giving up.'

OK it wasn't. But I was.

I sat down harder than I meant on a low chair. Hospital! Tests! And what about the bloody Bookfest? It opened this very Friday!

'Someone died?' Tony, one of the coaches, was standing beside me. For all he was six foot eight, I'd never noticed him.

My God, he could, couldn't he? 'Not yet,' I said.

'What's the trouble, then, pet?' He edged me towards a table and sat us down.

'You know this Big Brum Bookfest?'

'I ought to: we've got that Writers versus Players game a fortnight tomorrow. And I've got to teach some of them writers which end of the bat to hold.'

'Not Andy Rivers, at least,' I said, managing to grin. 'I taught him how to bowl leg breaks myself. He even had a trial with the Bears once.'

'Well, then. And will you be playing?'

What wouldn't I give to walk out on to Edgbaston's turf?

'I mean, there's nothing down about no women. And young Mike says you're a dab hand with the bat.'

'He might be biased.'

'Not about someone's batting,' Tony said positively. 'Come on, pet. I know you're not really a writer but aren't you running the show?'

My jaw dropped again. That was precisely what I might be doing. Running the show.

'Go back to the office again! Surely you've done enough for today?' Mike expostulated.

'It's to save me having to do one hell of a lot more. I don't have Martin Acheson's mobile phone number and it'll be on file in Brian's office. If I'm not to end up being temporary unpaid Bookfest director, Acheson's going to have to pull in a few favours and get some help.'

'Such as who?'

I spread my hands. 'There's a whole set of directors who must have administrative and management experience. They'll have to sort something out. It's their baby.'

He nodded. 'You're right. Otherwise we both know who'll have to adopt it.'

'Let's hope your concern is premature,' Acheson said, from the middle of a golf course somewhere near Wolverhampton. 'But I do admit, he didn't seem well when we met yesterday.'

'He was very unwell by the end of the day,' I said. 'Meanwhile, there are certain other developments you ought to be aware of. Would you phone me when it's convenient?'

Mike, who'd been freed by the ongoing rain to drive me into the city, made desperate flapping gestures. Quite right.

'Unfortunately I shan't be available this evening,' I continued, blowing Mike a kiss. 'And I shall be tied up for a great deal of tomorrow—'

'My dear girl, this is the weekend before the Bookfest! How can you possibly be tied up?'

I chose not to go into precise detail, but Mike, listening more closely, seemed to be suppressing convulsions. 'I'm just a volunteer, Mr Acheson. If it hadn't been for Afzal Mohammed the board wouldn't even have my limited amount of backup. Anyway, I'll leave my answerphone on, and you can always try my mobile.' I have him the number and rang off.

'There,' I said to Mike. 'That didn't take long, did it?'

At which point the phone rang again.

'Let the machine take it,' Mike urged, grinning. 'All that stuff about being tied up has given me ideas . . .'

I nodded, gathering up my things. But the voice that came through was that of Mrs Fairbrother, instructing me to phone her. OK, in her place I hope I'd have asked. But she must be under more strain than I'd like to contemplate so I obeyed.

'Look what you've driven him to! Just look! He's having a blood transfusion right now. And it's all your fault.'

All my fault? Mine? I was about to screech down the phone when she started to sob, with what sounded like increasing desperation.

It took her several minutes to calm down. All I could do was make sympathetic noises any time she might need them. At last, gulping audibly, she gained some modicum of control. 'I'm sorry. Not yours. The Big Brum bloody Bookfest. The hours he's been working. The pressure he's been under. That's what's done this.'

I couldn't disagree. However unfeeling I might sound, though, the important thing was to establish how soon he'd be back. To put himself under even more pressure, of course.

'I gather they're keeping him in,' I prompted gently.

'Keeping him in! The way he looked half an hour ago he'll be lucky ever to get out.'

Mike, unable not to hear, wrapped warm healthy arms round me.

'This sounds very serious,' I tried again.

'They won't tell me. Not yet. Tests. More tests. When he's stabilised they'll move him to the Queen Elizabeth. But every time he regains consciousness, he tries to get up. Got to get back to the Bookfest, he says.'

Which, by the sound of it, he never would. Not in time for the action, at least. All I could hope was that he'd be able to tie up all the administrative ends. After all, the Bookfest had taken in – and spent – more public and private money than I could imagine. It all had to be married to the original business plan. That meant book-keeping – even fully fledged accountants! I'd never had to do much more than check my restaurant bill. The thought of having to deal not with people but with money made me feel sick – but not sick like Brian. No, surely not!

'Tell him everything's under control,' I said, crossing my fingers behind my back. 'I've notified Martin Acheson. It's up to him and his friends now.' A voice inside my head added, 'And to you, Sophie.'

Chapter Twelve

My only consolation for being pulled into an emergency board meeting on the Sunday afternoon was that Mike looked like spending his afternoon in the field. OK, it was wonderful to watch him run for a ball or throw or, better still, catch. He had an ease, an elegance of movement that set me alight whatever he was doing – even taking rubbish to the bin, to be honest. But he was supreme when wielding a bat. Every movement—

But I digress. He would be fielding; I would be fielding questions. Or plaudits. Not that I expected many of those. Or, to be honest, very many board members to award them.

For one thing, the meeting was taking place not in central Birmingham but in Brewood, a suburb of Wolverhampton. Most Brummies, I'm afraid, consider that the only good thing to come out of Wolverhampton is the A4123 – a road once celebrated in an Auden poem, incidentally. We were to gather in Martin Acheson's house. Even if I hadn't been the star attraction, as it were, I'd have wanted to go; I loved seeing other people's homes. Perhaps that was why I liked bus travel through dark suburban streets – the little theatres of front rooms, with what should have been private dramas played out spot-lit for the public. I couldn't be the only person with a high nosiness factor, surely.

One thing was certain: Acheson's house couldn't have been rubbernecked from a bus. This was definitely a private-transport-only area. Big thirties houses were set well back from the tree-lined road, his, at least, with a semi-circular drive. I parked behind a Scorpio Estate on the road and walked. His garden was already bristling with flowers, and had had a good spring-clean. Yes, as kempt as a park. More kempt, in these days of municipal cutbacks.

Clutching the handset of a cordless phone, he opened the front door himself, with a smile that – disconcertingly – lit his face. He ushered me into the hall. For a moment he lost his poise – the call was clearly important, but he'd no doubt see it was discourteous to leave me hanging around. On the other hand, I was all too happy to hang. All those books! The hall was lined with shelves. There were sets in matching heritage-type bindings – great swathes of English and American giants. All Richardson, all Fielding, right through to hardback Anne Tyler and Margaret Attwood. No odds and ends picked up from charity shops. This was serious collecting of serious reading. All very disciplined. I wondered how he'd feel that authors weren't quite so amenable to discipline.

'My dear Sophie, I'm so sorry about that. Do come through. I thought we'd be most comfortable in here.'

'Here' was the dining room, a light airy place, the alcoves of which were full of yet more books. The dining table was laid out with coasters, water glasses and two types of mineral water. There were – yes – twelve places laid, as it were. Three were already taken: Puce Poet, Afzal, who smiled and patted the chair next to him, and the anxious young man whose minutes had provoked such protracted discussion. Marcus

Downing, the hard-working Afro-Caribbean poet arrived as I sat down, deep in conversation with ethnic jewellery woman. There was no sign of Councillor Roberts, who'd caused such chaos when he appeared last time, or of Councillor Burton, the one who, despite her continued nonappearance, had tried to cause even more chaos in the event-chairing arrangements.

Acheson plied us with water and took his seat in the carver at the end of the table. 'This is an extraordinary meeting with one agenda item only.'

I liked a man who knew where to put his *only*.

'As you all know, Brian Fairbrother has been admitted to hospital, with no firm diagnosis or prognosis yet. It is quite clear, however, that he will be unable to resume his work for the Bookfest for some days, possibly even weeks.'

I raised a hand. It was clear he didn't like being interrupted but I wanted to get my suggestion minuted before we got on to more substantial matters.

'If he's that ill, the very smallest gesture we could make would be to send him some flowers.'

'Good idea, Sophie: I'll get my secretary on to that.' He looked at the accountant, who scribbled accordingly. 'His prolonged absence means we need to find a replacement very rapidly.' He glanced around the table. 'Before I make any concrete proposals, I would welcome your input.'

He might have been a teacher posing a tricky question; everyone stared assiduously at the table. At last Marcus – checking, it seemed, that he wasn't treading on vociferous toes – raised a hand.

Acheson nodded.

'Chair. Ladies and gentlemen. I have two proposals to make. Each to some extent depends on the other. Firstly, I would suggest that Ms Rivers be asked to take over the running of the Bookfest as without doubt she is better versed in its ins and outs than anyone else. Naturally she would be paid an appropriate fee for this. Secondly, we must find someone experienced in this type of work to assist her.'

The minute-taking accountant looked up. 'And where will we find the money to pay anyone else?'

'Obvious,' said Puce Poet. 'If Fairbrother can't fulfil his contract, he loses it.'

'No!' I said. 'You can't do that. The man's run himself into the ground for you. Have you no idea of the hours he's put in? The meals he's skipped?'

'That was his decision,' she said flatly.

'His decision? You try to run a massive undertaking like this with just one man—'

'*Person*,' she corrected me.

'In any case,' the accountant said, 'he'd got you.'

'Only because Afzal here noticed he was swamped by work and only because Afzal knew I was available at the time. For goodness' sake don't add insult to injury by cutting his contract.'

'It's a risk people on short-term contracts just have to run,' the accountant said. He burrowed in a file. 'I fancy I have a copy of Fairbrother's here—'

'Stop,' I said. 'The board will be lucky if he doesn't put in a massive claim against you for workplace stress.'

'He wouldn't dare!' Puce Poet shouted.

Afzal shot out a hand. 'Enough. Sophie's right. We have moral if not a legal obligation to continue paying Brian. I'm sure no one would seriously wish to dispute that.' He looked at Acheson, who nodded and made a note on his jotter. 'The question arises, as Alan pointed out, of paying two people. Brian and Ms Rivers.'

'And a third,' I said. 'I'm not prepared to run the Bookfest on my own.'

'What about those students of yours?' Acheson asked.

'They can do clerical and reception work, but it would be wrong to impose responsibility on them for which they weren't ready. And, no doubt, blame them if things went wrong.'

I must have spoken even more firmly than I intended: Acheson held up his hands in mock-surrender.

'If I make so bold,' Marcus said, 'I do have some experience in this area. I'd be happy to come in, strictly as Ms Rivers' assistant, of course.'

Acheson looked hard at him. 'I thought you were finishing a collection for Bloodaxe.'

'I was. I delivered it last Friday, a couple of weeks before schedule. So if I can be of any assistance . . .'

Puce Poet glowered. I think her glower had been provoked by the mention of Bloodaxe; perhaps her own work appeared in a less prestigious imprint. But it remained. 'And what sort of experience might *you* have?' She sounded perilously like a memsahib questioning a native.

Mine weren't the only eyes opened in shock.

But the poet replied equably enough. 'Well, there was the Pan-Caribbean Festival. Five years I ran that. And then – yes, I ran Nottingham's festival for a couple of years. That was after I understudied at Edinburgh, of course. I did mainly the PR work there.'

Oh, to have someone other than Alexandrina! I beamed at him. I thought I caught a wink.

Acheson looked round the table. 'That would seem eminently satisfactory. Now, the question remains of remuneration. I suspect Ms Rivers and Mr Downing would be more comfortable if we discussed this without them.' He looked through the patio doors. 'The sun seems to be shining; would you care to stroll round the garden for five minutes – literally that?'

Downing and I smiled at each other, and exited.

'Marcus,' he said, offering his hand.

'Sophie.' I shook it.

We fell into step down a weed-free path.

'If you've got all that experience, I should be your assistant,' I said.

'If I'd got all that experience, you should indeed. But I was lying, Sophie. I've appeared at all those festivals, yes, and many others too. So I have a very fair idea of what needs to be done. And I'm prepared to learn.'

'What's your background?' I asked sharply enough to show I wasn't entirely happy.

'Libraries, actually. So I do know my way around the world of books. Book-*keeping*, though – I can't help there. Me and figyures, we strangers t'weach udder,' he said breaking into patois.

'Me too,' I said. 'But if we record meticulously all our outgoings . . . We don't have any incomings at this stage, of course. That tame accountant guy: surely he could be drafted in to sort the figures . . . Do you drive?'

'Ten years' clean licence. Don't joke about things like that,' he added, sensing my doubt. 'Come on, Sophie, we can do it.'

He grinned – what had happened to some of his teeth? I grinned back, but still shook my head. 'I hope you're right.'

We strolled in silence round the rest of the garden. Despite its weed-free neatness, it failed to impress me. Too many straight lines where I'd have had curves. Too many bushes with tightly pruned profiles. Benches put at just the wrong angle. There was a neat shed, which I'd have tucked away behind some handy trees, but which stood stark at the end of a dead-straight path. We peered through the window – every tool hung from a hook. The fertilisers and weedkillers stood on separate shelves. There were even colour-coded watering cans – at least, I assumed the red and green were significant.

'I wonder why he sent us out here?' I asked.

Marcus considered. 'Perhaps the rest of the house so tatty he ashamed for we to see it.'

We shared a laugh. 'All those books,' I said with wonder.

'Wonder what else he collects,' Marcus mused.

But Acheson was waving us back in. I was quite surprised to see no puffs of white smoke from the chimney.

'So I'm well on the way to becoming a bloated capitalist,' I told Mike, over supper at my house. 'They're back-dating the honorarium to the day I started, and it'll continue for another two weeks at least. And it's well over what my William Murdock salary would have been.'

'That's not saying much,' he said, quite unprompted.

'So what shall we do with it?'

'Deposit for a new car?' he suggested, topping up my glass.

'Or something extravagant by way of a holiday?' I beamed. For holiday, read honeymoon, even.

He put the bottle down and leant forward, resting his arms on the table. 'I'm paying for our honeymoon – right? So long as we have one. So long as we have a wedding first? When will it be, Sophie? When are we going to sneak off and do it?'

I bit my lip.

His face drained. 'My God, you haven't changed your mind?'

I was round the table in an instant. 'No! No! Of course I haven't.'

At last reassured, he asked, 'So why that hesitation?' He held me away from him and scanned my face.

'No hesitation at all about marrying you. I was just wondering – you know, the form of the wedding itself . . .'

'I'll do anything you want. You know that.'

I did. And, settling on his knee, I was just about to confess my fantasy when the phone rang.

'Take it,' he said resignedly. 'I'll load the dishwasher and then you and I, Ms Rivers,' he added, as I reached the phone, 'will have a serious talk.'

I blew him a kiss as I picked up the handset.

A male voice said, 'You make some very interesting decisions, Ms Rivers.'

It was just like old times, Ian and Chris sitting in my living room, asking me questions. Mike had decided my lawn was dry enough to mow, despite the gathering dusk. Then – I'd agreed without demur – we'd go back to his house.

'It's a pity you didn't let your answerphone take the call,' Ian said. 'I'd give a lot to get a voice analysis done.'

'On eight words? That was all he said you know, those eight words?'

'OK, it would have been better if he'd talked for ten minutes.'

'But as there isn't a recording, this is all a bit academic,' Chris cut in. He was only here because he'd been having tea – yes, it would be old-fashioned Sunday tea – with Ian and Val when I'd called Ian. 'Now, the caller to the Bookfest office had a strong Russian accent, as I recall. We'll know how genuine when the lab comes back to us on yesterday's

114

recording. I gather this man didn't?'

I shook my head. 'A light French one.'

'French!'

I nodded. 'Is someone playing around with us? I did wonder if the Russian accent was fake; it was ludicrously strong. And it can't be so hard to put on a French one, *n'est-ce pas*?' I might have been auditioning for a bit part in *'Allo, 'Allo*.

Ian managed a perfunctory grin. Chris didn't even bother to try.

'Have you had other calls in other circumstances involving accents?' I asked.

Chris hesitated. As of old, he and Ian exchanged a long glance. It was almost as if the younger, impulsive Chris were seeking permission of the older man. 'OK, Peter and Harvinder told me you'd guessed. Marietta Coe has been receiving phone calls, flowers, other unwanted gifts. And a copy of her wedding dress was set on fire. And – yes – some of the phone calls have been in a phoney French accent. On the grounds, it seemed to me, that French was the language of love. Her messages, you'll gather, have been nothing like as terse as yours.'

'What's she like?' I asked. 'I mean, I've read the press release and I've spoken to her over the phone. She sounds a decent, hard-working woman. Oh, and her fiancé works in a further education college, doesn't he?'

Chris hesitated, looking from me to Mike, who'd just pushed the door open. 'She's quite a short woman,' he said. 'Mid-thirties. Blondish. Blue eyes. Neat figure. Excellent legs.'

When the phone rang, Mike sprang to it.

'No!' Chris yelled. 'Let the answerphone take it, man.'

Mike hesitated but only for a second: 'I'm going to give that bastard a piece of my mind.'

Ian was across the room faster than I'd have believed possible, holding back Mike's hand. 'Just let us find out who it is first. Then you can give him the whole of your mind. Face to face, with a bit of luck.'

Mike turned slowly back towards me, every pore oozing reluctance. By now the welcoming message had stopped. The beep sounded. And the room was filled with my cousin Andy's voice. 'Hi, Soph. Just to let you know I'll be coming up tomorrow. A couple of things to do in Brum. Don't worry. I'll let myself in.'

Mike was the first to speak. 'When I was at school there was this teacher who was dead keen on literary terminology. Would that message be an example of bathos?'

Mike was very quiet when I arrived at his house. We'd gone in separate cars, since I might need mine the following day.

There'd be two things on his mind. Maybe three. Yes, almost certainly Chris's presence in my house would constitute a third. But he'd want reassurance on two big points: first, my personal safety, and second, my promise that whatever happened this would be the visit when I told Andy that he was the father of my child.

And yes, there might be a fourth issue, too. My hesitation over the wedding.

Last week, I could have started by saying, 'As soon as this Bookfest's over let's get married.' Now what I wanted to say was, 'As soon as this Bookfest's over, I want to start planning for the wedding of the year.'

I'd never realised that love could be like this. So many negotiations and concessions and anxieties and resolutions. I suppose my problem was no one had ever been anxious for me before – Chris apart, and at least he'd been in a position to protect me from danger, real or perceived. So much as I liked the idea of being cherished, part of me wanted to explode that I could look after myself. And though I knew I loved Mike more deeply – and yes, more painfully – than I'd ever loved anyone before, all he could do was take my declarations on trust.

We argued fiercely. We made up fiercely. When I woke in the night, we were still clutching each other like two lost children.

Chapter Thirteen

I hadn't realised quite how much Brian's daily assaults on Sheffield had irritated me. But I could feel myself relaxing as I let myself into a pleasantly quiet and empty office. OK, eight thirty wasn't quite so pleasant as nine thirty. But I could do the comforting routine things that used to get my head into gear at William Murdock: making a cup of tea; then systematically checking all incoming messages. On the grounds that no one had yet used it to communicate any threats, I opened the e-mail first. The first was an irritated one from the British consul's office in New York. Would I please intimate to Mr Myakovsky that threats of physical violence against consular staff were unlikely to ensure the speedy conclusion of his application.

I would. After a conciliatory reply, I sent Myakovsky a full and frank explanation and asked him to sit down and shut up. Then I scrubbed it. I was taking out my anger against Brian. So I tried again – more tactful but still firm: no duffing up HMC. The other messages were routine enough, and I answered them routinely.

Rolling up mental sleeves, I turned my attention to the voice mail. Yes, Ian's little machine seemed to have been working.

There was a sharp knock on the office door. It wasn't nine yet but one of my wonderful helpers was there already! Beaming I flung open the door to come face to face with a tiger lily.

It was one of a large bouquet supported by a library porter. 'They said to bring it here,' he told me.

'There must be some mistake.'

He groped amongst the foliage, producing a doll-sized envelope with a big flourish. There it was, in turquoise and white.

Ms Sophie Rivers
Bookfest Office

'Thanks,' I said inadequately.

'Nothing to do with me. I just brought them.'

'Well, thanks for doing that.'

'We're not supposed to. Not private things.'

God, was he expecting a tip? Did people tip, in this brave new century? I tossed a mental coin. No, I didn't tip.

He seemed to accept the inevitable, and toddled off, whistling the 'Marseillaise' under his breath.

The office had no receptacle capable of holding a dusty dandelion, let alone a young conservatory like this. The best I could do was . . . No, the best I could do was wait till my reinforcements came and nip out and get a vase. Now Brum was taking its place on the world stage, little shops selling touristy things were popping up all over the place. It wouldn't take me ten minutes to get something. Meanwhile, who had sent such an extravagant offering? Lilies, real carnations, roses, freesias. The scent was almost overwhelming, as if a whole chapel-full of flowers had landed on my desk.

I breathed in gently: yes, I'd like lilies at my wedding. The card, then.

For a wonderful woman

Hmm: that sounded nice even through the medium of some florist's ugly handwriting. Mike truly was the dearest man in the world. Fancy sending a peace-offering when if anyone had been responsible for last night's traumas it was me.

Another knock announced the arrival of Una and Tasleen.

'Goodness, you're keen,' I said. 'It's only just striking nine.'

We absorbed the boom of the Council House clock.

'Hey, someone thinks a lot of you,' Una said, sniffing the flowers and pouncing on the note. 'Where shall I put these? You can't leave them like this – they'll die.'

'Now you two are here I can nip out and buy a vase,' I said.

Tasleen coughed gently. 'I'm afraid you can't leave them in here anyway,' she said. 'Lilies bring me up in nettle rash. How about the ladies' loo?'

'It's right at the far end of the building from us,' I said. 'And shared by all the women admin staff. I'm sure it would be safe there, but . . .'

'It'd be safer in the gents,' Marcus finished for me. 'Not many men in that big office and it's right next door. Come your ways with me, pretty flowers.' He left as swiftly and silently as he'd come.

'That's another new team member,' I said. 'Marcus Downing, the poet.'

'I thought I recognised him!' Una exclaimed. 'My God, Sophie, how did you recruit him?'

'He volunteered,' I said. 'Hi, Marcus! Come and meet Una and Tasleen. But before you do, close that door. Security. If

121

you're ever in doubt, you can actually override the keypad outside and lock yourself in, see?'

They stared. Had I lost it completely, their silence asked.

I continued, 'I think it's time I explained to you women what's been going on . . .'

A quick check of the mail revealed nothing but nice flat envelopes, so at least when I asked the women to open the post I wasn't exposing them to a likely letter bomb. I gave them strict instructions not to separate envelope from contents till they'd checked the latter. I'd check the voice mail, and Marcus would be front of house for the time being.

'Sophie, I can keep an eye on that door just as well from this desk.' He pointed downwards at my usual one. 'And while I'm sitting there, I can call a few people I know and drum up support for some of these gigs where the numbers are low. Right?' He ran his finger along the chart where we recorded advance ticket sales.

'Right,' I grinned.

'And you get your arse at the boss's desk – right? 'Cause make no mistake about it, Sophie – you're the boss.'

I might have been the boss, but my work was quartered. OK, Marcus tripled our phone bill in one morning, but he also sold tickets for events which might otherwise have died, and he was promised space in several newspapers which I was quite sure Alexandrina had never heard of. Well, to be fair, neither had I. But Marcus not only knew of them, he knew the features editors. We were to have no fewer than four photoshoots between lunch and tea – the whole team together, I insisted. The morning flew by. The only time the gaiety stopped was when the phone rang. Whoever reached for it stopped, hand poised, and waited for me to take it instead. At last, however, Tasleen was so exasperated by having to summon me, she said something pungent under her breath and appointed herself switchboard woman.

She had no Russians, genuine or spurious, to deal with, and nothing to faze her. Until she put her head round Brian's door – my door! – and announced the Police were on the phone. Her capital, not mine.

The Police turned out to be Ian.

'You know, I called myself Sergeant Dale automatically,' he confessed. 'After all this time too. Anyway, I've been working from home, Sophie, on account of the gas man was supposed to be coming. Should have told you before.'

'No problem. Damn it, Ian, you're still a volunteer. And remember to charge us for your phone.'

'Funny you should say that,' he said, ''cause I've been on the blower a sizeable piece of the morning. Saying hello to old mates, and so on. Down in the Smoke, most of them. Now they say this Stonkin Mama lady's called wolf before. Publicity stunt. That sort of thing. She goes public with the threats, and hey presto she's an instant heroine, selling her books and CDs like the proverbial hot cakes. Two or three times she's done it.'

'You're sure she's not had death threats that simply weren't carried out?'

'You know me: I like to think the best of people. But there's certainly some evidence . . . Which you don't want to hear about. Well, I'm sure you do, but you're not going to. OK, love?'

'OK, Ian.'

'Now, the other thing is, young Chris was on the blower too. It seems this Marietta woman would like to talk to you about that short conversation you had with the man with the French accent last night. And, to be honest, about who's going to protect her and how for this Bookfest. If I collected her, unofficial, like, and brought her in, could you find time to give her lunch somewhere? I shall be, before you ask, at an adjacent table.'

'I'd rather you were at ours, Ian.' I meant it. I'd grown very fond of him.

'It'd be rude to keep looking round,' he said flatly, 'which is what I shall be doing. From behind my copy of the *Birmingham Post*. Where shall we eat?'

'There's that little café here,' I said.

'Or there's that new place in the Ikon Gallery,' he said. 'They do a decent sherry there, with the tapas. I'll book a couple of tables there. Charge them to the hospitality budget. I take it we have one?'

So there we were, this smallish, blondish woman with blue eyes and me, sitting opposite each other in a tapas bar in a corner of the Ikon Gallery. The Ikon is a gallery for modern art, based in a beautifully restored Victorian school. My older William Murdock colleagues remember it as housing a branch of another FE college. My bet would be it wasn't then the oasis of calm and elegance it now is. I might have been more at home with the students than with the present state-of-the-art art, come to think of it. But I never did score high for artistic taste, and I was always prepared to be proved wrong.

Ian certainly hadn't been wrong about this place as a venue for an informal lunch. Marietta and I had chosen a selection of tapas: assorted olives, fried courgettes, wonderful bread, to name but a few. After one glass of the bottle of heady house red I'd moved on to mineral water; Marietta, on the other hand, was making steady inroads into her third glass. Presumably this would be an afternoon when she didn't propose to write.

'I can't tell you how scary it is,' she was saying. 'Not that he ever did anything overtly violent. It was just so frightening knowing he was there, watching me. Sophie – it was like he was in my home with me. He knew about things I'd bought. Little things like CDs. And he knew about my clothes. Even my undies.'

Noting the past tense, I asked, 'How did it start?'

'Innocently enough. Well, a couple of heavy breathing phone calls. Then he started to – to talk pillow talk with this French accent. I laughed, first time. That seemed to get him angry. I certainly didn't laugh the next time.'

She took another piece of bread, tearing it fiercely.

'But then things started to arrive. Nothing overtly threatening. But things . . . I wouldn't want anyone else to give me. Well, would you want tampons through the post? The flowers were one thing, but the tampons quite another.'

'Flowers?'

'Hmm. I thought at first they were from my fiancé. But when I thanked him he said he hadn't sent them. It didn't do our relationship any good at all, Sophie – he's a bit on the jealous side. Not that I'd have liked it if anyone had sent him personal things.'

Flowers! Anonymous flowers! 'You talk of these things in the past,' I said as calmly as I could.

'Oh, I think involving the police may have scared him off,' she said, smiling for the first time. 'Day after day, week after week, I'd been pestered by him. And there was the wedding dress business. But suddenly, it's all stopped, as if someone's turned off a pneumatic drill. All that – and then a wonderful silence.'

Reculer pour mieux resortir? I wondered. But I didn't like to alarm her further.

'So you can see why I was so awkward about transport to the readings,' she continued. 'Which is why I wanted to see you today. To explain. And to apologise. And to thank you for asking your gorgeous cousin to look after me.'

Andy? Well, he had been gorgeous in his time. It explained why Stephan was such a good-looking boy, I suppose. And all of a sudden, I didn't want any more food, and it was all I could do not to reach across and have a swig from Marietta's glass. Andy would be waiting for me when I got home. And this time, not just for his sake and Stephan's, but for mine and Mike's, I simply had to tell him about his son.

She must have noticed something. She leant to top up my glass. 'You OK?'

I nodded. 'Just remembered something, that's all.'

'Can't be very nice, whatever it is. It's a big job for you, isn't it, this Bookfest.' She added, in a rush, 'I'm wondering whether to give up my job – to try to make a living from my writing. I might just survive. My fiancé – Miles – he says he'll support me.' She played with the stem of her glass. 'But it's a lot to give up, isn't it? The regular income. The freedom. Committing to one person.'

I found myself talking about me and Mike, but certainly not in terms of loss. All of a sudden we'd abandoned conversation for real girls' talk. 'And it was your wedding dress that made me decide I wanted a proper wedding!' I concluded.

'But' – her face clouded – 'having to give up your friends . . .'

As if Mike would ask such a thing! 'Giving up *friends*!'

'Well, men friends. Some of them.'

He might like me to see less of Chris, but he'd never think of telling me to. 'Anyone in particular?'

'There's one of my friends Miles really loathes. Hates him to phone, even. I have to sneak out if I want a quiet drink with him. Of course, he didn't like it when I told him I was going to marry Miles.'

So this was where she got the inspiration for her books – from her own life. 'Did he want to marry you himself?'

'Oh, that was never on the cards. It wasn't that sort of relationship.'

Did that mean it had been *that* sort of relationship? If so, no wonder Miles didn't want it to continue. And how would he feel if he found her 'sneaking out' for a quiet 'drink'? If drink it was! Mike and I these two weren't, not if my conclusions were even halfway correct. And I was sure they were: there was something about that tiny smile, that knowingness about the eyes, wasn't there? Financially reliable and nice Miles might be, but in bed he didn't match up.

'There's something more exciting about a lover than a husband, isn't there?' she reflected wistfully, almost as if that wedding dress had been meant to sweeten an occasion less palatable than it should have been. 'Anyway,' she added, pulling herself up straight and draining her glass, 'I shall have more chance to see – him. Shall I get another half-bottle?'

I shook my head. 'You don't think this . . . friend . . . of yours might be your stalker?'

'Of course not! He's as angry about it as I am!'

'And have you told the police team?'

She looked me straight in the eye. 'Absolutely not. This is strictly between us, Sophie. I can trust you. Can't I?

* * *

What with the photographers Marcus had organised and a stream of punters wanting tickets or information, the afternoon went remarkably quickly. So quickly I was late leaving. Not so late as Marcus, who called me back when I was halfway down the stairs.

'Hey, Sophie. What about those flowers I put in the gents' loo?'

I doubled back. By the time I'd reached the gents', however, Marcus was back in the office; I could hear him on the phone. So, establishing the place was unoccupied, I sallied in myself. All I wanted was to fish the flowers from a washbasin.

But they'd gone. No sign of them.

Marcus must have retrieved them before he called me. So I went back to the office. Yes, he was still on the phone, and no, not a stalk to be seen.

'Flowers?' I mouthed.

Covering the mouthpiece, he mouthed, 'Loo,' and pointed.

So if they weren't in a washbasin, where were they? Oh dear. Yes, there they were, looking remarkably good, stems deep in a lavatory pan. I only hoped he'd flushed it first.

Chapter Fourteen

So Andy was waiting for me when I got home and we had that Indian meal together. I was holding a lot back from him, of course, in my account of the Bookfest. Most of what had been going on in the last few days wasn't the sort of thing that I wanted overheard by someone at another table. So I diverted him by asking about Ruth's latest ventures. At last we walked back, nattering this time more easily, about people we knew from our shared past. This might be the very time, now he was mellowed . . .

But Mike's car was parked in front of my house: he'd cut back on the booze-up, then, to be there for me. He'd be disappointed I'd not told Andy about Stephan, but pleased – very pleased – that I'd told him we were to be married. If not how and where and wearing what. He probably wouldn't ask about the Andy business; he'd be in the next room, after all, and no matter how quietly we talked – and Mike and I always found so much to talk about – there must be constraint.

The two men shook hands with some appearance of pleasure.

'I hear congratulations are due,' Andy said, clapping Mike on the shoulder as if he'd just hit a winning six.

'I'm glad she's told you,' Mike said quietly. Then he

grinned. 'After all, it would have been such a waste to leave this in the fridge!' He disappeared, producing Moët and glasses.

'I thought champers did your stomach in,' Andy said sharply, looking at me.

'That was my William Murdock tum,' I said.

'Any news of Fairbrother and his tum?' Mike asked.

'The Bookfest boss, Andy. Off sick with what sounds like severe gastritis at very least.'

Andy looked at me sharply. 'So that means you are running the whole caboodle.'

'Just until Brian gets over this gastritis or whatever. Funny thing, though – I used to double up with pain every time it struck. He's been remarkably vertical, if he had that sort of pain. Anyway, he's in hospital under observation now. "Comfortable", they call it. So long as they ban visits from his kids, he should soon be on the mend. He's got a daughter from hell called Tabs – Tabitha, I suppose – who wrecks lives and phones.'

'Not much of a one for kids, are you?' Andy observed.

Mike's eyes shot to mine. I shook my head infinitesimally. He pulled a face.

'Not kids like that one,' I agreed. 'Though I'm sure there are nicer specimens.'

Andy held his glass to be refilled and sat down. 'Ruth's too old, of course . . . So there's no point in even thinking about the reversal operation.' He pointed gloomily at his crotch. 'We did wonder about in vitro or surrogate and all that. Then we thought there were enough of us in the world anyway. And they're such hostages to bloody fortune.' He swigged – good champagne, as if it were beer! – and stood up again. 'I'll be off to bed, if you don't mind. It's been a long day. But I thought

I might pop in to your office tomorrow – see if I can make myself useful.'

'That'd be great,' I said, wondering where we'd find him chair-space.

'Tell you what,' Mike said affably, 'Sophie and I will probably start tomorrow with a bit of a run. Care to join us?'

'Sure,' Andy said. 'What time? Sixish?'

'Sixish,' said Mike, with a hint of belligerence.

'Sixish,' I laughed. Nothing short of world war would get Andy out of bed before eight.

'I forgot to thank you for the flowers,' I said, as Mike watched me from the bed, taking off the last of my make-up. It was a process that seemed to fascinate him as much as its application. My conscientious skin-care routine had impressed him so much he'd started on a similar regime himself, on the grounds that his constant exposure to English and other summers would reduce his face to a lattice by the time he reached middle years.

'Flowers?'

'Hmm. That huge bunch in my living room.'

'You mean all those lilies and things? I thought they were from Andy.'

'Andy's not a man for flowers. Not for his cousin, at least.' Andy was actually very particular about the origin of any flowers he gave. It wasn't just the sheer nonsense of jetting non-essentials around the world, it was the impact of highly irrigated cash crops on local food-growing potential. But I was less concerned with ethics than with those flowers. 'There was a nice note,' I added.

'Not from me, I'm afraid. I'll get you some tomorrow.'

'Wait till those die: it'd be such a waste otherwise,' I said, my mind still on who might have sent the lilies.

He hitched himself up on his elbow. 'I can spend what I like when I like on you. You're my woman.'

'And you're my man.' I sat on the edge of the bed. 'Which is why I love having flowers from you. And don't like having them from anonymous admirers.' I told him what the note had said.

He sat up fully and took my hand. 'So who the hell sent them?'

'I had lunch with someone whose life was being made a misery by a stalker who started with anonymous phone calls and worked up to anonymous gifts. After months of harassment, the stalking's suddenly stopped.'

'And now someone sends you flowers.' He gripped my hand tightly. 'Are you thinking what I'm thinking?'

I wouldn't avoid his gaze. 'Probably. But it's far too soon to judge, isn't it? Let's see what tomorrow's post brings. Let's put it out of our heads for a while, or we'll be tossing and turning with insomnia all night.'

He smiled. 'Any tossing and turning, sweetheart, will be nothing to do with insomnia.' But I caught him looking anxious as I turned to switch off my lamp.

Not only did Andy sleep through our tepid attempts to wake him for a run, he was still spark-out when I left for work.

Mike did his best not to show concern, just as I tried to seem carefree when he was going in to bat against the world's fastest bowlers. I had to trust to his helmet, his padding and his immaculate timing; he had to trust to – what? My common sense? My intuition? My strong desire to stay alive?

The rain, which had held off while we were running, came on in good earnest as I started the car. I was almost glad, in a perverse, childish way. If I couldn't sit at Edgbaston and watch Mike score runs, why should anyone else? I told myself off at once. If there was one thing Mike hated it was a wasted day, the only consolation being that he got through an amount of reading that put me to shame.

Whatever rat-run one used into the city, there were inevitable snarl-ups somewhere. I hated myself for adding to them. I was perfectly happy to cycle or use a bus, but I needed to be more flexible than either option allowed this week. The pressure would certainly build though I now had three solid workers – plus Andy! – in support.

But it was I who happened to get there first and chanced to open the threatening letters. Oh, yes – note the plural. Stonkin Mama and Vladimir Myakovsky were the lucky targets. A first, for Myakovsky, on paper. White A4, but the paper was noticeably heavier than Stonkin Mama's correspondent's. But the two threatening letters had one thing in common – very blurred postmarks on the envelopes. I'd never made a study of postmarks, so I'd no idea what proportion of postmarks normally came out nice and legible. Perhaps the police had techniques for enhancing them. I hoped so. OK – both letters safely in their envelopes in the safe. No need to say anything to the others unless they asked directly.

The voice mail was a bit unnerving too. Another verbal threat against Myakovsky. Pray God he didn't get that visa. And, after several quite normal requests from Joe Public for information, there came the man with the French accent informing me that I had beautiful feet and he couldn't wait to suck my toes. Well, he'd bloody have to. For a good long time. I saved the tape on Ian's little machine and tucked that into the safe too.

No. I wouldn't panic. I wouldn't even get angry. I'd just

register that somewhere out there was a sicko and get on with my life.

So when Ian turned up, I naturally put my head on his shoulder and howled.

'I can't give up,' I said, before he even suggested it. 'Look how everyone's rallied round. I mean, look at you. You don't have to be here, but you are, and it isn't even nine yet. And Marcus and Una and Tasleen are giving it their all. I can't pull out, can I?'

'No, I don't think you can,' Ian said, producing a beautifully ironed linen handkerchief and sitting me down. 'You know I'm not one for advocating risks. But – apart from the unpleasantness – I wonder if this guy's all that dangerous. After all, he seems to have given up on Marietta.'

I nodded. 'I wondered if it was merely to lull her into a false sense of security. But do you think he's simple transferred his attention to me? And when he finds a substitute for me, he can move on to her?'

'Lucky woman, whoever she is. Let's hope so.'

'But we also have to accept,' I said, 'that some stalkers rape and even kill their victims.'

'They,' Ian said, 'don't have to reckon with me.'

I'd repaired my make-up and was at Brian's desk, sorting out schedules for the day. The two women were dealing with the rest of the post, and Marcus was already hustling. Ian sauntered back.

'I'll take the tape and those letters over to Smethwick soon as I've finished here,' he said. 'By the way, have you mentioned your stalkers to anyone?' He might have sounded casual, but Ian never asked casual questions.

'No one I shouldn't. Chris, Peter and Harvinder; Mike;

Andy. No, I don't think I told even Andy.'

'No one else? Just think hard.'

'What are you getting at? Someone getting a buzz from knowing I'm scared? So – oh yes, we're talking about someone I know well enough to talk to?'

Ian raised a hand. 'Slow down.'

'It's got to be one of the board, hasn't it?'

'You've lost me.'

I'd nearly lost myself. Surely I was off my head! Why should one of the board be doing this to me? Some dim connection was sparking between me and Marietta – someone must know us both – but I couldn't make it fire properly. 'No, it's a crazy idea. Isn't it? After all, you'd expect the board members to want to make the Bookfest a huge success. I mean, look at the effort Acheson put into the whole thing. And now Marcus. Though when I come to think of it, there are a lot of members with their own agendas.' I ran desperately through some of the characters involved. 'Tell me, do women ever stalk other women? Because most of the weirdos are women.'

'Maybe. But not in this case. Not unless whoever it is is a brilliant mimic. Men's voices, Sophie.' He shook his head at my dimness.

'Not an Afro-Caribbean man,' I said triumphantly.

'Not unless he'd got rid of his accent. Marcus only talks patois when he's a mind to.'

'Woman in cahoots with man?' I said. 'No?'

He shook his head. 'A man, Sophie. I'm sure this stalker's a man.'

And so, in my heart of hearts, was I.

There was a spate of calls only I could deal with. The first was from Acheson, asking for news of Myakovsky's visa.

135

'None yet. Though I'd say they may grant him one simply to shut him up. Him and Brian. Brian used to make a daily call to the visa people in Sheffield—'

'Of course. Don't you?'

'I thought too much pressure could well be counter-productive.'

'Nonsense. Think about dripping and stones.'

'Think about water torture,' I retaliated.

'Is that how you'd see it?' He sounded quite interested.

But I didn't want to discuss the finer points of psychology. 'I would if I were a clerk in Sheffield trying to get through a day's work!' I snapped. 'Anyway, a visa is irrelevant if Myakovsky's been put off by the death threats.' I flapped a hand at Marcus, who'd come in to alter some figures on our ticket sales chart and was hovering within earshot.

'Which I assure you he hasn't. I understand you've upset him, by the way.'

'Me!' How on earth had I done that? And how on earth did Acheson know? Brian would know if Acheson or one of his friends had pulled in a favour to get the Great Man to come to the provinces. But when could I ask Brian?

'You told him off for his lack of manners. My dear girl, one does not rebuke the great Myakovsky,' he said grandly. I wished he'd said it with a Russian accent. 'Now, what's the fall-back position?'

'If he doesn't come? Brian refused even to contemplate the situation.'

'I sincerely hope you've been contemplating it.'

I hadn't, had I? Marcus wrote in large letters on my scrap pad: CONTACTS – YOURS, MIKE'S, MINE. NO PROBS. Thumb up and grinning, I said blithely, 'I'm working on a number of contacts, Martin.'

'With all due respect, Sophie, what contacts does an ex-college lecturer have?'

I don't like it when people try to be scathing about my work. I said very quietly, 'My cousin is a UNICEF ambassador, my partner an England cricketer and my assistant a poet with an international reputation. Failing all those, one of my closest friends is a senior policeman. Believe me, Martin, I have contacts.' And I cut the connection. Not the wisest of moves, but even though I was now paid, I wasn't paid enough to be patronised.

My voice was probably still frosty when I took the next call. Andy. He seemed to have overslept – jet lag or something. Would he be any use if he came in?

'Why not? You could help Martin with some phone calls. And, Andy, bring your address book . . .'

So when Mike phoned, I was laughing enough to satisfy even him. When I relayed Martin Acheson's snide comments about my contacts, he was galvanised into action too. He knew several of the more controversial older cricketers who had autobiographies to puff. There was even one who claimed to have written a thriller, though he might have to bring his ghost along, since it was rumoured that he'd not only not written it, he'd not yet managed to read it.

'I'll have a list of possibles and their fees by lunchtime,' he promised. 'Oh, and, Sophie, don't agree to do anything, repeat *anything*, tonight. I want your sincere and absolute and immutable word on it.'

'What have you planned, then?'

'Something, my darling, I think you'll enjoy.'

Chapter Fifteen

Mike made so few demands, extracted so few promises like that, that when Martin Acheson turned up at five thirty, I told him I was about to lock the office and leave. It should, incidentally, have been locked at five.

'But you need to brief me,' he said. 'I thought over a quiet drink somewhere.' He smiled as if we were friends. Close friends.

'We'll have to take a rain check, Martin,' I said. 'I've got a prior commitment I absolutely cannot cut. I'll be in the office by eight thirty tomorrow. We could talk over the phone then.'

His smile evaporated. 'Sophie, you do realise you're running an international festival? You can't just take off wherever and whenever you want.'

'I believe Brian's contract requires him to be on duty every evening next week, and I shall be adhering to that. But tonight, Martin, I am going home.' Setting the alarm, I stepped out. If he didn't want to set it off, he'd have to follow.

'This is a rather unusual way of celebrating a major contract,' he said, stepping outside into the corridor but stopping immediately. 'Shirking your responsibilities at the first opportunity.'

I would not be intimidated. 'Don't give me that, Martin. You know a good worker when you see one. And a good manager. Thanks to me' – I set off briskly – 'you have three extra pairs of hands for your Bookfest, and a selection of celebrities willing and able to come in as substitutes for Myakovsky.' We started down the stairs. 'Two pop musicians, one with a title. Three cricketers, ditto. A novelist who won the Pulitzer a couple of years back. An ex-Prime Minister. And an ex-ambassador. Whom would you fancy? One or a selection?'

By now we were in Paradise Place. I wanted to cut back through Paradise Forum to the car park at the back of Baskerville House.

'This clearly warrants proper discussion,' he said.

'After due consideration,' I chipped back. 'So we could talk at eight thirty tomorrow. Or over lunch. Whatever. But now I've got to pick up my car. Goodbye.' I turned on my heel and strode away. As strides go, mine isn't impressive, on account of my lack of inches, but at least I cover a lot of ground very quickly if I put my mind to it. I got to the car in less than five minutes.

What a pity someone had got to it first. On another occasion what had been done would have made me smile, probably laugh out loud. Someone had fastened helium-filled balloons to the windscreen and rear-screen wipers and both wing mirrors. It was just the sort of thing Andy or even Mike would have done.

But somehow – I looked in vain for a passing child to palm them off on but ended up shoving them willy-nilly into the boot – somehow I didn't think they would have done it. Not this time.

* * *

Mike was tasting pasta sauce when I let myself into the house, Andy tearing up salad. Mike glanced at his watch.

'Traffic,' I said. 'I left spot on five thirty.'

'I bet that hurt.'

'I'd promised you,' I said, kissing him. 'And I actually felt quite pleased to be able to make a point. Acheson turned up wanting an instant meeting. I told him he couldn't have one. He rebuked me for insubordination.' An errant olive rolled from a collection on Andy's chopping board straight to my waiting hand. 'But someone else did something much jollier.'

'Like what?' Mike grabbed my arm.

'That'll burn.'

He turned off the gas. 'Well? Like what?'

'Like decorating my car with balloons. They're bobbing away in the hall even as we speak. And I think it'll take someone taller than me to retrieve them from the ceiling.'

'Right,' Mike said, gathering up the plates, 'tracksuit and trainers time.'

'But I had a run this morning.'

'I said trainers, not running shoes. And the less vivid tracksuit, I think.'

'Sir!' I saluted ironically and did as I was told.

Mike was in his Warwickshire tracksuit when I got downstairs. Something was definitely up, up enough to persuade Andy into one of Mike's spare tracksuits. And to leave the saucepans unwashed on the work surface.

'I thought some time in the nets was called for, pet,' Tony, the coach, greeted me, as we pulled into the Edgbaston players' car park. 'Thought you might be short of match practice, like. Young Andy here, now he turns out for the Lord's Taverners, I hear.'

Andy had the grace to blush.

'But way down the order and further down the averages, I also hear. So you can have a session too. And remember, lad, you're here to listen and learn, not to talk. Right?'

So there we were, on the training ground on Edgbaston Road, with real bowlers sending down real overarm deliveries. And I had to play them. For an hour, there was nothing in my head except that ball and Tony's yelled instructions. Nothing. If my concentration strayed for a minute, something got hit, the wickets or me. More often me. Painfully. But then it all came back, all the footwork, all the balance. And suddenly the timing. Yes!

At which point Tony made me take the pads and padding off, and threw me the ball. 'Leg breaks, I understand, young lady. So let's see your googly, shall we?'

Well, I'd taught Andy to bowl when we were both kids. But that was then. And my fingers were older and stiffer now.

'How was that then, pet?' Tony demanded, supping from the pint I'd bought him.

'Magic,' I said. 'Absolute magic. I feel a new woman.'

'You'll feel a very stiff woman tomorrow,' he said. 'You want a hot bath and a good rub from that young man of yours. And don't forget, lots of white spirit to toughen those hands. Or you'll be in trouble, match day.'

Laughing, I shook my head. 'I shan't be playing: I'm just the administrator.'

Tony didn't laugh. He shoved his index finger inches from my nose. 'You'll play, my girl, or I'll know the reason why.'

* * *

We were so drunk with fatigue or laughter that I didn't at first notice the little answerphone light flashing away. And when I did I said nothing. It could wait. I didn't have to press the play pad. It would still be there in the morning. So I got more bottles and cans from the fridge, and discovered an enormous hunger for cheese sandwiches. Andy responded with a desire for pickled onions. Mike watched with amusement: net practice was hardly a new experience for him.

At last he asked quietly, 'Which one of you is for the hot bath first? Andy?'

Giving a quizzical grimace, Andy took the hint. Mike put his arm round me and guided me to the phone. 'You haven't taken your eyes off it for more than five seconds ever since you saw it. Do you want me to check it out, while you're having your bath?'

'I'll do it now. But it would be nice if your arm were still there.'

The arm tightened. The other reached for my spare hand.

I touched the play button.

'I just wanted to bring a little joy into your life,' the French-accented voice said. 'I think you could do with some *joie de vivre*, living with that dull Englishman of yours. Don't you?'

'There's no need even to go over to Harborne, Peter,' I said, easing my assorted aches into a marginally more comfortable position at Brian's desk. 'If I give you my code number you can page the machine from Smethwick. Mind you, if you did go round, you could help yourself to some balloons.'

'Balloons!'

'That's what I said. Somehow they failed to give me the pleasure they usually do. As did the flowers someone sent me on Monday morning.'

'Ian told me about them,' Peter said grimly. 'What are you going to do, Sophie?'

'Do? Do what I always do. Stick to the job in hand and let you get on with yours.'

'That,' he said darkly, 'will be the day.'

It would certainly have to be today. There was a pile of mail, the voice-box overflowing, as it were, and I ought to open the e-mail. I ought to make calling Sheffield a priority too, if simply to establish that Myakovsky would not be getting a visa. But I couldn't do that for another forty minutes, until normal office hours. And I ought to check what time Martin Acheson wanted to speak to me.

There were plenty of arguments for doing that first, on the grounds that no one else in the team could tackle it. But, although I certainly didn't want to do it myself, I didn't like the thought of delegating to the others work that might involve them having to deal with death threats, albeit to other people. Though it had to be admitted that Marcus was big enough to look after himself and that he owed me for having blagged his way into a job for which he wasn't technically qualified. On the other hand, his PR work had proved brilliant. An unqualified success, perhaps? He'd certainly eclipsed Alexandrina, whom we'd neither seen nor heard from since the first half-day.

Yah. In fact, yah boo sucks. I thumbed my nose at her and her overbearing mother. And went further: I drafted a letter terminating her contract with effect from today's date. There! I stuck out my tongue as I signed it.

Well, being totally childish made me feel better. I whipped through the pile of post simply to check that there was nothing in an anonymous Jiffy bag. Negative. And no letters addressed to me personally. The Stonkin Mama and Myakovsky envelopes had been virtually indistinguishable from countless others, so I'd leave the rest of the mail for the women when they arrived. E-mail? Just a batch from writers confirming their arrival times, mostly but not exclusively at New Street Station. Some were bucking the trend and coming via Moor Street or Snow Hill Stations. I printed each out. Someone would have to do a careful tabulation to make sure each was met when and where they were supposed to be met. And someone must confirm their bookings, as appropriate, at the Mondiale. And run a last-minute check that all had books available to be signed. A local bookshop had undertaken to provide a bookstall at each event; I just hoped they wouldn't overstretch themselves. Perhaps checking them should be my job but I'd leave the rest to Una and Tasleen, whom I knew to be meticulous.

And now for the answerphone and voice-mail messages. Despite myself I was shaking. No, it was nothing to do with Myakovsky's Russian pals, or with Stonkin Mama. It was in anticipation of another intrusion into my territory by the Balloon Man. Or were the three as unconnected as I liked to think? Surely it wasn't logical for three separate people to be threatening one single festival. If the origin of Stonkin Mama's letters was conceivably a hoaxer, or the woman herself – how irritating that Ian was always so discreet! – Did that mean that the threats against me and Myakovsky were connected? Somehow the idea of three different nutters was more likely.

I was standing staring at the phones when there was a scratch at the office door. Delighted by the interruption, but now anxious about who might be outside, I opened the door to a shamefaced Marcus.

'Sorry, boss,' he said. 'I forgot the wretched key-code. Are you all right?'

'Fine. Except very stiff. Mike had fixed up an evening for me in the nets at Edgbaston. First time I've played anything other than back-lawn cricket with friends' children for years.' I clapped a hand to the small of my back. OK, the back wasn't hurting but the arm with the hand on did. Sharply.

'Any special reason?' he asked. 'I mean, most of us don't get the chance.'

'Just that they need bodies for the writers' team against the Bears at the end of the Bookfest. And someone suggested I should be on it. Here we are.' I fished from the file a sheet with the list of possible players and entered mine at the bottom.

'D'you think they'd like an extra man? I used to play when I was at Ampleforth,' he said, suddenly going into a clipped upper-class accent.

'Oh, ah,' I said, which is Black Country for *stop trying to con me: I've got you sussed.*

'Honestly. I mean, we're talking real ethnic minority here, Sophie. I did my GCSEs and A levels there. Except they might have been O levels in those days. And my degree at York.'

I flushed.

'Oh, it doesn't do my street cred any good if I let on,' he said. 'Any more than it would do Stonkin Mama's if people found out about the Cambridge connection. And what good's a degree in Sociology to a poet? I tells you, man, no good at all.' He reverted to his usual alternation between patois and ordinary Brummie West Indian accent.

I rather wished I didn't know about his public-school persona. And I certainly wished I hadn't heard his public-school voice. The one thing I didn't want was an assistant with a gift for mimicking accents.

Chapter Sixteen

It was almost a routine matter to fax the morning's hate mail – about both Myakovsky and Stonkin Mama – to Peter and Harvinder. Certainly I was cool and downbeat about it. Then it was time to cut the Gordian knot. Praying that Brian's constant hassling had so enraged Sheffield that Myakovsky's application was at the very foot of the bottom-most in-tray, I dialled and asked for the name Brian had ringed in red at the head of the very thick manila file. He'd meticulously noted the time, date and length of each call, with a summary of what he'd said and the official's response.

'Mrs Goldsmith? This is Sophie Rivers here, from the Big Brum Bookfest.' I spoke expecting a deluge of outrage. I got friendly warm South Yorkshire.

'Hello, love. We haven't heard from your office for a few days, now, have we? Everything all right?'

Nonplussed, I said, 'Well, Brian Fairbrother – my boss – I'm afraid he's not at all well.'

In an aside across a badly shielded mouthpiece she told a colleague, 'That nice man from Birmingham's been taken badly.' Back to me, she said, 'Poor man. What's happened to him?'

I resisted the urge to tell her it was excess of visa-related stress. 'Stomach problems.'

To colleague: 'Tummy ache, poor thing.' To me, 'Oh, the poor love. And you're helping out, are you, love?'

'Yes, indeed.' Yes, indeed! 'And I was just wondering where you'd got on Myakovsky's visa application.'

'Oh, things are moving very well. The Consulate should be able to hand it over tomorrow . . . What was that, love?'

Shit and shit and shit. 'Great,' I said faintly. 'You've been wonderfully helpful. Thank you very much.'

It occurred to me as I replaced the handset that Mrs Goldsmith had been a good deal more sympathetic about Brian than I had. OK, I'd tried between tasks to find out how he was but never managed to raise anyone in the Fairbrother household. The least I could do was try again.

It rang on and on – no answerphone clicked in. OK, Sophie – what now? His wife's mobile? But I'd no idea of her number, of course. I knew Brian's, but the use of mobiles was forbidden in hospitals. I couldn't even phone the hospital switchboard for news since I had no idea which ward he was in. Embarrassing as it might be, I'd just have to wait for Mrs Fairbrother to contact me.

Ian responded to the news of Myakovsky's visa with a cup of Earl Grey. 'Well, it's time to get the big-time players on to this. I mean, three, no, four people with Bookfest connections being threatened – even if we do suspect the threats to Stonkin Mama are spurious. I doubt if Peter and Harvinder will be allowed to continue with the case. They'll bring in a specialised group. Like for when Clinton and co. came for that Economics meeting.'

'I don't think even Myakovsky quite merits the attention of the G8 Summit,' I said bleakly. 'But I can see why Peter and Harvinder would be pulled out. Central Birmingham's scarcely their patch. What it needs is someone with an overall grasp of what's going on. If only the handover doesn't result in a lack of continuity.'

'I'll get on the blower to whoever it should be,' he said. 'I'll try to fix a meeting soon. Would you be free this afternoon?'

I rolled my eyes. 'Have to be, won't I? One thing you and the Expert ought to bear in mind is that one of Brum's great and good wishes to provide Myakovsky with accommodation at her home. As opposed to the Mondiale.'

He shook his head. 'Yes, I've been worrying about that. It really isn't a good idea. The Mondiale is geared up to events like this. Wonderful security system. That bloke Gavin installed it.'

'A mega-version of what he did to my house?'

Ian nodded.

'So Big Brother will be watching.'

'Not just Big Brother but all his sisters and his cousins and his aunts,' he said. He'd obviously followed an eclectic culture course since he'd retired. 'Gavin says he's still waiting to see you on the golf course.'

'He'll see his first flying pig first,' I said.

'I assume you'll be dealing with Councillor Burton,' I told Martin Acheson over a baguette at Brian's desk.

Acheson had made a fuss about wanting to take me out to lunch. 'Somewhere – rather special,' he'd said, with a smile I wasn't at all sure about. But the others were having to sacrifice their midday breaks to deal with an influx of ticket enquiries, and I wasn't going to walk out on them. When a CID officer phoned to confirm a meeting with me and Ian in the early afternoon, I felt more than justified in insisting on an office lunch. Acheson looked without approval at the healthy choice selected by Marcus, a vegan whose only concession to normality was to agree to buy us tuna or cheese, on the proviso he didn't have to sit in the same office as us. That seemed a reasonable price to pay, given my own reservations about peanut butter and the particularly nasty vegan ersatz cheese he himself favoured. Marcus had also bought mineral water and some fruit, so I felt we had a feast.

For a moment I thought Acheson was going to take my seat behind the desk – habit, perhaps. But he simply shifted it a little, and returned to his own side, where he rearranged his own chair. When his mental music stopped, we sat down.

I flipped open my notepad. If the man wanted to be briefed, he would be briefed.

'Councillor Burton?' he repeated.

'She made that fuss about providing accommodation for Myakovsky, and Ian Dale thinks he'd be much safer at the Mondiale.'

'Has Mr Dale seen Councillor Burton's house? Well, he should check it out before he makes hasty judgements.'

I thought I detected a slight emphasis on *Mr* and there was indisputably one on *hasty*. Why was he suddenly changing tack? 'What would he find if he did?'

'A very well-protected property. Electronic gates, sophisticated entry systems. That sort of thing.'

'In a private home?'

'In a private home.' He looked both smug and impressed.

I was intrigued but wouldn't let him see it. 'However good the security, I don't see how we can ask Ian to give up his time – and that of his expert colleagues – to look at it when we've got perfect accommodation already lined up.'

'Councillor Burton is already sufficiently offended by your failure to include her in any events.'

'Surely Brian explained to you that she was incommunicado—'

'"*Incommunicado!*"'

'Not answering phones, e-mails, whatever. All through the relevant period. We did everything to try to reach her. And then everything to find other people to chair events we'd had her pencilled in for. We can't pull out people who've volunteered their services, often at some inconvenience to themselves.'

He raised an unbelieving eyebrow, but I wouldn't give him what I began to suspect was the satisfaction of being argued with. At last he said, writing in his folder as if to minute it, 'I would prefer it if you and Mr Dale took the trouble to inspect her premises and report back to me. In fact, I told her she could expect you both this evening. Provided,' he added drily, 'you had no prior commitments.'

Why was Acheson suddenly so keen to support the councillor in this? Some sort of mutual palm-greasing maybe? Doubtless a man such as Acheson would find it useful to have favours to call in from councillors if he needed them.

I raised an eyebrow trained by years in the classroom and in college meetings to express a wide variety of emotions. Today's was ironic objection to Acheson's presumption – quite subtle for one eyebrow. I raised the other slowly, to include Ian in my objection.

To my delight Acheson started to bluster. 'Of course, I did warn her – and I realise Mr Dale is a volunteer – I'm sure some sort of emolument . . .'

Emolument is next in the dictionary to *emollient*. They have quite different meanings, quite different roots. But Acheson certainly meant this emolument to soothe – to soothe both Ian and me.

I bowed in acknowledgement. 'Ian certainly deserves something for all the trouble he's already gone to. But it will have to be offered tactfully.'

Acheson nodded. He dusted the last crumbs from his fingers and declined the offer of fruit.

'Tea or coffee?' I asked, pushing away from the desk. 'The tea's better.'

'Tea it shall be then. Where are you going?'

'To make it.'

'Surely one of your staff—'

'They volunteered to run the Bookfest, Martin, not to make my drinks.'

When I got back – I hope he was impressed by the alternatives of milk and lemon – he was on his feet checking our wall charts. Good. One picture would save a thousand of my words.

'The advance bookings are much healthier, aren't they?' I observed. 'Marcus has worked wonders drumming up support. And he seems to have pressed the right button in the media. We've got regional BBC coming to film for their arts slot, plus a lot of coverage from Carlton and cable.'

He lowered his voice. 'I just wish he'd look the part. You know. His dreadlocks. That knitted cap. It's not what people expect.'

'It rather depends which people,' I said. Dreadlocks and woolly hat were so much part of Marcus I hardly registered them, any more than I noticed Tasleen's clothes. 'In fact, I rather think they're an asset, you know. After all, this is a multicultural festival for a multicultural city.' I smiled. But I wasn't taking any racism from anyone.

'So where precisely are we at now?' Acheson asked, with an audible change of gear.

'The women are dealing with writers' travel and accommodation arrangements, so everyone can be met and escorted to either their venue or their accommodation. Tomorrow we take delivery of the sponsored car – another fine photo opportunity. We've got permission to have it driven up into Chamberlain Square, and I want the whole team to be photographed with it.'

'Who'll man the office?'

'The office will be temporarily unstaffed,' I said. 'Five minutes. No problem.' Rather belatedly I added, 'It would be good if you could be in the photos. After all the whole thing was your brainchild.' It was. I'd goofed. I should have invited him from the outset. Perhaps a smile would mollify him.

'I'll see what I can do,' he said, apparently not displeased.

Acheson was only just leaving – he'd spun out our discussion of administrative trivia way beyond its natural length – when the CID officer was announced. As soon as I saw her – Detective Inspector Bishop, her card said – I knew that Acheson would find an excuse to stay. DI Bishop was, after all, the sort of woman for whom I would expect most men to hang around. She was about five foot seven, no more than size twelve, a natural blonde, I'd say (as one who knows what isn't – quite – natural), with blue eyes and a stunning complexion. She was the right height and build for a most elegant trouser suit.

Ian, arriving half a minute after her, caught my eye and winked. 'I'd better get another chair,' he said, with amused tolerance.

We were just discussing Councillor Burton's offer of

hospitality when Una tapped on the door and beckoned me. Excusing myself, I slipped out.

'We wouldn't have interrupted you,' she whispered, 'but we thought you ought to see the midday post. No, nothing nasty. Just a bit funny, really. Though I wouldn't like it done to me.'

'Show me,' I said. For the first time in six months, something stabbed my stomach.

I followed her into my former office. On the desk was a file of photocopied images of women doing different things – driving cars, digging the garden, cooking a meal, sky-diving, whatever. The funny thing was that all the women had my face.

'Except it isn't funny at all,' I told Chris over the phone.

'Of course it isn't. Particularly as—' He stopped abruptly.

'Particularly as?' I prompted.

'Hell! I'm not telling you this, Sophie, and you don't want to know anyway. But Marietta Coe was involved in – a possible incident – today. Oh, it may have been a simple accident, quite innocent. But someone drove at her as she was crossing the road. About fifty yards from her house.'

'Could she say anything about the car?'

Chris managed a bark of laughter. 'Sometimes when you talk I think I'm listening to me. As it happens, she didn't clock more than the fact it was big and fast. She isn't even sure it was an attack. A lot of drivers of big, fast cars ignore pedestrian lights.'

So Marietta hadn't just been jaywalking.

'As for your stalker,' Chris said, 'I promise you, Sophie, we'll get him. Have you told the Bookfest people?'

'Not yet. Not,' I added not quite ironically, 'without police permission. Actually, I'm supposed to be in a meeting about security right now. I just thought Peter and Harvinder ought to know. And, to be honest, you, since you seemed very involved in the Marietta case. Any news of the paraffin yet?' I added, trying to lighten the mood.

'None,' he said. From the sound of his voice I had not succeeded.

DI Bishop – Claire – and Acheson had a tacit contest to see who would stay in my office the longer. Claire clearly wanted to talk to me; Acheson clearly wanted to talk to her. He looked, in fact, as if he wanted to do a good deal more than talk. Claire won, though she had to resort to the rather crude observation that Acheson must want to be on his way.

I shut the door behind his unwilling back.

'More tea?' Ian asked, leaving Claire and me together.

'You're in a very interesting situation,' Claire said. 'You've managed to get this writer you didn't want, you're supposed to be putting him into accommodation neither Ian nor I wants him to take, and, I gather, you're now being stalked. And you've got a sleaze-ball of a boss. What is it that stops you packing up and heading for Mauritius?'

Ian returned with the tea. The question was presumably rhetorical anyway. She took the tea and smiled at Ian. 'What I'd like is for you to be unable to check out Councillor Burton's home tonight. I'd like to check it over.'

'Can I come too?' I asked.

'Why on earth . . .?' she asked.

'Because I like – I don't know – being nosy. See how other people live. It's like going round a stately home or something. I always want to see the bits you're not allowed to see.'

Claire grinned. 'Well, I somehow suspect that that'll be the situation with Councillor Burton's residence. We shall see the bits they want us to see.'

'We can ask to see the rest?'

'I can. You can't. You're only there to see if the place is luxurious enough for your honoured guest, remember. You can ask about tea-making facilities but not about window locks. OK?'

I'd heard houses referred to – ironically, as Claire had done – as residences. I'd certainly seen them described as such in estate agents' ads. But I'd never seen one that actually described itself as one. But this one did. Beside the wrought-iron gates, tipped with gold paint, a marble tablet, its deeply incised lettering touched in gold, declared, 'PRIVATE RESIDENCE'.

Neither of us could see a gate handle, and Claire was edgy about leaving her car stuck across road and pavement. At last we spotted a discreet grille, about three inches by two. Claire spoke into it, suggesting the gates were opened immediately.

They were.

We drove in and they closed behind us.

Chapter Seventeen

We'd joked, hadn't we, about stately homes? And here we were outside one.

'Wow,' Claire said, 'I didn't know Brum had anything like this. Hang on – I thought Mrs B was supposed to be Labour!'

'Well,' I said, 'this *is* part of the Calthorpe Estate.'

'Calthorpe Estate? You must remember I'm an immigrant.' For a moment she turned on a Liverpool accent.

While she cut the engine and we unclipped our seat belts, I got into didactic mode. 'Early in the nineteenth century, Birmingham had to expand. The old town was around the Colmore Row, Newhall Street area. But as the factory owners got rich, they wanted appropriate homes – well away from the stinking masses. So a clever entrepreneur bought up a lot of land in Edgbaston and built some very pukka houses. All either big or bijou but posh. Not a pleb for miles except the servants. I'll give you a guided tour afterwards, if you like – there are some lovely buildings.'

Claire pulled a face. 'Thanks but no thanks. I've got my man's tea to cook.'

I felt a pang. Warwickshire had started an away match this morning, and Mike wouldn't be there when I got home. Nor tomorrow nor the day after. He'd try and make it for the

Bookfest reception, but I knew he couldn't guarantee even that.

'Fine,' I said. 'Anyway, checking this over will take hours.' Funny, anyone would think I didn't want to go home. I always wanted to go home. Didn't I? I didn't now, not if I was to be assailed by *soi-disant* affectionate messages from someone I didn't want to know. And then I remembered. Andy would be there to support me. Except that would present a whole lot of problems in itself.

'I'm afraid it will,' Claire said, getting out. 'Christ, I hope they haven't got any bleeding guard dogs.'

So did I. But there wasn't any baying, and, more to the point, no silent rush of feet, so we might be all right. I gestured to Claire to attack the sort of bell pull that might have summoned Mrs Fairfax when Jane Eyre turned up at Rochester's place. I looked up. Plenty of attic room for concealing mad wives. Or Russian writers.

The outer door opened to reveal a woman in her late fifties, neatly dressed and well made-up.

'Councillor Burton?'

'Councillor Burton is expecting you,' she said, stepping back to hold open for us a vestibule door with, I noticed, bevelled glass. It was hard not to gasp at the perfect proportions of the hall. Mike, with his love of history, would have known who'd designed it, who'd made the lovely occasional furniture standing around.

Coughing slightly – we must both have been gawping – the woman ushered us into what she called the drawing room. Again, it was like stepping into a National Trust room, with a couple of newspapers artlessly left on a coffee table to show the punters that the aristos really did live here. This room was full of chinoiserie. I was full of covetousness.

Neither of us wanted to sit down until invited. But if I, at five foot one, felt overlarge and ungainly, maybe Claire felt the same. She sat down on the extreme edge of a spindly legged chair, looking as if she was waiting to see her gynaecologist. I settled for a sofa, trying to cross my legs elegantly but probably failing. Through the deep, wide windows, I could see a garden as spacious and beautifully maintained as the house.

The door opened and in bustled a pigeon of a woman, whose heavy breasts and thick ankles must have been a source of deep distress to her, so out of place were they in these surroundings. Her clothes were wonderfully cut, and I suspected that the sort of chin that often went with a chest like that might have been subject to the surgical variety of cut. The rest of her face was remarkably wrinkle-free (tucks or good cosmetics?), but I couldn't, from the state of her hands, put her age at anything less than sixty. I wished I'd done my homework beforehand: the lives of councillors are scarcely private property.

'Detective Inspector Bishop,' Claire said, getting to her feet. 'And Ms Rivers from the Big Brum Bookfest.'

'Do sit down,' Councillor Burton said. 'Now, may I offer you some refreshment? The sun's low enough in the sky for me to offer you gin? A cocktail? Wine?' Underneath the cultured voice was a distinct south of Watford twang. It had been Brian who'd quipped about Watford: still no news of him. I'd try his home number again tonight, if I had a chance.

Belatedly remembering my manners, I said, 'A glass of white wine would be perfect, Councillor Burton.' I didn't somehow think she'd think any the less of me for accepting.

She nodded, looking at Claire, whom I'd effectively stymied, of course: if that was the right term. One day I'd have to take up Gavin's golfing offer, if only to enrich my vocabulary.

Though not, perhaps, my wardrobe.

'Mineral water, please.'

We'd both given orders as if we knew what we wanted would be there. Well, one would, in a room like this. But one would also have a pretty fair idea of who would be running round with bottle openers: not Councillor Burton, anyway.

She touched a button at the side of the overmantel and then sat down. She didn't manage an elegant crossing of the ankles, either – her legs must have been even shorter than mine. 'Now, I understand you wish to discuss Mr Myakovsky's accommodation. What—'

'Not so much accommodation,' Claire said, 'as security. And I may as well point out, Councillor Burton—'

'Iris, please.'

'Iris. I may as well point out that it is not simply Mr Myakovsky's safety we're interested in, it's yours and your family's. Not to mention,' she added, 'that of this property.' She looked around to emphasise her point.

'Well, you've seen the gates, of course.'

Claire nodded.

'And we've got security lights everywhere. Shutters to the windows.'

Claire glanced up from her notebook. 'Steel?'

Iris looked aghast. 'My dear – the original shutters.'

'What about the windows themselves? Locks? Double glazing?'

'Inspector, this is a Grade One listed building.'

'Alarm system.'

'Of course.'

'Fire escapes . . . no fire escapes? Security cameras?'

'*Cameras*? You mean, in the rooms?'

I didn't like the look of the colour mounting in Iris Burton's cheeks. 'I think the inspector means outside.'

Claire glanced up. 'I mean both. Mrs Burton – Iris – I have to tell you that in my opinion you should call in a firm of security experts first thing tomorrow.'

'You mean the house isn't safe for Mr Myakovsky?'

'I mean, Iris, that the house isn't safe for you.'

Each succeeding room was as beautifully decorated, lit and furnished as its predecessor. Only one thing missing, from my point of view: books. There were hardly any. OK, you wouldn't expect pulp fiction to lie on Sheraton shelves, but there weren't any classic novels either. Upstairs, perhaps, in less public rooms? But I got diverted from books to domestic arrangements. They'd had dressing rooms to convert into en suite bathrooms, so damage in the name of sanitary progress had been minimal. All in all, if anyone had asked me where I'd choose to stay, I'd have chosen this. But then, my life wasn't at stake.

Was it?

Claire came to a halt at the bottom of a cantilevered staircase. 'Have you lived here long, Mrs Burton?'

To my amazement, she blushed. 'Only two years. This is Perry's second marriage, you see. It's his family home. Old money,' she nodded.

'What does your husband do?' Claire asked, with commendable cool.

Iris almost flinched at the crudity of the question. Clearly one did not have to 'do' anything if one had old money. But surely hers wasn't old. 'He was in the armed forces,' she said.

Claire's eyebrows – though not, I flatter myself, in the same league as mine – were expressive. She said quietly, 'I'm even more surprised at the lack of security, then.'

I fished in my bag. 'I wonder if you should consult a friend of mine. I know he's worked for some very high-risk people.' I did not add, *me included*. I scribbled his phone number on a page torn from my diary.

Iris took it, but did not look impressed.

'How long have you been involved with this Bookfest?' Claire asked suddenly. I glanced at her: she had registered the lack of reading matter too?

'Oh, since its inception. I mean, I was in at the very ground floor. A moving force.'

'How are you involved, apart from looking after Mr Myakovsky?'

Iris beamed at her: 'Oh, I'm there simply at Mr Fairbrother's disposal. I'll help in any way I can.'

But not if it involved going to meetings, responding to urgent phone messages asking for her help – or even keeping up to date with Brian's illness.

Claire nodded. 'It must be wonderful, knowing all these literary people: poets, novelists . . .' She tailed off. She was leaving the punch line to me, bless her.

'Knowing someone like Myakovsky well enough to have him to stay,' I said. 'How did you meet him?'

Iris blushed, but not becomingly. 'Oh. I've never met him. But he's an old acquaintance of Perry's. Old friend.'

Claire nodded. 'Well, I'm very grateful for your time, Mrs Burton. Very grateful. I'll have a word with my colleagues, and Sophie will no doubt have a word with the board. Bother – it looks as if it's coming on to rain.'

Claire drove me back into town, although it took her out of her way and I'd happily have gone by bus.

'What do you make of all that?' she asked, as we picked

our way back to the Five Ways island. 'And why do they call this Five Ways when there are six roads? And why does that silly bleeder signal right and keep straight on?' She wrenched the car out of his way.

Thinking we'd had enough local history for one day, I answered the first question. 'I make a woman doing something to please her husband,' I said. 'Not big readers, either of them, though. Unless they keep books tucked away in those wonderful ormolu chests.'

'And if he's ex-military, how does he have a house as big as that with so little security?'

'If it does have so little security,' I said slowly.

She slowed for the Broad Street exit. 'Eh?'

'Just because Iris knew nothing about it, doesn't mean there wasn't any. Oh, no nasty metal blinds, I grant you. But hidden cameras are just that.'

'So you can film intruders nicking your silver? Nice one, Sophie.'

'All the same, I'll bet five pence she doesn't phone Gavin.'

'Gavin the Golfer? Holes in one a speciality?'

'That Gavin. But he seems to know his job.'

'I'd like to know more about Perry's job. And his relationship if any with Myakovsky.'

'Not to mention,' I added, 'his relationship if any with Martin Acheson and the Big Brum Bookfest. With all this security scare Acheson's really sticking his neck out to please Mrs Burton, having Myakovsky staying with her. But maybe what he's really doing is pleasing Perry.'

Chapter Eighteen

My car was sitting patiently in the car park, where I'd left it, unsullied by balloons or indeed by anything else. Was it neurotic to bend down and peer underneath it? Not that I knew what I was peering for, but surely I'd have spotted anything truly out of place.

There was a pair of feet beside me. Claire's. I straightened quickly, feeling foolish. But her smile reassured me.

'You're right to take precautions like that. If you ask me,' she added quietly, 'what we need is a complete team devoted to this: the stalkings, the death threats, the Bookfest. It's not good enough for individual officers to be investigating individual incidents; it's time for a more global approach. I'm going to have a word with Them Upstairs.'

I refrained from commenting that it was about time too. 'Makes sense to me. Unless you're going to spend all your time phoning the lads at Smethwick to find out how they're getting on, and they you. How flexible can the police be?'

'We'll just have to find that out, won't we?' She smiled, waited while I started the engine, and watched me on my way.

It's a good job the roads were pretty clear as I drove back to Harborne: I was so busy agonising that the post or answerphone would provide further evidence of someone's intrusion into my life that I forgot to worry about an overdue tête-à-tête with Andy. And when I remembered that, I forgot about the other matter. The combined effect was a regrettable lack of concentration: one of those scary journeys where you get home and can't remember which route you took.

The other problem was food, of course. Andy had a cavalier attitude towards domesticity. No, he had a selfish attitude towards things he wanted, like food and drink, which he'd blithely finish without bothering to replace. Or even leaving a note telling someone else to replace. So it was quite possible that he'd grazed my fridge bare – not that there was ever much in there these days, with my life divided between Harborne and Bournville.

But there was no sign of him when I opened the front door. Penalty points, Andy, for not locking it, but bonus points for remembering the burglar alarm. And double bonus points for leaving a note on the kitchen table: 'OUT OF MILK. DON'T START COOKING. BRINGING A TAKEAWAY.'

Overwhelmed by Andy's transformation, I picked up the post and idly shuffled through it. The letter with an Australian stamp was from the mother of one of the cricketers Mike had played against last winter. Her son was currently Sussex's overseas player, and she hoped I'd look out for him. No problem, and a nice stamp for Oxfam. Then there were no fewer than three offers of loans, and one for a new credit card. All into the paperbank sack. And then a couple with printed adhesive labels – exactly the same sort that had brought the death threats to Stonkin Mama and Myakovsky. Exactly the same as used by businesses everywhere, come to that. I breathed out hard and opened the first: a circular about a summer concert. The second was a catalogue for sexy underwear. From Mike? Or a random mailing? Or . . .?

All right. Answerphone time. And nothing. Absolutely nothing. So why did I have to sit down hard at the kitchen table and hold my head in my hands? It didn't make sense, did it? To be rattled when he did something, to be rattled when he didn't. Perhaps, though, he thought my morning's post at work had been sufficient. That and – possibly – the underwear catalogue.

At this point Andy bustled in, carrying a brown paper carrier bag already stained with curry. 'Can you keep this warm while I get the rest of the stuff?'

I busied myself with plates and lager. He brought in two Safeway carriers per hand, and then went back to lock the car.

He came back looking singularly grim. 'This was on the driver's seat,' he said, dropping a bright turquoise envelope bearing my name on to the table alongside the bag of poppadams. 'The thing is, why should anyone drop it on the seat of a hire car? If it's your stalker, he knows what car you drive. Why choose a rented Mondeo?'

'To show how much he knows about me,' I said flatly.

The envelope wasn't sealed; the flap was tucked in. I flicked it open and fished out a greetings card. No message, of course. At least, not on the inside.

Andy wrapped an arm round my shoulders and peered at it. 'Klimt,' he said. 'But what's the subject? Looks like some woman wearing gym-knickers!'

'Dream on. That, unless I'm very much mistaken, is Leda being raped by the Swan.'

Supper was a sombre affair, Andy dragging moodily on the lager and stabbing at his balti with chunks of roughly torn naan. He seemed to be taking this even harder than I was.

'Hell, Sophie,' he said at last, 'it isn't as if you're famous or anything. Just an ordinary woman, doing an ordinary job, for Christ's sake. Makes it worse, somehow.'

I wasn't sure of his logic but didn't have the energy to disagree. Or to talk all that much at all. Soon Mike would phone – our nightly ritual phone call whenever he was playing away. A lovely long one. Neither said much that was important. He'd talk about the day's play, or, if rain had prevented play, about the book he was currently reading. I'd talk about my doings too, which had until recently entertained him. But today would not be so good. It was no good censoring anything. He'd pick up from the sound of my voice that something was wrong, and hated me to minimise problems. It was the only thing we'd ever had a row about: I'd tried to make light of what had happened while he was playing in Australia, and he'd accused me of trying to protect him.

The phone rang. I pounced. Ruth for Andy. She and I had a short natter, and then I pointed at the handset and at the living room. Andy might as well take the call in there. He responded with an ironic grin. But he pointed at his watch and gave a thumbs up: yes, he knew the importance of my call to me.

I'd tidied the kitchen and had a shower by the time Andy and Ruth had finished. This time Andy's grin was apologetic. He in turn pointed to the living room. 'I'd meant to unpack the Safeway shopping myself. I take it you found the malt whisky?'

'There's no need,' I said, showing him the pantry shelf groaning under the weight of exotic drinks Mike had had pressed upon him.

'Take it as a gesture, woman. I never said thank you for getting me out of that fraud shit. How did you do it?'

'Tell you later.' I had my call to make.

Some time later he sauntered back to join me, by now sporting a spectacular black silk dressing gown, heavily embroidered with oriental birds. He'd obviously showered too, and was looking sleek. He settled down in an armchair opposite the sofa I was occupying, and refreshed my malt while I bade Mike a tender – OK, a soppy – good night.

The curtains drawn against a suddenly stormy sky, the low lights, the drink and the dressing gowns – we could have been in for a night of seduction. Instead, I took a bracing swig, sat up straight and decent, and said, 'Andy, there's something I have to tell you.'

At this point, naturally, the front doorbell rang. Long ago, at another time when I wouldn't have wanted to open my door to a stranger, Chris and I had devised a little rhythmic code: it was that code pressed now. So, while not knowing whether to curse or heave a sigh of relief, at least I could open the door in confidence.

'I wanted to chew something over with you,' he said, without preamble.

'Go on through. I'll get another glass.'

What he'd make of the sight of Andy, also in dishabille, I didn't know. But I could hear them talking amicably enough, possibly about chess. Anyway, Chris was sitting on the floor when I returned, his long legs stretched in front of him. Yes, he knew he looked good in uniform, didn't he? In fact, sitting like that, gently flexing his ankles from time to time, had been his opening gambit in our short relationship – as opposed to our long friendship.

I passed him a good tot of malt. If he did what he'd often done in the past, relaxed so much he fell asleep for the night, at least Andy would chaperone us. There was less need, of course, to protect my reputation these days now Aggie, my neighbour, was no longer there to keep an eye on things.

'This guy's really becoming a pain, then?' he asked, toasting us both silently. 'Andy's shown me the card.'

'Any more news of Marietta Coe's near miss?' I asked.

'Marietta Coe?' Andy put in. 'Isn't she the woman whose launch I'm supposed to be hosting? And I'm ferrying here and there?'

'The same. She, like Sophie, has been subjected to some harassment. Hers seemed to have tailed off, indeed stopped, much to everyone's relief. But some guy in a big car failed to stop at a crossing. She was so rattled she reported it. But now she thinks it might have been a coincidence.'

'And what do you think it is?'

'Who can tell? She couldn't tell us the make of the car or any part of the registration.'

'Colour?'

He shook his head. 'Something dark. Which covers a multitude of sins.'

'For Christ's sake, wouldn't you clock things like that?' Andy demanded.

'Some people remember everything in an incident, some nothing. That's why we have SOCOs and CCTV and—' Chris broke off, shrugging. He waited while Andy sloshed. 'Glenmorangie? I thought you favoured Irish, Sophie?'

'Present from Andy,' I said quickly. It would do no one any good if Andy announced it was a thank you present for eliminating evidence in a possible case against him. Not since it was Chris's case. However well the two men got on in theory, Chris had never forgiven Andy for putting me in a position where I'd had to break the law to save Mwandara, Andy's African hospital. He'd never quite forgiven me for breaking it, either. Thank goodness the more damage we inflicted on it, the more our friendship had deepened.

Carefully disposing my bathrobe, I sat down. 'You don't think the stalker might just have transferred his attentions from Marietta to me?'

'Does it work like that? Trouble is, I don't know enough about the subject. You read all the new legislation and see how it will affect police operations, but you don't always register the fine detail. I know what charges to bring, what evidence we need but I don't know anything about the psychology of the stalkers. Apart from the popular stereotype, of course – seedy, sad men unable to make proper relationships.'

'What about women stalkers? There are enough of those, for Christ's sake,' Andy said.

He said it with such bitterness both Chris and I looked up. 'You've been stalked?' Chris asked.

'In the States. This beautiful woman. She could have had any man she wanted, in real life. But she wanted a fantasy me. She even thought she was pregnant by me! We called them fans then, not stalkers; you can tell how long ago it was.'

'There are ex-lovers, too,' I put in, not wishing to pursue the phantom pregnancy idea, not until I'd made it clear that Stephan was entirely real. 'Not that Marietta and I share any of those, as far as I'm aware.' My face stiffened.

Chris noticed, of course. Saying nothing, he just raised the eyebrow the far side from Andy.

'The funny thing is,' I made myself say, knowing that however casual I tried to be, both men would pick up the tension I was trying to conceal, 'Marietta and I do have a couple of things in common. Not a lot. But we're both in our thirties, both blonde, and so on.'

'Your features are nothing like . . .' But Chris's brave

assertion tailed off. He stared at me.

'And there's something else. You, Andy. She had a teenage crush on you.'

'So what? So did lots of other kids.'

'So nothing, I should imagine.' And then I said, at the same pace as the thought wormed its way into my brain, 'If the stalker knows me as well as he seems to, there is – just – a possibility – and I know this sounds crazy . . .'

'Go on,' Chris said. 'Your crazy often turns out to be good sharp intuition.'

'Well, this is really crazy. I hope. And I've got nothing at all to base it on. That nice policewoman in charge of Bookfest security – Claire Bishop – do you know her?'

Chris shook his head with forbearance: 'West Midlands Police is a very big service, Sophie. But that's not the point, is it? What are you trying to tell me?'

'If Marietta's a smaller, younger blonde, how about a taller, younger blonde? Chris, what if Claire's at risk?'

Chapter Nineteen

At this point, Andy had got bored with police detail and wandered off to bed. I could see Chris relaxing slightly. At last I could ask, 'So what was it you wanted to chew over with me?'

He transferred himself from the floor to the chair Andy had been occupying. The whisky was well down in his glass, so I pointed to the bottle, covering my own glass. He poured a couple of fingers, and then sat back in apparent contentment. But he was forward again, elbows on knees in a moment.

He'd begin in his own time; I waited.

'It's taken me a long time to get into this job,' he said at last. 'And I think I'm just beginning to get to grips with it. Dealing with the budget, lobbying for more funding. Balancing the needs of glamorous departments against socially vital ones. And against government demands. I feel I'm – yes, into it at last. I fit the chair. I fit the uniform. I may even be starting to make a mark . . .'

'But?'

He grimaced. 'But I've been offered something else.'

Just as Andy had predicted!

'Already?'

'Already. A move I'd have given my teeth for last year. But I'm not sure about it now.'

'Do you have a choice?' In my limited experience, the police service tended to wish changes on to its personnel.

'Yes. But it's pretty clear what they'd like me to do. And in many ways it's what I'd love to do.'

'So what's the problem?' No doubt he'd get round to telling me eventually what the job was.

'Well, I don't feel I've finished in Smethwick. And I'm enjoying being there.'

Trust Chris to put duty before pleasure. 'You like being cock of your own dunghill?'

'Oh, I'd be cock of my own dunghill in the new job. But only for the time being. It's a new appointment, you see. Across the region. Taking responsibility for the new murder investigation unit. A really élite operation. Me at the top, then a team of DCIs heading up teams that would go in whenever there was a major incident.'

'But only ones involving death?'

'There aren't many more serious crimes than murder!'

'What if they're only death *threats*?' I slid in. I had a vested interest, after all. 'Would they be covered by these élite teams?'

'Depends how serious they looked.'

'How would you judge?'

Chris held up a hand in surrender. 'Sophie, give up. You've made your point. Your present case is certainly being taken seriously.'

'Which present case – the death threats or the stalkings?'

'How about the death threats *and* the stalkings?'

I subsided, flushing with guilt. 'Chris: I'm sorry – I know I hijacked the conversation. Let's get back to your sheep. You want a job. They want you for the job. I can see you don't want to leave a job half done, but you were a wonderful detective. Now you've got all those management skills on top of experience in CID, I'd have thought you were the natural choice. If that phrase hasn't been entirely hijacked by food advertising.' I grinned. 'You might even be the healthy choice!'

'But – and here's the problem – only the temporary choice. The job would be up for grabs at interview in a few months. There's no guarantee I'd get it.'

I looked back on my years of teaching. 'Isn't the one in post the one with the strongest chance of getting the job?'

'Or is it the bright bloke who's been on the most courses at Bramshill? I'd hate to be taken away from a job I'm beginning to enjoy only to end up doing neither that nor the one I really want.'

'What might you end up doing?'

'Running a bigger nick, maybe. Or a specialist area like traffic!'

'Just remember,' I said, reminding him of his worst fear, 'you could be in charge of the detention cells at Steelhouse Lane.'

For the first time, I was the last to arrive at the Bookfest office. I'd been invited by the Mondiale for a final check on arrangements, plus a rapid review of security. Ian and I were met in the foyer by the woman into whose charge the Bookfest launch and accommodation had been put – a middle-aged woman called Nesta. She radiated confidence and anticipated questions with a calm smile. Ian consented to drink coffee while we waited for a late arrival – Claire Bishop. It was very good coffee. But then, everything about the Mondiale seemed very good. We said nothing at this stage about alternative accommodation for Myakovsky. I was leaving Claire to offer what I hoped would be an unbiased opinion. And, please God, to take the decision out of my hands, and field the flack from Iris Burton and Martin Acheson. He'd just have to find some other way of buttering her up – or was it her husband? – and let me get on with organising the Bookfest.

When Claire arrived, breathless but in her way as confidence-inspiring as Nesta, Ian and I excused ourselves and walked down Broad Street to the office. Ian sniffed disparagingly but predictably at the statue in Centenary Square but drifted over to the fountain, splashing on the paving stones.

'I've always thought it was the one thing Birmingham was missing,' he said, standing just out of range. 'Other great cities have a river. All we can manage is the poor old Rea.'

'And a lot of canals,' I reminded him.

'Oh, all that stuff about us having more canals than Venice! But canals – OK, I know they're doing them up and making everything lovely' – he gestured back to the ICC and the canals beyond it – 'but they're not . . . they don't . . . they can't compete with a strong-flowing open river. Val and I are thinking of moving to Tewkesbury.'

'Ian!'

'More *were* thinking, I suppose. After all the floods . . . well, we've not got much risk of being washed away up here.' He'd never so much as hinted about this dream before. But there was something about the way he tried to brace his shoulders that told me he was reluctant to let it go.

There was a reception committee waiting for us at the Bookfest office. Peter and Harvinder from Smethwick, Martin Acheson, Marcus, and Tasleen and Una, all crammed into the office that had become mine. The expressions on the faces ranged from frightened to stolid, with irate somewhere in between.

I looked from one to another, knowing that any minute Claire would be along to join the fun. It was like being back at William Murdock, except with adults. Someone had better take charge. That someone was me. I stepped behind my desk and coughed.

'Yes?' I said, looking at Marcus – he was after all, my deputy.

'A little local difficulty,' he said, in a voice that might have been leading assembly in his old school hall. No trace of Brum or patois.

'Which might be?'

'I don't feel a public rehearsal of all that has been said would be appropriate,' he said. 'It would make more sense for us to proceed with what was scheduled for today. I'll brief you on the other matter later.'

If he could be smooth, I could be managerial. 'That seems to make sense. Una and Tasleen, could you get on with that arrivals and departures database and chart we were talking about? And if I were you, I'd print out and enlarge the names of people to be met at the station, so we can stick them to some card and wave them in the station foyer. Marcus, what was it you wanted to do this morning? Yes, you were going to take the car and leaflet locations in Handsworth – right? Oh, and the universities – one last push to increase the audience for that social anthropologist!' Brian had been eclectic in his choice of speakers. 'Can all that wait till we've spoken?'

'No problem. I can always keep myself busy.'

As the office cleared, I turned to Ian and the police officers. 'Peter and Harvinder, would it be better to wait to say what you've got to say until Claire Bishop joins us? She shouldn't be more than five minutes. Or are you in a hurry?'

'I'll get the kettle on,' Ian said.

Peter and Harvinder drifted after him, closing the door firmly behind them.

I gestured Acheson to a chair, sat down myself, donned my listening face and waited. For, I fancied, a bollocking. Not that I had any idea why I might merit one.

'I cannot understand,' he said, 'that someone in your position should leave the office in the hands of two – two—'

'Entirely capable young women,' I concluded. 'Them and my deputy. Who were no doubt doing what they were supposed to be doing: checking incoming communication. I'm not at all sure why the police are here, however. Or you. Could you brief me?' I smiled, almost sweetly.

'The black woman called them.'

'Ah. More threats?'

'It seems whoever it is might have extended his scope. It seems that you yourself are now a liability.'

I leant back in my chair and laughed in his face. 'You mean someone's threatening me! Oh, that's old news, Martin. Anything more?'

Anyone else might have been decently nonplussed. Or even diverted into asking why I hadn't seen fit to tell the board. Not Martin Acheson. 'I understand that you visited Councillor Burton's home last night but did so without Mr Dale – whom I'd expressly asked you to take.'

'He was outranked, Martin. Ian was only ever a detective sergeant. I was accompanied last night by a detective inspector. It's she for whom we're now waiting.' My students would have known that when I got grammatical, I was at my most irritated.

'Why was I not informed?'

'Because, while you are the chair of the board, you have, I understand, no executive powers while you have a paid employee in post.' It sounded good, even if I wasn't entirely sure of my ground. I was saved from possible exposure by the sound of raised voices outside the door. Claire, with a bit of luck. 'What I can't quite understand is why you agreed to make the change in the first place, when everything had been set up at the Mondiale. A word from you would have silenced Councillor Burton.'

'To preserve something of the Bookfest's rapidly evaporating budget, of course. This is a publicly funded festival: it is incumbent on us to reduce our outgoings to the minimum – and now we are, in effect, paying two directors' salaries, not to mention a deputy director's, it is also incumbent upon us to take advantage of every generous offer we receive. Especially from a leading local politician, I would have thought.'

'Of course. I quite see that.' I sounded particularly soothing, not believing a word of it. 'It'll be sad if we can't take it up, won't it?'

'Can't? Won't!'

'DI Bishop is an expert in her field.'

'A bit of a girl,' Acheson sniffed.

'A senior officer,' I said firmly.

A woman who had, after all, made it to inspector after ten years in the police service while Ian had still been a sergeant after thirty. I'd often wondered if he'd have pressed harder for promotion if he hadn't been in Chris's squad.

'Right,' I said, determined to turn the discussion to something more positive, 'I wonder if we could just go over the arrangements for the reception tomorrow. Everything is set up at the Mondiale. You'll be making the keynote speech, Martin, and welcoming the civic dignitaries. And then at six forty-five, you'll organise us to the Rep, for the opening gig.

Provided Myakovsky gets here in time.'

'And if he doesn't?'

'I told you: we have a choice. I'd have thought we have to narrow it down to two: either Tom Phipps, the cricket umpire who's written those lovely children's stories since he retired, or Sir Gareth Whatsit – you know, our ex-UN ambassador. I agree that neither of them's an adequate substitute . . .'

'Couldn't your *contacts*,' he sneered, 'have produced someone more appropriate?'

Numbering on my fingers, I ran through those Andy had tried and failed to get: the Booker prize-winner was touring Australasia, the Pulitzer prize-winner suddenly hospital-ised . . .

'Flip a coin,' Acheson said, holding up an irritated hand.

'Ambassador, then. I'll get Andy—'

'Who will be puffing his autobiography next week, I see. I hope the press don't pick up a rather strong smell of nepotism.'

My, we were cranky this morning. 'As you well know, he was booked by Brian before I came on the scene. You also know he's donating his purely nominal fee to his African hospital trust, and that any profits from sales go to the same trust. More to the point, his event's a sellout. And he's staying on to help with the logistics of the Bookfest.'

Martin's face expressed pure boredom, then coalesced into malice. 'Anyone would think,' he said, leaning towards me, 'that Andy Rivers was much closer to you than a mere cousin.'

Chapter Twenty

This was the moment for a *deus ex machina* if ever there was. And who should fill the bill but Ian, tapping at the door and putting his head round it simultaneously.

'Thought you should know, both of you,' he said in the sort of voice he must often have used to break interesting news to Chris, 'Stonkin Mama's pulled out.'

'She's bloody what?' I demanded, leaping to my feet as if to wring the messenger's neck. I'd have liked to wring Martin's too, but still didn't know how to react to his insinuation. If that was what it was. Surely I was just overreacting – or would have been had it not been for Ian's eruption.

Martin had risen too. 'Pulled out? At this stage? What about her contract? How dare she?'

I was about to add a soprano line to his bass aria of abuse, but – probably as it had in the past stopped Chris open-mouthed to complain – something about Ian's face told me to hold my tongue. 'What's happened?' I asked, my voice much more controlled.

'Her boyfriend's tried to top himself,' Ian said quietly.

'And?'

'Didn't quite manage it. But they've sectioned him. And she's too shocked to do anything, poor lass.'

I waited. There was a lot more story to come by the sound of it. Acheson didn't know Ian as well as I did, of course, and was still chuntering about contracts and professionalism and replacements.

'Thing is,' Ian continued, so quietly that Martin had to shut up in order to hear, 'he tried to kill them both. By driving off a cliff. Down south somewhere. She managed to stop the car, God knows how, and then fought him for the keys. Then he tried to take a running jump, as it were, but some off-duty copper managed to bring him down. Had to knock him out to calm him down.'

'But that's not why Stonkin Mama's pulled out, is it? Not the whole reason?'

Ian shook his head. 'Seems her boyfriend was a bit of a writer. Well, he wrote letters, more to the point. Anonymous ones. On his computer. And printed labels for the envelopes. A development of what I told you the Met suspected when all this started. Began doing it as publicity for her – then it seems to have become an obsession.'

I sat down. Ian did likewise, but Martin remained on his feet, apparently still furious at the disruption of his precious Bookfest.

'Are you saying he's responsible for all this anonymous mail we've been getting?'

Ian shook his head slowly. 'Not all of it, Sophie. He kept copies on his computer. But they're all about her. Nothing about Myakovsky. Nothing at all, I'm afraid,' he added in response to my next – but unasked – question.

'But he could have wiped them – that must be the answer,' Martin said. 'Must be. Must be. Yes!' He banged his fist on to his open palm.

''Fraid not, Martin,' Ian said. 'You've heard of forensic

scientists – well, we've got forensic geeks, too. They check the machine's hard disk – whatever that is,' he added, smiling disarmingly. 'And there's nothing about Myakovsky. Not a sausage. But you leave it to us – to the *police*' – he corrected himself hastily – 'to look into all this. What you've got to worry about is finding a replacement at short notice. Can't have those punters disappointed.'

I straightened. 'Time for a meeting, then.'

Ian nodded. 'But not a meeting about replacement poets. We've got Peter and Harvinder outside, remember – and Claire Bishop's just arrived.'

And suddenly Martin's face was as sunny as it had been furious before. But his delight, I was sure, was not for Peter and Harv.

'So it's my conclusion,' Claire said, every inch a DI, 'that whatever the material advantages accruing to the Bookfest and indeed to Mr Myakovsky's comfort if he stayed at the Burton home, there would be a considerably enhanced security risk, and I would not therefore recommend such a move.'

Peter and Harvinder nodded. So did Ian. I looked from each in turn to Martin Acheson He shrugged. 'Will you contact Mrs Burton, Sophie?'

I smiled. 'It would come better from you, Martin. I'm sure we can rely on you to say the appropriate thing. And she'd take a reminder about her security systems better from you than from me.'

Claire nodded emphatically. 'Please urge her to get proper crime prevention advice. She's sitting on a burglar's dream.' She gathered up her file and her bag. 'I'll be off, then. But I'll see you two down at Steelhouse Lane – in, what, half an hour?'

Hello, hello, hello what were the police up to then? It might seem to Joe Public the obvious thing to do to put together three such well-informed officers, but the exigencies of police protocol, not to mention in-trays, didn't often permit such logical moves.

'Ma'am,' Harvinder said.

'Sure,' Peter said, super-casual; he wasn't about to be outranked by an equal, was he? 'Soon as we've had a word with Sophie and her team.'

Oh dear. Acheson bridled visibly. I was afraid he wouldn't shift, but Claire held the door open for him with a friendly smile, and he rose to follow her.

We listened to their voices until the outer door shut them off.

'As might be expected,' Peter said, 'there are no threats against Stonkin Mama today. But there's one against Myakovsky, very explicit and very upsetting to the women who opened the letter. But not as upsetting as the implicit one against you. You're not going to like this, Sophie.' He looked at Harvinder, who shook his head sympathetically and produced from his briefcase a small Jiffy bag. He handed it to Peter.

'They shouldn't have opened that!' I exclaimed. 'I gave them explicit instructions not to open anything that could be a letter bomb!'

'Not all Jiffy bags contain bombs,' Harvinder said reasonably.

'And your Marcus had a good feel and decided it was OK,' Peter said, deadpan. 'In the event, he was right. But you still won't like what he found.' He slid a hand into the bag and came up with scarlet lace. 'The knickers are crotchless, the bra peep-through.' He waggled a finger through a cup to demonstrate. 'Nothing wrong with the suspender belt. I suppose you and Mike haven't . . .? Quite. Well, you could take them home and try them, Sophie, or, if you prefer, we could log them as evidence.'

'You can wipe that snigger off your face, young man,' Ian said. 'Log them as evidence indeed! I'll bet my pension they'll never find their way into the locked evidence room.' His face cracked slightly. 'Wouldn't have in my day, anyway. Not till they'd been round the canteen and locker-room at least twice.'

'Ho, ho, ho. Very funny,' I said. Then found it wasn't. 'Just go and get rid of the bloody things, will you?'

And then I had to call them back. 'Hang on: what are you doing meeting Claire?'

Peter touched the side of his nose and grinned enigmatically.

I stuck my tongue out.

As soon as they'd left, Marcus brought into my office some very good coffee and cake. 'From home,' he said in his usual voice, sitting opposite me. 'My missus.'

'Thanks.' I was getting to a stage where I no longer risked consuming every calorie regardless, but I couldn't resist his offer. My fillings expressed some dismay, but the rest of me was glad of the blood-sugar. 'Hmm, thank your missus. This is very good.'

He nodded almost absently. 'What I'm beginning to think is that I ought to resign from this job.'

'What?' To my irritation, my voice cracked. 'And leave us stranded?'

'I've done all I really needed to do. Well, I will have done by the end of the week. And those women are as sharp as needles – they can pick up any loose ends.'

'But I thought you needed the money?'

'More than one way of skinning a cat. You're going to need

a poet. Well, ma'am, may I introduce Marcus Downing, the poet?' He got to his feet, giving a low bow.

'Of course. Of course! Hang on, though, Marcus.' I brought Stonkin Mama's contract on to the screen. Then his. 'She's only got three gigs. You'd lose a couple of hundred quid. More.'

'But add in travel expenses for the gigs and think about the free time.' He settled down, crossing one leg over the other so that one ankle rested on the other knee.

I thought. But my mental arithmetic didn't make the two add up. 'You've got a perfectly good job here.'

'Which I lied my way into. OK, man, I've done a bloody good job. But it all these bloody meetings and all this . . . all this shit, man,' he added in a whining patois.

I still couldn't make sense of what he wanted: to give up a week's salary for the fee for three one-and-a-half-hour gigs. But then, I wasn't a poet, and what to me sounded completely crazy in economic terms might have made absolute sense to him in creative ones.

'You should have raised this when Acheson was here,' I said at last. 'You know I can't make that sort of decision without a modicum of consultation.'

Instead of responding to my implicit criticism, he smiled easily. 'You don't like him a lot, do you?' He drank the last of his coffee and put the mug on my desk.

'You don't have to like bosses. Just respect them.'

'But you're not sure whether you respect him any more.'

Why was he probing like this? 'Just because he wants our pet international star to shack up with a councillor instead of in a hotel doesn't mean I don't respect him. It was just that particular idea that struck me as weird.'

'If you ask me, he got de hots for you, lady.' Back to patois for the second half of his sentence.

'I didn't ask you.' Any other day I'd have pointed out that Claire was now flavour of the month. 'Look, Marcus, I'd like to drop this. I feel really peevish and crochety this morning, and it seems to me it would be more profitable to examine the bigger issues. If you want to convince him that your suggestion's the best thing for the Bookfest, we'll have to list: possible alternatives; the likelihood of getting anyone at this stage; the aspects of your current job that someone else will have to pick up; and – yes, your suitability as a stand-in.'

He stood up – to attention, in fact – and sketched a salute. 'Sophie – the Miss Whiplash of the Big Brum Bookfest.' Then he produced a conciliatory grin. 'Must be all those years of teaching, Sophie – you do authoritative very well.'

While Marcus popped out for lunch, I went into the office he shared with the women. They had produced a huge wall chart showing who had to be met where, by whom and where they had to be taken.

'All we need to do now is fill in the who's meeting them column,' Una said.

'After lunch,' I said. 'Which you deserve.' I glanced at the stack of name sheets they'd produced to be waved in station foyers. 'You haven't half shifted the work this morning.'

'Better to work than to worry is what my grandma always said,' Una said.

'Have you seen that thing they sent about Myakovsky?' I asked. Why on earth hadn't I thought of it before?

'Those policemen took it away as evidence,' Tasleen said.

Una snorted, ferreting in a drawer. 'But I got a photocopy first.' She passed it across, with exaggeratedly finicky finger movements. She dusted the tips off afterwards.

'A case of one picture telling a thousand words, as Una's grandma might have said,' Tasleen observed. 'Isn't that from the Tarot cards?'

'The Hanged Man,' I nodded. 'But I've never seen one actually eviscerated before.'

'Hanged, drawn but not yet quartered,' Tasleen said. 'God, and you English people claim to be civilised.'

Una's head went back: 'I don't think this sort of violence is the prerogative of the English.'

I jumped in. 'I don't think sadism's anyone's prerogative, more's the pity – and the British certainly can't claim to be any better than any other nation. But I didn't want to talk about violations of human rights. I wanted to talk about a suggestion Marcus has made. It would very much involve you two.'

'Oh,' Tasleen said, sitting back and opening a pot of yoghurt, 'that crazy idea about him resigning so he can do the poetry gigs? Resign and good luck to him, that's what I say. We can cope.'

'It would have been nice to have an extra driver,' Una said, pointing to the chart. 'One or two days we're going to be really hard-pressed.'

'My brother-in-law's a minicab driver.'

'Oh God, Tas, what a cliché.'

'Well, he is.'

'So he'd have to charge, wouldn't he? And we're supposed to be watching our budgets, right?'

I didn't like the edges sharpening on their voices. Too many hours in a small dark office, perhaps.

'My cousin Andy'll do some driving,' I said. 'And I bet Ian would too. And I've e-mailed all the members of the board to enlist their help. If it rains, Mike might even—'

'You can't rely on rain,' Una put in. 'We're running to a

tight budget here, Sophie, as you should know.'

'OK. Go and have some lunch. And, like I said, we'll fill in the chart later. And give this Marcus business some thought. I don't want to tell Acheson anything you don't agree with.'

They left together, but I could hear them bickering along the corridor. I sighed. Then I realised I should have gone to the loo before they left. Never mind, the office would just have to be unstaffed for a little while. I even left a neat note – the classic 'Back in five minutes'.

When I got back, there was a single red rose waiting for me. It was fastened to the door with a drawing pin.

Chapter Twenty-one

'Hey, that's a bit of all right, isn't it, Soph?' this voice called, posh Brummie overlaid with estuary English. Steph. My son.

I was just about to drag the flower off and trample it underfoot, but I stopped, and turned to face him.

'Someone on the pull, eh?' he asked. 'Or is it just Mike getting all romantic?'

I grinned. Though I still pulled the rose from the door, I did it quite gently. I pressed the keys to admit us, and pushed open the door. He stepped inside and stood, hands in baggy jeans pockets, looking around him.

'There's my office. In you go.' I followed, bringing with me a seething mass of emotions. The one uppermost was relief that I wasn't going to be on my own, for a while at least. Steph was no one's idea of a macho man, but I'd bet he'd be no pushover either. In fact, though he was thin, there were a lot of whippy muscles in the arms sticking out of a deplorable T-shirt. Several deplorable T-shirts. Steph was firmly locked in the grunge era, despite – or perhaps because of – his adoptive parents' affluence.

He didn't sit, but, hands still in pockets, stalked round, looking at the wall charts and fetching up by the window, which he peered out of, sniffing disparagingly.

'Bit claustrophobic, isn't it? I mean, look at all that crap out there. Haven't they ever cleaned it since the place was opened?'

'What the eye doesn't see . . .'

'All the same. So what are you doing here, Soph?'

'Working here. I assumed you must have heard. How did you find your way up here otherwise?'

He snorted. 'Saw you the other day, didn't I? Right up the escalator and all. I thought I'd pop in and take you out for a coffee or something. Then I met this bloke from college. So we went and shared some draw and knocked around a bit, then this afternoon I remembered and I came looking properly.'

I didn't care for the timescale of all this – he must have wasted so much valuable time. I suspected he rarely went to the college classes he was supposed to go to, and I longed to drag him by the back hair into one of my A level classes at William Murdock. That would have shown him what work was. And as his tutor I could have held his nose to the grindstone as long as he needed external as opposed to self-discipline. But he wasn't my son, except biologically, and soon, I suspected, William Murdock would no longer be my college, not the way the rumours were going.

'I suppose,' I said casually, flourishing the rose, 'you didn't see anyone who might have left this? No, you can't smoke in here! We're part of a library for God's sake!'

With great reluctance he stowed his tin and his lighter. 'Not specially. Hey, you can't throw it away.'

'Know someone who'd like it?'

He blushed. 'Might do.'

I shoved the stem into an envelope. 'Be my guest.'

'Ta.' He wriggled. 'Suppose you don't fancy a bite?'

'Got to wait for the others to come back,' I said. 'Then I'm all yours. So long as it isn't a McDonald's.'

'That Italian place you usually take me to?'

'Ciao Bella? Doesn't open at lunchtimes. We'll find somewhere else, though.'

He dug a watch out of his pocket. 'Dunno. Supposed to be meeting this guy . . .'

'What I'd like to do is feed you and get that watch fixed,' I said, 'before you lose it.'

'Only plastic.'

'All the same.'

'Right, better be pushing off, then.' He hung back. 'Hey, if you're into throwing money away on watches, you couldn't lend me a few quid? Only I'm a bit short this week.'

I dug in my purse. 'Any special reason?'

'Fine. Speeding.'

God, that motorbike of his. I knew it was too powerful for him, knew his parents should have had more sense. I opened my mouth to say something, then shut it again. If ever there was a clone of Andy, Steph was it. So maybe he'd turn out all right one day. Maybe. I flicked a tenner at him, then reflected I'd have spent at least that much on lunch for him, plus a jazzy watch. I flicked out a second too. And my last fiver. I had a feeling I'd have made a pretty crap parent.

I was staring dismally into the middle distance when there was a knock on the office door.

'Sophie? It's OK, it's me. Andy.'

It seemed to take a long time to unlock the door. Not a good impression to give Joe Public, Sophie.

'I've come to take you to lunch, Sophie,' he said, stepping in and kissing me. 'By way of apology for not doing anything else for a bit.'

'Lovely,' I said. 'But you'll have to wait till the others come back. In the meantime, come into my office and sit down. There's something important I have to tell you.' Five minutes ago I could have shown, not told, him.

Both phones started to ring. I'd have ignored them.

'Sounds like it'll have to wait,' he said briskly, 'whatever it is. Which one shall I take?'

I pointed to the women's office. I'd better remember I was the boss and that I was supposed to be working, not having an emotional crisis.

By the time we'd sorted the phone messages out, the women were back, and Peter was popping his head round my door. I gestured him in and shut the door.

'You OK?' He looked concerned.

'Family problems,' I said, without thinking.

'You and Andy? I'd have thought you were getting on like a house on fire. He's certainly got those women out there eating out of his hand.'

'Just something's cropped up,' I said. 'But enough of me. What have you and Harvinder been doing down in Steelhouse Lane?'

'Talking to important people and then walking across to Lloyd House.'

While Steelhouse Lane was a police station, Lloyd House was the administrative centre for West Midlands Police.

'To talk to even more important people?'

'Quite. Who are thinking – but only thinking, so far, mind you – of pulling Harv out from Piddock Road nick to work with Claire Bishop on the stalker/protection side of the Bookfest. They'll let us know later today.'

'Not you?'

'You want to give Chris a heart attack? Both of us pulled out? As it is, they've still got to talk him into letting Harv go and upgrading a temporary replacement.'

'I can't see Chris ever standing in anyone's way if there's a chance of him or her getting some good experience.' No matter how he felt about the proposals for his own future.

There was a tap at the door. Una.

'Sophie, we brought this in for you. In case you didn't get time to go out, see.' She produced a baguette and an obscene-looking pastry.

Perhaps boys just took longer to grow up than girls.

So no excuse for a lunch with Andy, who, in any case, soon got bored with whatever he was doing in the other office and popped his head round my office door to wave me goodbye.

I covered the phone mouthpiece. 'Andy, we really do have to talk. There's something very important—'

He shook his head. 'It'll just have to wait, I'm afraid. There's a bit of a problem down in Devon. The farm manager says he needs to see me. I'm going down there now. No! Don't panic! I shall be back on the road by nine tomorrow.'

'But—'

He stepped into the office. 'When did I ever let you down?'

he demanded, dotting a kiss on my forehead, and leaving before I could tell him.

Back to the phone. It really was quite an important call. It was from Myakovsky's American agent. Yes, the visa had come through. But no, Mr Myakovsky would not be on the flight he'd hoped to be on. The visa had come through just half an hour too late. Meanwhile, she was checking all available flights for the next few days and would be back with me as soon as possible. The auguries, she added, were not encouraging.

As soon as I'd cut the connection I was stabbing Andy's mobile number. Time for him to call in one or two of the favours he claimed he was owed. I had to fill not just the opening slot, after all, but probably – yes – three others in the following three days.

To do him justice, Andy dropped all talk of his farm, and came straight back into the office. 'I'll fix up Gareth for tomorrow,' he said. 'And I'll sort out a variety of others for the smaller gigs. Actually, I bet Ruth could fix up a novelist or two.' But it was clear he wouldn't have a quiet space to work so he shrugged and headed for my house and my phone. He, like me, regarded mobiles as brain-fryers, for emergency use only.

Tomorrow! It was all so horribly close! One thing, I didn't think there'd be any argument about where Sir Gareth Thingy stayed, but I'd confirm it after I'd spoken to Acheson, due any moment to take delivery of the Mazda in Centenary Square. Not just him: the multicultural team without which we'd have no Bookfest. I sent the women down to greet the press and the driver, and put out a call for Marcus, who'd been gone far longer than I'd have expected.

Acheson arrived as I put down the phone. It was clear that from his wardrobe of good clothes he's chosen a particularly fine suit. No wonder he preened when he caught sight of his reflection in the rather dirty window. Then he walked over and peered into the balcony that seemed to fascinate so many people.

I ran a comb through my hair, dabbed on some lipstick and ushered him out, not before checking, rather ostentatiously, that the answerphones were on. I also set the alarm.

The car and photographers were already in place, surrounded by a mêlée of citizens. A couple of snappy suits marked out the solicitors who were funding the car. A rather more sober suit declared the Mazda marketing manager. It didn't take long for the suits to coalesce together, talking boys' talk, no doubt.

The photographer, a young woman with a modish haircut and well-worn jeans, managed to disperse the citizenry and arrange Una and Tas to her satisfaction, and then added me.

'Hang on,' I said. 'Wait for Marcus!' He was running frantically up the broad sweep of steps from the fountain to the library entrance. God! I still hadn't discussed with Acheson the possibility of his taking on Stonkin Mama's gigs! 'And what about the chairman and our sponsors?'

'I'd like one of the team on its own first,' she said. 'And then one of' – she consulted her notebook – 'Ms Rivers and the sponsors.'

Acheson must have noticed an important omission. He was over in a trice, leaving ribbons of conversation trailing behind him. Executive powers or not, this, his body language said, was his show and he was going to run it. It was easier to let him get on with it. If only the media had thought so too.

* * *

'Well,' I said, making tea and coffee, 'that all went very well.'

'Fancy the TV people turning up!' Una said. 'I wish they'd let me lie across the bonnet, like at the Motor Show.'

Tas raised an amused eyebrow. 'You'd look great on a Jag, Una. But that Mazda's rather little – not much room for lounging.'

True. They'd loaned us a 121 – the Mazda equivalent of a Fiesta – but I wasn't going to start looking gift cars in radiators. And since we were going to be ferrying one writer at a time, it wouldn't have been very green to have anything larger. What was far more important was that Una and Tas were again at ease with each other. We couldn't start the last day of the run-up with the team at odds.

I was tidying up at the end of the day – OK, it was seven thirty, but I wanted to know everything that had to be done was done. I checked things off for one last time: Andy's contacts coming up trumps; all the travel and accommodation arrangements checked; Marcus officially leaving the team tomorrow so he could take over the Stonkin Mama gigs. Yes. And one other thing to tick off: a call confirming that the security for the whole event had indeed come together under the leadership of Claire and Harvinder – a bit of flexibility I'd never truly expected of the West Midlands Police. One of them would be in at eight thirty tomorrow to talk to me and Acheson. I didn't see why he was needed, but he no doubt required mollifying after the afternoon's media slight.

Right. Time to go home.

There was a knock on the office door.

More startled than I liked to admit – and why? The library was, after all, open till eight – I swallowed hard.

'Who is it?' I asked, with more confidence than I felt.

'Me!' came Andy's voice.

Right: this must be the moment.

'We thought you might need an escort,' he continued.

We? I opened the door.

'And I thought you might need an extra pair of hands,' said Ruth. Andy's wife.

Chapter Twenty-two

We naturally headed for Ciao Bella, my favourite Italian restaurant, run, oddly enough, by a lovely Pakistani couple who employed a genius of a chef from Casablanca. By the time Ruth and I had been kissed and fussed over by all three I'd almost forgotten why I'd wished she hadn't turned up. No, of course I was glad she was there. I just kicked myself harder than ever for not making a moment to talk properly to Andy. It was, after all, up to him whether he told her – as and when he knew himself, that is – that he'd once been so out of his mind with an improbable mixture of chemicals that he'd once raped me. And – unlikely or not – I'd conceived after my very first sexual encounter.

'Poor Sophie: you're looking like I used to feel after a bad day at school,' Ruth said, pouring me a liberal dose of the house red. 'Go on: slurp it down. Andy's on the wagon tonight.'

He pulled a face. 'It's really your turn.'

'You haven't just flown in from Somalia,' she said. 'I'm running on borrowed adrenaline, so I hope you'll both excuse me if I simply keel over.'

'So long as you give us warning and we can clear a space first,' I said. 'It'd be terrible to waste any of Abdul's pasta . . .'

When the jet lag finally swamped her, it made a thorough job of it. She could hardly sit upright in her chair. It would have been cruel to keep her from her bed any longer so we declined coffee, and, taking an arm each, led her from the restaurant.

The only minus side to Ciao Bella, in the humble opinion of the more decrepit amongst us, was that at one end of Fletchers Walk was a rock club, which attracted a lot of hard-looking bikers. Apart from being apparently stone deaf – you can hear and, indeed, feel the music many yards away – they might well, of course, have been absolute pussycats. But they caused many a *frisson* of alarm amongst the older members of the chamber music society of which I was a member. Some of the club's clients also turned up on less conventional wheels – like the roller-bladers just now at the far end. Or the pair of skate-boarders caracoling towards us.

It's easy enough for one pedestrian to flatten herself against a shop front; it was tricky to negotiate the dormant Ruth out of the way. Not that the skate-boarders themselves managed to gain a specially straight line, although the amount of arm-flailing suggested they were at lest trying.

But not trying hard enough. Ruth and I went down; one of the youths went flying. The other managed to stop – indeed, tried apologetically to help us to our feet. But when Andy suggested – in rather emphatic terms – that he might as well go away, he took the hint and pushed off.

It was I who spotted a Post-it sticking to Ruth's jacket. I peeled if off, holding it where Andy and I could both read it.

DEAR HEART, (it said in neat capitals)
   I WANTED TO BOWL YOU OVER, WHISK YOU AWAY TO SOMEWHERE SPECIAL.
   XXX

Ruth took it, holding it at arm's length. I always forgot how much older she was than Andy till she reached with exasperated sighs for middle-aged-looking glasses. Not that she bothered with specs now. Andy flicked it from her hand.

'Not for you, Ruth. That's clearly for Sophie.'

He was right, wasn't he? Whoever my stalker was had found a new means of delivery.

We compared notes, literally, Claire and I. We were sitting in my office, drinking good coffee – I'd at last got round to replacing Brian's. Big Brum boomed eight thirty as she laid her little polythene bag beside mine. She'd put on rather more make-up than I'd seen her in before.

YOU MOST BEAUTIFUL OF WOMEN
    I WANT TO BOWL YOU OVER, WHISK YOU
AWAY TO SOMEWHERE SPECIAL
    XXX

'Let's be positive,' she said, making an effort to straighten her shoulders. 'At least now we've got something for Forensics to work on. From fingerprints to handwriting analysis.'

I compared the two. 'Bad news for you, Claire. Your note's in the present tense, mine's in the past. I'd say he's transferred his affections to you.'

'How reassuring,' she said drily, biting her lip. She looked me straight in the eye. 'You haven't forgotten Marietta Coe's near miss, have you? I'd be careful how you cross the road for a bit, Sophie.'

'I always am. As a matter of interest, how was your Post-it delivered?' I knew, of course.

'You know the underpass under Great Charles Street? This stupid kid on a skate-board cannoned into me. By the time I'd sorted myself out and made sure he hadn't nicked my bag, he was nowhere to be seen, naturally. Just this on my jacket.' She pointed. Her hand wasn't entirely steady. Funny, a woman as senior as she at that age must have seen stomach-churning crimes and dealt with them with the minimal turning of hair, but she seemed as thrown by this incident as I'd been by mine.

'Just as a matter of interest,' I said, not wanting to stretch our growing friendship too far too fast for professional comfort, 'has Marietta had any unconventional postal deliveries?'

'Funny you should ask,' she said. 'I was just going to ask if I could use your phone.'

'Be my guest. I'll go and check the mail.' We smiled at each other: yes, we would come through.

I'd barely started – having commandeered the desk in the other office – when the phone rang. Just to see what happened, I let it continue. I could always answer it if it seemed interesting – a request for tickets, say.

It wasn't a request for tickets. It was our Russian friend. Nipping sharply into the other office, I beckoned urgently. Claire was beside me before he'd finished his second sentence. She picked up the receiver herself.

'Good morning. Big Brum Bookfest here,' she cooed. She'd have made Martin Acheson a much more receptive receptionist than his current one. 'How may I help you?'

'When you meet that bastard's plane, remember you will not be unwatched. It is not just Myakovsky who dies, it is all who succour him.'

'I'll expect to see you at the airport then.' But she was speaking to thin air. 'So they don't know about all the visa problems and travel glitches.'

'Or they do and it's a bluff?'

'Equally possible. How's the Stonkin Mama fan club? All closed down?'

'As far as I can see. Ah.' I picked up a Jiffy bag addressed to me. 'But mine might not have done.'

This time the Jiffy bag was A4 – bigger than the one that had brought the unwanted underwear.

'Aren't you going to open it?'

'Would *you* want to?'

'I'd have to see what was inside. Call me nosy but I couldn't not.'

How recently was it that Chris had called me nosy? But I certainly didn't want to stick my nose into this package. I passed it to her silently. Then grabbed it back. 'What if it's— OK, I know I'm overreacting, but I've had a letter bomb before.' I pushed her hands away. 'Please – no risks. This could be my version of a fast car on a crossing!'

'OK. Point taken. But I'm sure you're . . . well, Peter told me about the stink bomb affair.'

'Did he tell you about the genuine bomb I once had? The one that would have taken off both hands and probably blinded me? *That's* why I'm overreacting, Claire.'

She gently wrested the package from me and scooped me into the other office. 'I think you could use another coffee. And maybe – maybe I will get someone to take a closer look.'

She clearly thought I needed nannying, but I insisted on making the coffee while she used the phone again. When I heard her ending the call, I pushed through and put the mugs on the desk.

'So has Marietta had any Post-its?' I asked.

'There was no reply. Just her answerphone. A message saying she'd be away from the phone for some time.' Claire spoke almost absently, as she stirred sweeteners into her coffee and popped the little tin back into her bag.

'Really?' I said, cool as I could manage. 'Perhaps she's decided that nothing as prosaic as a phone call should bring her down from the Parnassus of her launch tomorrow. Plus all the library events next week, of course.'

Claire was already speaking into her radio by the time I'd finished speaking. One day, I thought, I'd remember which occasions provoked which communications medium.

Then she looked at me shamefaced. 'D'you think I was overreacting?'

'Suppose I listen to the answerphone message too?'

Some people change their messages every day, and do so with casual aplomb. Others record their message as if it's a once-and-for-all commitment, stumbles and all. Marietta, who hadn't struck me as lacking in confidence, seemed to belong to the latter group. Which was nothing in itself, of course. I left what I hoped sounded like a friendly, upbeat message, hoping to see her at the opening reception.

'Well?' Claire asked.

All I could do was resort to a cliché. 'Better safe than sorry,' I said.

By the time the others arrived, Claire had discreetly passed the package to a uniformed cop.

'Today it all falls into place,' I told everyone, trying to sound optimistic and full of leadership potential. 'We all know what we have to do. We all have mobile phones. If anything goes wrong, no one has to do anything without support from me or Marcus. OK?'

Una burst out laughing. 'You make it sound like some *noir* movie, Sophie, with us as the undercover cops.'

I didn't say it out loud but I certainly thought it: *That's just what it feels like, sister.*

The question was, would the sudden amazing weather make any difference to last-minute bookings? Would a summer-like sun encourage people to venture out to a reading they might not have bothered with in the rain or would they be too busy with the results of their pillages of the local garden centres? Certainly it had an interesting effect on the first writer to be met at the station. Gus Cesar – I didn't want to know what the Gus might be short for – was an old friend of Marcus, so it was he who set off, shirt-sleeved and beaming. But he didn't come back. Not for a good hour. Hour and a half.

'Train must be late,' Una said.

'We're supposed to phone in when that happens,' Tas said. 'They've probably gone off to the cricket together.'

'Warwickshire are in Yorkshire,' I said more curtly than necessary.

'OK. You know what I mean.'

'Sure. Sorry to bite your head off. Trouble is, I'm just waiting for things to go wrong. Talking of which, neither of you has taken a call from Brian Fairbrother? I thought he might have tried to wish us well.'

'Tell you what,' said Tas, anxious, I guessed, to have me out of their hair, 'you could always go and try phoning him.'

To my amazement, Elly answered the phone first ring.

'We've been wondering how Brian is,' I said, after introducing myself.

'How would you expect him to be?'

'Mrs Fairbrother, that's precisely why I'm phoning. I have tried to contact you but you don't have an answerphone and I don't know your mobile number – if you have one, that is.'

'What do you mean, no answerphone! It's always – ah . . .'

Tabs' little fingers, no doubt.

'Anyway,' I continued, 'how is he?' I suppressed my desire to know why on earth she hadn't seen fit to be in touch with us.

'Very far from well. Very far. In fact, they say he'll be on slops for another week or so.'

'How is he in himself?'

'How would you expect him to be?'

I was getting very tired of all this. 'The thing is, Mrs Fairbrother, it's not unreasonable for employers to have regular up-dates, not to mention, by now, a self-certification form.'

'Do you think I've had time to think of that?'

'I'm sure you've had infinite numbers of more urgent things to think about. But you must appreciate that—'

'I certainly don't appreciate your attitude. Firstly you don't care enough to find out how he is, then you harass me over piddling pieces of paper.'

God, I was glad she wasn't my solicitor!

'Mrs Fairbrother, keep calm, please. Just tell me when you expect Brian to return to work. And also when we can expect a sick note.' Damn it, he wouldn't need a sick note if it weren't for me! The man would be getting his cards from us.

'Sick note! And what would you like on it? Poisoned?'

'Poisoned?'

At which point Marcus put his head round the door and grinned.

Chapter Twenty-three

I flapped a hand to keep him quiet.

'Poisoned!' I repeated. 'Are you sure?'

'That's what I— What is it, Tabs? No, darling, you—'

There was a terrific clatter. And an irritated buzzing. Then silence.

I could have screamed with exasperation. It was no good throwing the phone down: it might do to mine whatever Tabs had done to her mother's. My head told me the woman was teetering on the edge that Brian seemed to have gone over; my heart wanted to report her allegation to Claire, to Peter, to whoever. Now. Despite the fact that I knew that the hospital authorities would have notified them already, or at least someone in the West Midlands Police, if there were any substance in her allegations.

What my mouth wanted to do – and did – was say to Marcus, with a mildness my students would have known was dangerous, 'You've been a long time.'

'Yes, man.' He lounged back against the doorjamb. 'Well, we goes back long time, Gus 'n' me. Long time, man. Anyways, he want to walk, not to take a cab on a lovely day like today. So that what we did. Walk all the way from de station to de hotel.'

'Which must have taken all of fifteen minutes. Come on,

Marcus: we're all on edge today, and we don't need someone disappearing for upwards of an hour.'

'Sorry, Sophie. Had to have a coffee with him.'

Coffee? Maybe, but more like a couple of strong spliffs. Now I came to think about it, I could smell the pot on him.

'Anyway, I'm back now. What next?'

Talk about being demob happy!

Before I could blister at him, the phone rang.

'It's all on the schedule in the other office – remember?' I said, reaching for the phone.

The voice at the other end of the phone was Claire's. 'You won't like this, Sophie, but there's no sign of Marietta at her house. And one of the neighbours says she saw her going off in a taxi, clutching a suitcase.'

'Oh, my God. Hang on – going off on her own? Not at gunpoint or anything like that?'

'No.'

'Any idea how big the suitcase was?'

She muttered as she read whatever it was in front of her. 'Ah! Small case.'

'Have they spoken to her fiancé yet?' Or, of course, her ex-lover. If he was ex.

'Not yet. Still trying to find his name – it'll be on file somewhere. I'll get back to you, Sophie. Soon as I can.'

There was no time after that for anything except work. I did insist that we all broke at some time or other for lunch, even if it was to do no more than buy a sandwich. I was eating mine at my desk when there was a tap at the door – Ruth, with a bunch of red roses.

'Mike told me your last lot of flowers had been less than welcome,' she said.

'Mike! Is he home?'

She shook her head. 'He phoned Andy and got me. He was seventy-three not out a few minutes ago, by the way. It looks horribly, he says, as if play will go on all day.'

I bit my lip; there was little chance he'd make it to the reception, then.

'Anyway,' Ruth continued, 'he wanted Andy to get some on his behalf, but I volunteered. I thought Andy needed a decent haircut if he was going to support that novelist – what's her name?'

'Marietta,' I said automatically.

'He's started to refer to her as "the lady novelist".'

'As in "never has been kissed"? Well, she's not like that at all. She's an attractive young woman, engaged to be married, works full time for Sandwell Council and writes big thick books which keep even an old cynic like me entertained.'

'Since when were you a cynic, Sophie? Hell, no vase. Do you want me to go and get one or is there a loo we can keep them in?'

'Not unless Marcus is here,' I explained.

'Cue for all the jokes about crap ideas and being flushed with success. OK. I'll nip out and get one. I always used to hate an office without flowers. What's wrong?'

I might have known she'd notice. 'It's just that we've lost Marietta Coe. And I'm terribly afraid we shall have a dratted Russian turning up just at the most inconvenient moment.'

'A Russian? Not Myakovsky? Oh, Sophie, can I meet him? I mean, meet him at the airport or wherever? I could practise my Russian.'

I don't think I'm really management material. Being a manager must mean setting everything in motion and then stepping back and – managing. I think what I am is a control freak. As the reception began, I wanted to do everything, from announce the guests to pour their wine, plus, in one or two cases, write and deliver the speeches. Oh yes, all the civic worthies put in their three penn'orth. Not just the Birmingham ones. Solihull and Sandwell had sent along their mayors or mayor-substitutes. Sir Gareth offered a few neatly turned words, I replied, and then the bubbly flowed. Including some into the glass of none other than Marietta Coe, closely attended by a short young man with close-cropped brown hair. As soon as she saw me she came over and air-kissed me.

'Miles,' she said, touching his arm. We nodded at each other.

She leant intimately towards me, looking and smelling as if she'd spent a day on the preparations. 'I'm so sorry!' she said. 'I'd got more and more frazzled and I just had to do something. So I booked myself in for an all-day beauty treatment – seaweed, mud, massage, the lot.' She looked at me. 'Shall I give you the address?'

'I'm looking that good, am I? OK, Marietta, just have a word with Claire, here, will you, so she can pull out the search teams and the sniffer dogs.'

Claire, who was talking to Ian, had made every effort not to look like a police officer: she was striking in a turquoise silk suit. Unfortunately it rather clashed with a bluey-green dress I'd thought was smart until I saw Marietta's black number. I suppose the three of us must have presented an interesting combination if the press were so keen for us to pose together. Claire, however, had other ideas, and melted away, like a serene-looking Cheshire cat. In her place materialised Martin Acheson, who, though he'd been chatting affably with two of the country's leading novelists, was happy to put an arm round Marietta and me, simply, of course, to oblige the photographer. Then Marcus replaced him, probably at my suggestion. And Tas and Una replaced me and Marietta. I doubted if the photographer would use any of these shots; he rapidly went cruising in the direction of the great and the good. Whether Andy counted under either heading, no one cared, least of all the press chap, who snapped him in practically every permutation of guests. From time to time, Ruth caught my eye and raised an ironic eyebrow.

And so, in a loose procession, to the Repertory Theatre, where Sir Gareth had already been taken by Claire and her colleagues. No one knew any reason why anyone might want to take a pot shot at a former ambassador, particularly one with such a fine record on environmental and human rights issues, but the police were, not surprisingly, taking no chances. Marcus and I were responsible for making sure that the guests had their tickets and that they were in their places on time. Una and Tas, suddenly looking incredibly young and vulnerable, could sit back and scoff the last of the nibbles or come to the Rep or simply go home, as the mood took them. I'd given them cash for taxis whatever they chose. In the event they decided to come to hear Sir Gareth.

So it was an absolutely full house at the Rep that watched the spotlight go up on a central lectern on the big stage and let their voices fall into an expectant hush.

Which lasted and lasted.

I didn't need my bleeper to get me backstage fast.

What I found was Sir Gareth locked in an amused embrace with a bulky middle-aged man in a loud suit.

'It is I,' said the other man, breaking away, and turning towards me, arms outstretched, 'running to your rescue, my dear Miss Sophie.' His accent was almost identical to the one

I'd heard too many times. Only this one must be genuine. 'It is I, Vladimir Myakovsky.'

Mike was waiting backstage at the end, and revived me with the hug I'd needed all evening. 'So they got two for the price of one, I gather.'

'They did indeed. I only panicked once: when Myakovsky demanded champagne in his carafe, not water. But Gareth insisted on sharing it, so neither of them got plastered. Well, Gareth wouldn't because he only took two sips. Myakovsky didn't because it seems to take a good deal more than half a bottle of bubbly to get him drunk. But we're about to find out. We're all bidden to his suite at the Mondiale for more drinks.'

'"All"? So no one would notice if I toddled off home?'

'I would.' I came down to earth quickly. 'What's up?'

'Nothing, I'm just a bit tired.'

'What did you get, then? Oh, Mike, this must be the first time I haven't asked you.'

'It is, actually. But I forgive you. You've got more than enough on your plate to worry about me.'

'I should never have too much on my plate to worry about you. Did you get that century?'

'A hundred and fifteen. I carried my bat: ran out of partners when that twerp Butler sent a real dolly of a catch back to the bowler.'

'All that effort in vain! You poor love.' I reached up to kiss him. 'And – oh, Mike – thank you for those roses.' I kissed him again. If it had been up to me we'd both have skipped the party and had one of our own.

'You know,' he said, 'I think I'm sufficiently revived to make it to that booze-up after all. If only to make sure he doesn't try and play your little balalaika.'

* * *

Myakovsky wasn't entirely convinced when I told him that for me running the Bookfest and downing champagne by the bottle were incompatible. But there were enough people – and more to the point, I suspected, enough attractive women like Marietta and Claire – still happy to party all night to mollify even him. Marcus was certainly up to it, and his mate Gus. Not to mention Martin Acheson, deep in colloquy with Sir Gareth. The entire board seemed to be there, tongues a-slaver.

Assisted by Ruth, practising her Russian, Myakovsky and I had had to have a short earnest discussion about who was paying for the booze, which culminated in his flourishing a wallet crammed with cash. His treat, he insisted. I had a further conversation with the hotel staff about the limits to which his hospitality should be taken. At last I could leave everything in the competent hands of Claire, whose champagne looked suspiciously like mineral water. Ian's almost certainly was.

Good night, ladies. Good night, sweet ladies . . . And tomorrow, was, of course, another day. I must have had more of that champagne than I'd realised . . .

Chapter Twenty-four

'On a morning like this,' I said, taking a cup of tea up to Mike and spreading the *Birmingham Post* across the bed, 'you wonder why you ever worried about anything. Look.' I pointed to the photographs inside, and a splendid review by Terry Grimley of our first event.

'It's because you worried early on, my love, that everything's come together so well. Now all you have to do is sit back and take the plaudits.'

'For two minutes, at least. But we've got the children's events down at the Midlands Arts Centre today, and someone ought to see that no little darling strays from the Centre into the lake or gets nibbled by a goose.'

'Are you scheduled to do that?'

'No, I think it's Una—'

'Does she have a phone to reach you if necessary?'

'Of course—'

'So leave her to do it. Don't let her think you're peering over her shoulder; it's bad for her morale. What else is there to worry about?'

'Gus – he's got a day school at the Ikon Gallery. He'll call Marcus if there's a problem. There are a couple of library events – Tas is dealing with one, and the other's a woman who used to live up here. She says she can handle everything herself, from getting there to laying out the chairs if necessary.'

'Don't tell me,' Mike said, reaching for the sports section, 'she's an ex-teacher.'

'Spot on. Then there's the cocktails for Marietta. Andy'll pick her up and act as MC. But we must all be on show for that because half the board don't intend to turn up. Snobs. Then her reading, then the after-dark poets.'

'Sounds as if you could do with some nice therapeutic exercise,' Mike said, pushing the paper to one side.

But I was glad to discover he didn't mean a five-mile run.

'It's a good healthy turnout,' I said to Ian, as we surveyed the guests gathered for Marietta's launch. This, like the previous evening's reception, was to be held in the Mondiale, before a reading at the Rep. She wasn't to be in the main auditorium, however, but in the smaller studio theatre.

'I wish I could say it was a case of the more the merrier,' he muttered. 'Still, I hear they've persuaded Myakovsky to have a bodyguard. His publishers have coughed up. Don't want to lose a good layer, I suppose. Oh,' he added, in response to my startled eyebrows, 'as in goose and golden eggs, Sophie.'

'Could you possibly mean anything else?' I responded blandly.

Marcus, to my amazement, had brought a drum along – presumably to herald announcements with a resounding roll – and was wearing a wonderful African shirt. Acheson was in bright plumage too, but confined his to a silk tie. To my pleased surprise, the distinguished novelists who'd come to the opening reception were here again; presumably there was a brotherhood amongst writers themselves that didn't obtain amongst their readers. Acheson was soon laughing and joking with them, but seemed to me to be checking the room for someone who'd not yet arrived. There were more of the board than I'd expected, most of whom were busily assuring her publisher and agent that Marietta was the best thing since sliced bread. At the last minute who should stroll in but Myakovsky, complete with the solid-looking individual predicted by Ian.

Myakovsky darted across the room, followed by his new shadow, who was deeply preoccupied with looking meanly into the middle distance. 'So where is she, this beautiful writer of the most erotic prose?'

Where indeed? We had the drinks, the canapés, the books, the posters, the assembled masses. But no Marietta Coe.

No Andy, of course, either. Ruth looked anxiously across at me. I reached for my mobile phone.

Before I could dial, Claire appeared at the door, gesturing frantically.

'I didn't worry at first,' she whispered. 'You know how she did that bunk yesterday. I thought she'd done it again. I thought she'd gone back to her fiancé's last night. I thought anything. But she's gone.'

'Andy?' Ruth demanded.

'It was he who alerted us – couldn't make anyone hear at her house. I sent him on to her bloke's. Do you want to make an announcement?'

I looked around. 'I think we should leave it five more minutes. She might have got the idea from Myakovsky of making a dramatic last-minute appearance. And – to be honest – I don't think anyone's noticed she's not here. Not yet. Listen to them.' I was suddenly revolted by the bray of voices, by the glasses held out as if by chance for yet another slurp of publisher's champagne. Well, a decent New Zealand substitute.

'And then?' Claire prompted.

'We'll get her publisher over here – you'll have to tell her the truth -- and get her to say she's indisposed. That's all we can do. At this stage. Hell – Ruth, go and keep Andy out of here. One look at his face and everyone'll know something's wrong!'

They might have gathered something from the speed at which she left the room, had anyone dragged his or her attention away from the mêlée.

I feared the worst when Harvinder appeared and caught Claire's eye. They had a whispered discussion – her firing questions, by the look of it, and him replying. The result was a negative I couldn't miss: I slipped over to them.

'It's time to get her publisher, Sophie,' Claire said, incredibly grim.

'You've – found her?'

A curt shake of the head. 'Just lost my career. My first big case protecting someone, and she disappears. I know it's not much fun for you, Sophie, losing one of your stars, but for God's sake you don't want to make a career out of running things like this, do you?'

'After this? I'd rather go and teach in a school under Chris Woodhead's perpetual gaze.'

While Claire broke the news to the publisher, I did some nifty backstairs work with the Rep management. The main house was only half-full. If our punters wanted, they could fill empty seats, provided we could come to some financial accommodation later. Knowing Acheson would want the matter referred to him, I none the less accepted: our cancellation insurance should cover the cost.

What amazed me was that I could still think and act like a woman in control. Inside I was gibbering with terror. Maybe Claire was too, though she seemed to personify police calm.

* * *

'Do they usually react like this when someone goes missing?'
Mike asked, holding my hand as I waited at Steelhouse Lane
nick to be interviewed.

'I wouldn't have thought so. Doesn't it usually take some
time before you can officially become a Missing Person? It'd
be because of the stalker, wouldn't it?' I wished for both our
sakes I hadn't said that.

'Who has recently turned his attentions to you.' His grip
tightened.

'And to Claire herself. I should think her days on this case
are numbered. They wouldn't want to put her at any more risk
than they have to.'

'And you? Sophie? And you?'

'I'm sure the police are busy working on that even as we
speak. Meanwhile, thank God I've got you.' All four hands
were now welded by terror.

I'd got plenty of other company too. Most of the people
who'd been to Myakovsky's suite were there: Marcus,
Acheson, a crop of board members, everyone who might have
seen Marietta leave.

'Mike, Marietta's fiancé. Did you meet him last night?'

'How would I know him from Adam?'

'Oh, he was better dressed. She introduced me to someone
called Miles. But neither seemed to be behaving in a
particularly fiancé-ish way.'

'If by fiancé-ish you mean looking at her lovingly and
protectively, the nearest you have to that is that smart bloke
over there. He kept accidentally touching her, the way I
accidentally touch you. Acheson, is it? Oh, and she was
dancing with Marcus at one time. It was he who rescued her
from Myakovsky, as I recall.'

'Rescued?'

'He was showing her how Russian bears hug. Only I'd never have thought bears would be quite so interested in whether the huggee was wearing a bra.'

'Perhaps the fasteners get in their teeth. Shit, oh shit, oh shit. Mike, why did I ever get involved in all this?'

'Because, my love, you're you.'

The last person I expected to see – but probably the person I most wanted to see – striding into Steelhouse Lane was Chris Groom. He was talking to another officer with lots of pips on his uniform but Chris himself was in mufti. I freed a hand from Mike's and pointed. 'See who I see?'

'What's he doing here?'

'He must have accepted that move to whatever it's called – the Murder Investigation Unit.'

Mike looked blank.

'The thing is, Mike, whatever it is he'll do it well. And if it's to take overall control of the Marietta business—'

'And the you and Claire business—'

'And that too. Mike I know you can't be happy if he does take charge, but remember two things. One, I'm in love with you and he knows it. Two' – I managed a grin, even a little chuckle – 'don't you think Claire might provide a happy substitute for me? Once he's given her the bollocking of her life, I think he could get very protective towards her.'

'He's much too old for her,' Mike grumbled. But I could feel him relaxing, all the same.

Until the commotion by the front desk. A distraught young man with short brown hair was demanding to know where his girlfriend was. The civilian behind the desk put things together painfully slowly. What some of us already knew, and everyone else realised much faster than she, was that this must be Marietta Coe's fiancé. Miles.

'He doesn't look like a man who's just killed his woman,' Mike whispered.

'True. But then, appearances often are deceptive, aren't they?'

What was quite clear, however, was that I was being singled out for different treatment from the rest of the group. It didn't alarm me. I wasn't there just to give information about an event. I was going to have to talk about the next week's events, not least those involving me. And decisions were going to have to be made at a very high level.

So I was surprised when I was shown into an anonymous meeting room to find Chris, Claire and Harvinder present, but no Martin Acheson. Almost as Chris closed the door behind me, however, he opened it again to admit Ian Dale.

Chris went to the head of the table. 'This is much too big and impersonal but it'll have to do,' he said, gesturing irritably at the room, high-ceilinged and pompous. 'You'll have gathered I've been asked to take temporary responsibility for the new Murder Investigation Unit. This will incorporate the small team set up to investigate links between the stalking of three women and the death threats against two authors. We can now eliminate one of those death threats from our inquiries. It's quite clear that it was Stonkin Mama's boyfriend who was writing the letters, though we have to wait to see how much collusion there may have been between him and the victim.' Chris paused for breath. I'd never seen him so uneasy or so formal. 'Tonight we have to make some swift decisions. We have, I think, to treat the disappearance of Marietta Coe with the utmost seriousness – hence its allocation to the MIU. But we also have two more women who are a much more integral part of the Bookfest and its security who may well be at risk themselves.' He smiled formally at Claire and me. 'As far as you're concerned, Claire, we can simply order you off the case and move you into secure accommodation. That may well be what' – he broke into a genuine smile – 'Them Upstairs decide. I'm sure you'll have a view you'd like me to put to them, however. But we have no similar power to protect Sophie, and she is, after all, in control of a whole series of events which can scarcely be cancelled.'

I was glad he realised that. But I was trying to work out how much I could do from what I assumed must be the comparative safety of the office, as opposed to a more hands-on approach.

'Claire: just between ourselves – and I do want to insist that this meeting is absolutely confidential – how do you feel about being pulled from the case? I don't want you to see yourself as having in any way failed. It's clear now – it's amazing how efficient hindsight is, isn't it? – that we should have insisted on round-the-clock protection for Marietta, which is what you recommended on every occasion. What I don't see is how we can accord that protection to you, if you're a major player in the investigation. And, believe me,' he smiled, 'you are going to be protected.'

She returned his smile, tentatively at first, then with some warmth. Very nice. Then I remembered: she'd got a bloke, hadn't she? Damn and damn. 'This is going to be a big operation, isn't it, Gaffer? There must be some useful role I can play in the incident room. And yes, I'll accept whatever protection you think appropriate.'

He smiled and made a note. 'That would be my

recommendation, Claire. Now, Sophie – what are we going to do about you?'

'Much the same, I suppose. We must be able to reschedule our tasks so I can be basically office-bound. I can't just pull out altogether, not with Brian still off sick. And who's to say whether the stalker mightn't turn his attention to Una and Tasleen, the work-experience volunteers?'

'Going very much against type, Sophie,' Ian said. 'I'd go for a man who prefers blonde, blue-eyed women. In fact, I'd like to check the marital and relationship histories of all the men involved – see if a real pattern of obsession emerges. Sorry, Gaffer.'

Chris grinned. It was good to see the two men working together again. 'Point taken. I'll get someone on to it, in fact.'

I said quietly, 'There's someone else you should try to locate. Marietta had another "significant other" . . .' I explained.

Chris tore his hair. 'There's nothing about that in her file!'

'She told me that time we had lunch. Swore me to absolute secrecy. And no, I've no idea who. None. Sorry.'

'Jesus Christ! OK. Someone else to check out. When we find out who he is. Does Miles know?'

'He knows there's someone in her past – I gather he wasn't happy about it. But I've hardly spoken to the man. And it's not the sort of thing you talk about at a drinkies do.'

'Which brings us neatly back to tonight . . . Where was I? Ah – the volunteers . . . What do you want to do about them?'

'The thing is, Chris,' I said, 'I'm really only an employee of the Bookfest board. Shouldn't . . . ?'

'Shouldn't what, Sophie?'

I bit my lip. 'I was going to say, shouldn't Martin Acheson be party to any discussions? But—'

'But what? Go on.'

My gesture felt very helpless. 'I don't know. It seems to me that there must be a connection between the stalker's targets and the Bookfest. And since, as Ian reminded me, there is every indication that the stalker is a man, the fewer men who are privy to our discussions the better. Including, of course, Martin Acheson and Marcus Downing.'

Claire nodded. 'I was thinking the same thing myself. It seems to me that much as they'll hate it, we ought to ask Tas and Una to pull out. Just in case. And – since Sophie can't be left on her own – that their place is taken by one of our colleagues. Armed for preference.'

'But Tas and Una will be meeting and escorting celebs next week; hardly using the office at all,' I said. 'Which, of course, makes them all the more vulnerable, doesn't it?' But even their safety faded into insignificance as another thought struck me. 'Chris – were any threats ever made against Marietta's fiancé? As a way of getting at her? Because of all the places to be a sitting target I'd have thought a cricket field one of the worst.'

Ian laughed grimly. 'At most of the county matches I went to last summer, anyone in a stand would stick out like a sore thumb. Those lads are playing in nigh-on empty grounds.'

'Even so.'

Harvinder spoke for the first time. 'As far as I know, no threats were ever made against him. He's along the corridor just now, isn't he? Why don't I go and have a word?' He was on his feet and out of the room.

I wondered why he'd been so quiet; but he always was a man to keep his own counsel.

Chris looked at his watch. 'It seems to me we should adjourn till tomorrow. Claire, can you make arrangements to move into safe quarters for a while? Sophie, I think you and Mike should check into the Mondiale for tonight: the security there's even better than at your place.'

'What about Andy and Ruth? They're staying with me.'

'I should think,' Ian said at his driest, 'that young Andy might just be able to afford a room there himself. We can always have a whip round if he can't.'

'I have to be in the office tomorrow, Chris. There's a lot going on then.'

'You won't be on your own, Sophie. I can promise you that.'

Chapter Twenty-five

So it was actually a police officer who made the discovery.

Gwen Harvey had picked me up from the Mondiale on another gorgeous morning. It was just the weather for the outdoor storytelling events in parks and open spaces all round the city. Just the weather for cricket, too, though it was a very gloomy Mike who set off for the County Ground.

'She'll be fine, love, don't you worry,' Gwen said, pushing him out of the room. 'She'll be all right with me.'

I forgave him for appearing doubtful. Gwen looked like a woman who'd be happier carrying a Sainsbury's bag than whatever weapon she was packing. She was fortysomething, running slightly to fat. It would be kind to say she was having a bad hair day, but I suspected the need for restructuring serum and conditioner was more chronic than simply acute. Clothes sense: not a high score there either, even remembering that her jacket had to be large enough to conceal her gun. What was her game, this woman in what was almost certainly still very much a man's world? Why didn't she look the tough part she undoubtedly played?

However, since we walked the short distance from the Mondiale to the library, I was glad she didn't mimic the macho mean peering that had characterised Myakovsky's minder. She didn't need to, anyway: the Sunday shoppers hadn't arrived in the city yet.

'Eh, I don't think much of this place,' she said, stepping into my office. 'No natural light.' She headed for the window. 'And this – what does this look out on to? What a dreadful—'

There was something about the way she broke off that told me I oughtn't to look. But I did. And there, on the maintenance walkway, amidst the Christmas lights and nub ends and all the other detritus of Paradise Forum, lay the abandoned body of Marietta Coe.

The police allowed me to phone Tas and Una to tell them there'd been a break-in at the office and not to try to come in. They had their appointed tasks, anyway, and didn't need to do more than keep in touch by phone. As far as the punters were concerned, I recorded an answerphone message referring them to my mobile phone. Then the police took over. The whole suite became a crime scene. I'd have loved to stay and watch; I'd always wanted to see a SOCO team extracting those minute scraps of evidence capable of convicting a killer. But my stomach decided otherwise. However much I tried to see something other than the naked body, the figure '1' burnt – with a cigarette, they reckoned – on to its abdomen, I failed. The poor woman must have died a slow and painful death – nothing serene about the agonised face, the clenched fist, culminating in what looked to me like a broken neck. I tried to think about Mike, about Aggie, tried to think about any bloody thing except that damaged body. But my stomach decided to be sick. Fortunately there was no one in the gents' loo. I had a sneaking suspicion that no one would try to get past Gwen, however great his need.

It was only as I straightened up that I remembered what Elly Fairbrother had said. About poison.

No one had poisoned me. Had they? No. I recognised my William Murdock tum. All too well.

Why on earth hadn't I thought of it before? OK, Elly was a woman whose thought processes could scarcely be described as rational, but I should have told someone what she'd said. OK, I'd been busy to the point of frantic. But an accusation like that should have been raised at Chis's big meeting. I must tell someone right now. Probably not one of the people here, though. They were all too busy. I didn't know any of them, anyway. Why wasn't Harvinder here? He was part of the team. I could have talked to him. Meanwhile, I – I had nowhere to go.

'Yes, you have,' Gwen said briskly. 'You have your room at the hotel. Or your own home. Or that nice lad Mike's place. Or even back to Steelhouse Lane, if that takes your fancy. Actually, that might be best, come to think of it. We never had a statement off you last night, did we? You were too busy chin-wagging with Them Upstairs.'

So to Steelhouse Lane it was.

Steelhouse Lane was a big nick, not at all the almost intimate friendly place I was beginning to find Piddock Road. And I knew no one. Except Chris, who would no doubt be agonising whether he should tie up ends in Smethwick or start unravelling problems here.

Then I saw Harvinder, who turned a corner of the corridor Gwen was taking me down. His face lit up in a smile reflecting mine. But he was called back by someone.

It wasn't a lowly constable who appeared in the interview room Gwen and I were put in. It was Chris, who looked around with some distaste.

'This must be very hard for you,' he said at last.

'That number on her – the big number one hadn't gone unnoticed,' I said. 'I take it that's one detail that won't be released to the press? Because I don't want Mike to know about it until you've got whoever did it.'

'"You?" Come on, Sophie, whatever happened to "we?" You're usually – well, rather keener than some people to shove your oar in.'

'I think I've caught a crab.'

Chris picked up the reference and grinned; Gwen didn't, and looked shocked. Maybe I'd explain later. If I could be bothered.

'Look, I've got to talk to the DCI who's being put into place. When you've got this out of the way, I'd welcome a chat.'

'Chris, you're detecting again. Are you sure you ought to be? Aren't you supposed to be the administrator in charge of the MIU, not a mere foot soldier?'

'You're obviously feeling better! Perhaps if we met in my coffee break . . .? Then I shan't be depriving the service of any of my admin. time! Morning, Davinder.' He waved a friendly hand at the incoming constable – a stoutish Asian woman in her twenties – and left us to it.

'Chris! Was that who I think it was?'

'Hello, again to you, Sophie, and welcome to my new abode. Would you like a cup of tea?' Something must be up. Chris only insisted on courtesies when he was in optimistic mood. 'Do sit down.' He touched the back of a chair the far side of his new desk.

'I'd love a cup of tea, please, Acting Detective Superintendent Groom. That is your title, I suppose?'

'For all practical purposes you can dispense with the

"Acting" part.' Switching on an electric kettle, he turned to me and rubbed his hands together. Yes, he was beginning to enjoy himself.

'Anyway, was it Dave Clarke I saw leaving this very room?'

'Detective Chief Inspector David Clarke, Sophie.'

'That randy little – little inspector making it to DCI! Wow!'

'And not just DCI. DCI in charge of your particular case, Sophie. Such is the wisdom of the West Midlands Police. And me, actually,' he added. 'He's a good cop, Dave.'

I nodded. 'Less . . . conventional . . . than you in his methods.'

'That was then. I don't want to know about now. So long as he gets results.'

'So why— Thanks!' I took a mug of tea made to perfection. 'So why does a fraud expert head a murder inquiry?'

He pulled his chair to the side of the desk. 'Because Fraud is being slimmed down and much of its work dispersed to OCUs like mine. Remember? And because Dave's a very good cop. If,' he added with a wry grin, 'occasionally unconventional.'

'And always randy. OK.'

Chris looked pointedly at my hands, which I discovered were still shaking. 'You don't have to make this effort, Sophie. You do jolly and upbeat very well, but you don't have to. You've been working under an enormous amount of pressure, from what I can gather, and now you've had a dreadful shock. Doubly dreadful: not just seeing . . . the body . . . but seeing its implications. I gather you gave a wonderfully crisp account to Davinder.'

'Good sharp woman. I didn't have to correct any of her spelling.'

'There you go again. Now, just simmer down and relax.

That way you'll come up with the really useful stuff. Right? Here.' He passed a plate of assorted biscuits. 'Sorry I couldn't bring Bridget over, but I'm sure you can cope with the packet variety.'

I nodded. 'The tum's bad. Chris! Chris!' I pushed the plate aside. Now I had someone to say it to it seemed so foolish. 'Brian Fairbrother, the Bookfest boss—'

'That's actually you, these days, but never mind.'

'He threw up back at Piddock Road. Harvinder was very kind to him—'

Chris nodded: he knew Harv was kind. He pointed to the plate of biscuits; I took a couple, but parked them on the desk.

'He was rushed to hospital because he was vomiting blood. It must have been serious because they kept him in and ran tests. I don't know what's happening to him now. I've tried to talk to him or his wife but got nowhere.'

'You've heard *nothing*? But shouldn't he be getting in sick notes by now?'

Oh yes, Chris *had* become an administrator, hadn't he?

'Quite. But I did get through yesterday morning. Only to have the call cut short by the most repellent brat you could imagine. But before the hell-child wrecked the entire BT network, her mother mentioned poison. Alleged, perhaps I should say, that Brian had been poisoned. I know I should have mentioned it earlier, but—'

'You've been a touch busy. In any case, there are procedures for hospitals to notify us of such incidents. All the same . . .' He made a note, his handwriting so clear I could read it from where I sat. 'When was he taken ill?'

'Friday tea-time. He'd just thrown up when you and I spoke on the phone. And then again at Piddock Road. When I spoke to his wife on the Saturday morning, he was having a blood transfusion. But, as I said, we heard nothing more till I finally got through yesterday.'

He stroked his chin. 'Who would have a grudge against the Bookfest?' he asked suddenly. 'Big enough to want to put its administrator out of action? Maybe big enough to try to deter its leading international guest?'

'Maybe big enough to bump off its leading local guest?'

He snorted. 'Marietta's stalking started months before she was booked for the Bookfest. But there must be a connection. I've got a whole team working on it.'

'And the stalker's suddenly transferred his affections to the substitute administrator and even more suddenly to the police officer responsible for security!'

Chris looked me straight in the eye. 'This rather limits the field, doesn't it?'

I was afraid he was going to say that.

'Who stood to gain most if the Bookfest administrator pulled out? And who would know about Marietta, you and Claire resembling each other?'

'And,' I added, making my mouth form the words, 'who has terminated his contract with the board after . . . after bending the truth to get it?'

'We're talking Marcus Downing here, aren't we?'

I thought of his cheerful efficiency, the enormous amount of work he'd put into raising our profile. And I thought of his feeble excuse for giving up after only a week. Surely a grown man would be more responsible than to throw up good money simply to have more time to himself? Then there was the pot he'd smoked with his mate. It wasn't the pot that bothered me. No. To my knowledge, he was the only person associated with the Bookfest who smoked.

Nodding, I managed to say, 'We're talking Marcus

Downing.' And my ears filled with a harsh rushing and my eyes flooded with huge yellow blobs and I started to pass out.

I had to hand it to Chris. He must have moved very quickly. Before I knew it my head was between my knees and he'd produced his smelling salts.

I gestured them helplessly away. 'You've still got them,' I said, groping for tissues to dab my streaming eyes.

'Looks as if I still need them,' he said. 'Get those biscuits inside you fast. That's better.' He didn't replace the smelling salts bottle immediately, but left it there, as a silent reminder of what would happen if I didn't eat.

I did. Silently. And took another. By which time my brain started up again. 'But how could Marcus possibly have poisoned Brian? The only one who could have done that was Acheson, surely, when he gave us drinks at his office? And if Brian ended up so ill, why didn't I? Acheson doesn't smoke either, so far as I know. Plus – and this is a big plus – the Bookfest is Martin's baby. From conception to delivery.' I wrinkled my nose in distaste at my own metaphor.

The phone rang. Chris responded without haste but still managed to pick it up third or fourth ring. 'Good,' he said. 'Excellent. I'll see you as soon as you get back.'

All really helpful: I took and ate another biscuit to make the point that I really wasn't listening.

'Dave,' he said. 'About the post-mortem on Marietta. At least being just the administrator I'm spared that treat.' He checked the top on the smelling salts and returned them to the pocket where they always lived. 'So Acheson has the opportunity to poison Brian – if poisoning it was – but not the motive, and Downing has a motive, but no real opportunity.'

My phone chirruped. I switched it off. 'What now, Chris?'

'You and Gwen go somewhere safe. The SOCOs and Dave's

team will do all they can. And if, while you're sitting quietly, you get any brilliant ideas – or even, Sophie, any mad panics – use that.' He pointed to the mobile. 'Any idea where you'll be?'

I thought hard. 'How about being quietly anonymous, watching the cricket at Edgbaston?'

Chapter Twenty-six

Gwen peered about her in disbelief. 'When you see cricket on telly the ground is always packed! Where is everyone?'

'The match doesn't start till two. They've got a strange system of slotting Sunday games in the middle of the four-day county games. Sometimes. Sometimes they run a county game across the Sunday. Sometimes there's no play on a Saturday, just when you'd have thought the punters would have wanted it. An arcane system.'

She peered at me over her sunglasses. 'I still think you'd be better off in bed.'

'Got to be able to take phone messages, haven't I?' I patted my mobile. 'And I get precious little chance of watching Mike play, especially on a gorgeous hot day like this. Hey, we've got no sun hats – they'll have them on sale in the shop.'

Gwen grimaced. 'What about some food, too?'

'Oh, there's plenty of that available. Come on, I'll leave my jacket across these seats here.'

'Leave something like that lying round? Sophie, love, is that wise?'

'This is a cricket match,' I said loftily, and stomped off. Then I had to stomp back and get it. Gwen was right, wasn't she? I grinned my acknowledgement.

The customer ahead of us in the shop was a tall, elegant man, whose accent and demeanour defined him in my terms as an old buffer. No, I didn't know him, but it dawned on me so fast I could hardly wait to switch my phone on that Chris might not have been alerted to the connection between Acheson and Perry Burton. One of his team must talk to Brian about who really wanted Myakovsky to stay at the Burtons' house. I was sure Brian had insisted it was Acheson who wanted the move, which never had made sense. And now I came to think of it, it made even less sense given that Mrs Burton hadn't, as far as I could recall, been at either of the receptions so far. Though I could imagine her avoiding low-profile but essential Bookfest jobs, I didn't see how she could possibly have stayed away from a nice glittery evening teeming with famous figures. My brain made one of its silly leaps. What if Mrs Burton had only got herself on to the board to make her interest in having Myakovsky to stay seem authentic?

I paid for the head-gear – OK, Gwen could claim on expenses for hers if she preferred – and, stepping into the sun, tapped away. As I did so, my phone reminded me I had a message. Tough. Chris first.

I had to leave a message. Only then did I see who wanted me.

Marcus. One of de storyteller was late getting to Handsworth Park, man, and he 'bout to do a bit of a warm-up, like.

Oh dear: Marcus and his accents.

'You don't want to use those things, pet. They rot your brain something shocking.'

I jumped. Far more than usual.

'You OK, pet?' Tony put his hand on my shoulder and peered down at me.

'More or less. Tony, this is Gwen, a friend of mine. Gwen

Tony, one of the Warwickshire coaches. Tony, love, could you be an angel and tell Mike I shall watch as much of the game as I can? He wasn't expecting me here at all, but I'd like him to know.'

He nodded: 'Lad needs a bit of cheering up. Said he was worried about something.'

'Tell him from me she's OK,' said Gwen, 'and he's to go and get whatever he's supposed to get – a lot of wickets?'

'Ah,' observed Tony, 'I can see your friend here's a real fan, pet.'

We were walking back, complete with food, drinks, scorecards and the promise of fat ice creams for pudding when Gwen stopped.

'I don't care what the medics say,' she said, looking at me even harder than Tony had done. 'I reckon the best thing for shock's a good stiff brandy. There must be a bar somewhere.'

'Practically next to where we're sitting.'

'Right – just along here?' She took my arm. 'In we go.'

'But what about tomorrow?' Mike asked. 'And the day after, and the day after that? It's all very well protecting her – yes, and the rest of us – but we have lives to lead.'

We were having dinner in our room at the Mondiale. Mike and I, Gwen, Chris, Andy and Ruth, that is.

'If you want to have a life to lead, Mike, I think you'll have to put up with all this. When people close to you are involved, you'd like everyone clapped safely behind bars. But we have to work within the law, and that means no arrests until we've evidence to back them.'

There was a smart rap at the door. Gwen opened it cautiously. I heard Ian's voice first, then another man's voice, vaguely familiar. Andy was on his feet in a rush, almost dragging whoever it was inside. Not from panic, but from pleasure, by the look of it, as he hugged and slapped on the back a big slab of a man. Ruth spilt her wine as she pushed away to join them.

'Griff,' I said to anyone who needed to know. 'Used to do a bit of security work for Andy in the days when he was the Main Act and the Money. Saved his bacon – and Ruth's, a couple of times. Ex-Met,' I added to Gwen, who nodded and mopped at the wine before she sat down again.

'Yes, well,' Griff said, introductions over. 'So Andy can forget this ferrying business, can he? Now he's got no one to ferry? Poor lass,' he added.

Andy coughed. 'Not quite. It wasn't just Marietta I was going to chauffeur. There was someone I had to meet at the station – we got Gareth safely back on his train, Sophie – and I'm due to chair a learned discussion about the historical origins of the Arthurian Legends. Someone's done new translations of both Wace and Gildas, and the guy who revised Nennius last year's not happy.'

There was a digestive silence.

'Someone else meets whoever it is at the station. Wherever you and Ruth go, I go too,' Griff said.

'Andy and I aren't joined at the hip,' Ruth objected. She turned to me. 'Are you simply cancelling the poor woman's readings?'

'I don't see what else I can do. It'd be simply bad taste to shove anyone else in. Not to mention impossible at this stage. How do you want to deal with Andy's own big night, Griff?'

Griff stared at me. 'Without you, if you don't mind. Look, if you two have finished, I wouldn't mind going to talk tactics. Coming, Ian?'

'I'm sticking around here for a bit. I've an idea the Gaffer's about to give us the latest news – and I don't mean that the Bears won again.'

'I have got the preliminary report from the SOCOs,' Chris admitted, at last, pushing aside his empty coffee cup. 'The first – not surprising – piece of information is that Marietta died in the Bookfest office. Sorry, Sophie, but in your chair.'

'She was . . . tortured . . . first?'

'Burnt with a cigarette and then her neck was broken over the back of the chair.' To hear Chris speak, he might have been discussing the possibility of overnight rain. Many of his colleagues faced with similar trauma became raucous. But I couldn't imagine any situation where Chris would allow himself to do that. 'We haven't found her clothes yet.'

Mike jotted on a paper napkin. 'So someone got her to walk into the office. Which implies someone she knew. And someone she associated with the Bookfest office.'

Chris and I exchanged a glance. What if her lover and the stalker were one and the same, despite what she'd said?

'Someone who was able to communicate with her at her home address and get her to come along to the office,' Mike explained, as if he needed to.

'There's no evidence of any letter or phone call to that effect having been sent to her,' Chris said. 'Oh,' he continued, responding to my eyebrows, 'we were monitoring both. God, the media'll crucify us, having let a stalker get his prey.' He put his head in his hands, as if unbelievably he was just realising the full enormity of it.

Mike's bracing return to the fray might have been designed to take his mind off things. 'Someone associated with the

Bookfest office,' he repeated. 'It'd have to be a man. Well, do you see Sophie, Una or Tasleen as killers? No, a man. Acheson, for my money.'

'But it's his festival!' I objected.

'Acheson?' Chris asked, his voice neutral. 'Why Acheson, not Downing?'

'Because – because I'm biased. He couldn't keep his eyes off Sophie at the second reception. I suspect he'd have had his hands where his eyes were, given half a chance.'

I shook my head. 'He's always been the soul of courtesy.' Then I thought back. 'At the start, he did seem to like me in short skirts. And there was often a . . . a twinkle . . . in his eye when he spoke to me. But latterly he seems to have changed. Once I became in a sense his employee he became quite – demanding, in work terms, that is. Gave no quarter, whatever a quarter is in that context.'

'A lot of bosses like to boss,' Gwen observed.

'And he wanted Myakovsky to stay chez Burton,' I said, illogically but relevantly.

'I haven't been able to get that checked out yet,' Chris said. 'I don't want to – to interfere with the case. Tread on Dave Clarke's toes. Not when he's new in post. Later on,' he grinned, 'I shall jump all over them in hobnailed boots. But not yet. If this is to be a long case, I want to be responsible about overtime—'

'Not budgets again, Chris!' I expostulated.

'The same. Plus – and I'd say this was more important – my colleagues' time and energy. If they're to go into overdrive when I want them to, then they'll need something in reserve.' He looked at his watch. 'Now, if you'll excuse me, I have to go to talk to the DCI of one of the other MIUs. He's got some bodies and needs some support,' he added with a restrained anger which told me it must be a truly unspeakable crime.

'Anything to do with our case?' Mike asked.

In his place I'd have kept quiet.

'Not unless you think Marietta's killer might have killed four children under two and buried them under their mother's conservatory.' He leant across and kissed me on the cheek. 'Try to sleep. Gwen here will be handing over to – who is it, Gwen?'

'Tom Horner,' she said. 'Good job you'll be here, Mike.' There was a loud rap at the door. Winking, Gwen got up to open it. She found, not an armed colleague, but a basket of flowers and fruit. A girl bellhop in a jacket three sizes too large for her and shoes to match stepped from behind it.

'The porter found this in the lobby,' she said. 'And it's got your name on it.'

Chris and Gwen banged their heads together in their efforts to check it.

'Bastard,' said Chris. 'Bloody cheeky bastard, too. No, nothing nasty. Just this envelope – and a note.' He eased it out with the back of a knife. 'You can look if you don't touch,' he added. 'As somebody no doubt said to somebody else.'

The paper was good-quality A4.

'You don't think he might have overreached himself this time, do you?' I asked. 'It's the same weight paper, I'd say, as those sent about Vladimir Myakovsky.'

It was better to think about the paper than about the message:

'Farewell, my lovely.'

Eventually Gwen took the flowers, promising to leave them at St Mary's Hospice the following morning. 'Be nice for them to have something that doesn't look as if it came from someone's funeral,' she said. She clapped her hand over her mouth. 'Oh, Sophie, I'm sorry.'

Chris slung an arm round her shoulders. 'Don't worry, Gwen. We're not planning a funeral for Sophie yet a while. Not if I've got anything to do with it, anyway.'

Chapter Twenty-seven

Tom Horner was all that Gwen wasn't, and seemed to take as one of his life's tenets that he get up as many noses as he could in the shortest of times. I'd enjoyed the company of many police officers, at all levels, and was used to a certain amount of swearing; Mike lived a very masculine life with its attendant vocabulary. But both of us were disconcerted by the sheer profusion of f- and c- words. Where anyone else might have used an 'er' sound to fill a momentary gap, he plugged it with an obscenity. It was as if he were playing a private round of that radio parlour game *Just a Minute*, which required no hesitation – though come to think of it, he'd have been penalised for repetition and almost certainly deviation.

After a prowl of inspection round the rooms – designed, since Gwen had already checked them out and no one could possibly have gained access since without several witnesses, to show off his magnificent physique – he took up station by the door.

For all his verbal bravado, he looked a bit shocked when Mike and I retreated together to the bathroom. As if he were 007 defeating listening devices, Mike turned the shower to maximum – and then sat beside me on the edge of the bath, howling with laughter.

'You're supposed to be impressed,' I said, no longer bothering to stifle my giggles. 'You're supposed to realise what a poor shadow of a man you are beside him. You may have scored more runs than any other England player in Oz last winter; you may, come to think of it, have scored more runs than most of the England players put together; you may have scored the first first-class century this season and be out of sight at the top of the batting averages – but to him you're a mere civilian wimp!'

'And my balls aren't as big as his!' Mike sobbed on to my shoulder. 'God, he must have monster balls to have to walk like that.'

At this point the conversation degenerated sharply.

Before I left for work the following morning, I paged my home answerphone.

'A quid says the stalker won't have bothered, since he knows I'm here,' I told Tom, who grunted and squared his jaw, withdrawing to the window and favouring it with a basilisk stare designed to show he'd be completely deaf to any private communications.

In fact, there were only two messages. One was from my former neighbour, Aggie, just saying hello, the other from Steph, saying it would be nice to do lunch and he'd pop up to the office, like, sometime.

'There's your opportunity,' said Mike. 'Invite Andy as well and let them see for themselves – no explanation, no nothing.'

'No tact, either.'

'Life isn't always tactful.' He sighed. 'For a woman with more than her fair share of bottle, Sophie, you're not making a good fist of this, are you?'

I shook my head. 'A lot of kids'd be proud to have a dad

like Andy – his music career, his charity work. Right on. But I'm not sure Steph would see him like that. Steph's no fool: he'll wonder why I didn't tell Andy I was pregnant straight away—'

'And he won't be the only one! Andy—'

'Was hardly on this planet for a year or so after Steph was conceived. I told you: he simply wouldn't have taken it in. And I'm terribly afraid if he had, he'd simply have thrust a fistful of fivers at me and told me to do something about it.'

Mike held me very tightly. 'What do you think he'll make of Steph now?' he asked, at last.

'Hard to tell. Steph's not everyone's idea of a perfect young man – apart from the fact he doesn't have Andy's musical talents, he's a spitting image of Andy at that age. Which might not endear him to Andy at all.'

'Not Andy in his pillar-of-the-community mode, at least,' Mike laughed. 'Will you be going to his launch, after what Griff said?'

'I'll take Chris and Dave's advice, not Griff's. I might have given the Arthurian origins discussion a miss this evening, but the numbers are still so low I ought to paper the house somehow. I suppose you and your mates wouldn't like to make a collective appearance?'

'You suppose right. Though I'd like to see what sort of a fist he makes of it. What about the launch? I can't imagine you staying away.'

'It'd be very strange not to be there – maybe even stranger to be there and hear bits of my childhood read aloud. I wonder why he hasn't given me a copy yet . . .'

I was glad to see there was a new chair in my office. No

carpet, but a new chair, courtesy, I presumed, West Midlands Police – more specifically, Chris Groom. The schedule in the other office told me that the women would be out and about all day, collecting writers from whichever stations they were arriving at, delivering them to their venues and packing them off again at the end of the gig. It would be the responsibility of whoever chaired the reading to feed and water them. My mind returned to Mrs Burton and her intermittent enthusiasms.

I turned to Tom. 'What time does Gwen take over from you?'

'Ten.'

'Fine. Now, I want to check something in the library. I take it you'll be coming with me?'

'Right.'

'Fine. Now, I wonder if you'd mind trying to be as unobtrusive as possible – not like what you are at all, just an ordinary reader.'

He stared.

'They don't get too many gun-packing minders in Companies House,' I said.

'I thought you said the library.'

'Companies House lives in the library basement,' I said. 'Follow me.'

It was a long time since I'd had to check company records, but it all came back quite quickly, and it took only minutes to establish connections between Burton and Acheson. For a start, Peregrine Burton was on the board of Acheson's company. And quite a lot of other companies. Some – big electronics ones – I recognised. Others I didn't. I wrote them all down. Then I thought it might be worth getting print-outs of all of them. if a company is registered as, say, Zero Communications it doesn't give much indication of what it's actually trading in. I'd need *Kelly's* or something for that, wouldn't I?

Clutching my spoils, I called Tom to heel and we set off back upstairs. Reference section, this time, to check on Acheson in *Who's Who*. He wasn't there, not surprisingly, but Burton was. I photocopied the entry. If I'd had time I'd have tried to discover the Army equivalent of the Navy list, but, looking wistfully at *Kelly's* too, realised that Tom was getting restive – this was, after all, a very public space – and that I really ought to get back to the office and actually do what I was paid to do. In any case, I'd phone Chris – or more properly Dave – to get the police to it. Sighing, I abandoned my search.

I let us back into the office and got Tom to brew coffee while I started the day's routine. Post first. There wasn't much and what there was was strictly routine. OK. E-mails? One from Claire, to my surprise. My package, she said, had caused some hilarity amongst those who'd opened it – the stalker had moved on from lacy undies to a full-scale basque. With the sort of police humour I've never been quite able to relate to, Claire had got some poor rookie constable to price it up at Rackhams. Imagine having the sort of money to splash around simply to make someone miserable. Oh, and to satisfy whatever fantasies drove you. Meanwhile, in the fastnesses of Steelhouse nick, she was beavering away, as I no doubt was. Despite being ferried by an armed colleague to and from a protected location she still felt she ought to look over her shoulder all the time. She could imagine how I must feel. Oh, and did I know they were pulling both Martin Acheson and Marcus Downing in for questioning today?

It had better not interfere with the gig he'd taken over from Stonkin Mama!

I e-mailed her back, asking what underwear or other gifts sent to her colleagues had had to blow up. And as I did so I had a weird thought: could whoever had lured Marietta to her death possibly have e-mailed her? As an experiment, I printed off Claire's message to me. No. No good. It came with the name and e-mail address of the originator, of course. Drat: another idea bit the dust. So no phone message, no letter, no e-mail. Carrier pigeon, no doubt. And an instruction to swallow the message.

I drank the coffee Tom had made and settled down to deal with the phone messages.

They started with the usual requests for tickets and information. Then there was one that made me summon Tom. 'You failed to heed my warnings,' this Russian accent intoned, 'about Myakovsky. Oh, he has a minder now. But who will mind the minder?'

'*And who,*' Tom began, to my amazement, to sing, '*takes care of the caretaker's daughter while the caretaker's busy taking care?*'

'You think it's an Englishman, not a Russian?' I asked, trying not to sound eager.

'It's not how he says it but what he says, isn't it? That's what you want to worry about. You want to get a forensic linguist on that. D'you want me to drop the tape off at Steelhouse Lane for you on my way back home?'

I did. Yes, Tom might be right. A forensic linguist was just what we wanted. In fact, we'd wanted one some days ago. What had happened to the analysis someone was supposed to be doing of an earlier message? I'd e-mail Dave – yes, I'd remembered – to ask. Meanwhile I had to trust to Tom's common sense and my instinct. The trouble was, who was putting on the accent? And was it Marcus, who I knew was a clever mimic? Or another man, one who could feign a romantic French accent to go with the romantic flowers and *soi-disant* romantic undies?

Gwen turned up with an ironic glance at her colleague, and a bag containing her knitting. 'My secret weapon,' she said, touching the needles. 'Now, will the clicking disturb you?'

'I'll let you know,' I said. 'I may be doing some clicking of my own. But that'll just be my brain cells getting into gear.'

Now the Bookfest was underway, there was very little need for anyone to be in the office. But I had this old-fashioned notion that if I was being paid to be doing Bookfest work, that was what I ought to be doing. Even if it meant hunting round to find Bookfest work. Simply being in the office to deal with last-minute enquiries seemed, on the face of it, the only thing I could do. I wasn't qualified to do anything with the occasional invoice except file it. No one had got round to authorising my signature on Bookfest cheques, for one thing. So, with a squeaky clean conscience, I settled down to read those print-outs and discover all I could about Peregrine Burton.

I'd have liked any of it to resonate with me. I knew less than nothing about matters military. Was his education – Wellington and Sandhurst – significant? Or his choice of regiment? Certainly his hobbies looked innocent enough: ornithology and genealogy. No, nothing there to get my teeth into. His commercial interests varied from insurance to security. I didn't like the sound of that one. Not considering his house's lack of same.

What about Acheson? No, not a lot to go on there. He wasn't on the board of any companies of which Burton was a director, and, from his neutral accent, I'd be prepared to bet he was the product of a local state school rather than a public school.

All very frustrating. And all the more frustrating to know that back at Steelhouse Lane, the police would be getting all the information I wanted to know. Some of which, if I was lucky, Chris might later share with me.

The phone! Just a punter wanting tickets for a gig today. I referred her to the appropriate library and returned to my great thoughts, or rather, the lack thereof.

'It's another nice day,' Gwen said at last. 'You don't want to go and watch some more cricket?'

'Love to,' I said. 'But I can't just skive off, can I?'

'Suppose not.'

Unable to sit still, I made some tea. Gwen sniffed at hers with apprehension.

'Earl Grey,' I said.

'No milk?'

'Tastes best with lemon, but we've got no lemon. And only powdered milk. And I don't suppose you fancy nipping out to the shops.'

Not sure if I was joking or not – well, neither was I, come to think of it – she sniffed again, wrinkling her nose as she inhaled the bergamot. 'Try anything once, I suppose.'

'Except,' I said, not sure whom I was quoting, 'incest and country dancing.' I was sitting staring at Gwen's knitting when the phone rang. It was one of our authors, a woman who wanted to know when she'd be paid.

'Cash-flow crisis,' she admitted, apologetically.

I could have told her I'd no idea, given my financial restrictions. Then I had another idea. I could take the cheques round to Brian Fairbrother's for him to sign. It was a reasonable excuse. And it would mean I could talk to him about this poisoning allegation.

'Look,' I said to the writer, 'why don't you fax your invoice through to me, and I'll see what I can do?'

Chapter Twenty-eight

While I was waiting for the writer's fax to come through, I gathered together everything Brian would need: invoices, cheque book, envelopes. Oh, his address – I had to get that from the phone book. I even printed off the address labels (I'd put together a database of writers myself, even if I'd never got round to doing one for the great and the good) and stuck them on to the envelopes. Stamps . . .

'No franking machine?' Gwen demanded.

'Too small an outfit,' I said.

'Shame, I've always wanted to play with one.'

The phone rang to announce the arrival of the fax. I gathered it up, stuffed it in the folder with the others, and prepared to close the office.

Gwen hesitated. 'I'd rather we OK'd this with DCI Clarke. He thinks you're in a controlled environment.'

'Makes me sound like some rare plant.' I passed her the phone.

She still hesitated.

'Ah. You mean you'd rather *I* cleared it with Dave. OK. Know his phone number?'

I got Dave's answerphone. He'd hear a cheerful message that Gwen and I had urgent business at Brian's Moseley house, and that we'd phone in again as soon as our mission was accomplished. I also left my mobile number.

Gwen gave a sudden grin, shedding ten years. 'A nice ordinary bit of police work at last,' she said.

'What makes you think it's police work?'

She grinned again. 'Ian Dale and I had a bit of a chat.'

As I left the office, I hesitated. Should I phone Brian first? What if he wasn't in? No, forget it; it would be nice simply to get out into the fresh air.

'Someone's not short of money,' Gwen observed, as I pulled up outside a detached house in the heart of Moseley.

'Must be his wife's earnings – she's a solicitor.'

Brian's was hardly a mean salary either, though people who regularly worked short contracts must need a good fee to keep them going over lean periods. That or a cash injection from the Criminal Injuries Board, to which I owed at least part of my present liquidity. It was terrifying having no monthly pay cheque, and I wouldn't like to have to live off my wits for long. But equally I was secretly dreading my eventual return to the William Murdock treadmill. Mike was more than happy, he said, to support me. As long as he was earning. But the life of a cricketer is limited, and he'd been older than most when his talent had finally been recognised. How much longer as a big earner? Three, four years?

Impressive though the Fairbrothers' house was, it had been neglected. Maybe worse, if the other two children, like Tabs, were positive agents of destruction. No. They couldn't be like Tabs. Parents wouldn't ever have a Tabs as an eldest or a middle child. A Tabs would always put the full stop on child-bearing. Wouldn't it? Or did I mean she?

A couple of open windows suggested someone might be at

home. Even if it was only the woman I spoke to the morning Brian was hospitalised, I might get some hard news. It would be nicer if it was Brian himself or Elly, though I didn't imagine the latter would greet me with unalloyed pleasure, especially if it meant inflicting work on Brian. I might even ask for a sick note – that would really enrage her.

On the whole, it might be better if it was the home help: she might relish a good gossip, and what I must not forget was that Gwen would probably be an expert in extracting gossip. She wasn't, as she'd observed, just an armed police officer. She was an experienced policewoman.

She stood ironically aside for me to ring the doorbell, which seemed reluctant to respond.

'It's one of those battery ones,' she said. 'And the batteries only last five minutes. Try the knocker.'

I pointed – the knocker had been removed. I banged on the door with my fist.

No response. I put my ear to the letter box; yes, I was sure I could hear movement. I yelled, and applied the ear again. Silence.

I tried again. 'Brian, it's Sophie!'

This time I was rewarded by the sound of footsteps. I stood back from the door, not wanting to hassle him with further peerings or listenings.

I could hear him by the door, but he did nothing but stand there. There was a spyhole; I positioned myself in front of it. 'Only me and a friend.'

The door opened. A grey-faced, unshaven Brian gestured us in. He was ill, all right. How many colleagues had I seen with that haunted look, that cringing posture? Stress, depression, whatever you called it – trying to run the Bookfest solo had taken its toll.

He led the way through a hall nearly as wide as my living room, but cluttered with enough large plastic toys for a playgroup, to a kitchen I'd have given my teeth for, provided that I could spend a week cleaning it first. No disrespect to their Mrs Thing: this wouldn't have responded to the superficial cleaning her no doubt tight schedule allowed. Not if she was expected to do all the washing-up piled up in the sink as well.

Brian swilled a couple of mugs under the tap. 'Coffee?'

Gwen and I spoke as one. 'No, thanks.'

'You'd better come through into my study then.' Hunched dispiritedly, he left from a door in the kitchen I'd assumed led to the garage. In fact, it led through a utility room into what might once have been the rear end of a superb garage, but was now a remarkably well-appointed office, complete with fax, computer a generation newer than mine and bookshelves that would have kept a bibliophile happy for months. But there was only one chair, so he trailed back to the kitchen, returning with two stools I wanted to wipe before I sat down. I introduced Gwen, reiterating simply that she was a friend.

'You've had a bad time by the look of it,' she said.

He nodded.

'Your wife said something about poisoning?' I asked.

'The tests were inconclusive,' he said, in a dull voice of someone who's said the same thing a number of times before.

'Poisoning?' Gwen repeated. 'Brian, how awful. How could that have happened?'

'God knows. Sophie – remember I just started throwing up?'

'That's right. On the A4123. And at Piddock Road nick.'

'And at intervals through the night. There was . . . blood.' He shuddered. 'So I had to have a transfusion, and all these

X-rays and scans and things. Acute gastritis, that's what they said in the end. But one of the kids thought it might be Paraquat.'

'Kids?'

'Oh, you know how they all look about fifteen. A registrar, or something.'

Gwen frowned. 'I thought Paraquat always came with an emetic these days. Ah! The vomiting.'

'Quite. But it was too late by then. All the – the evidence' – he managed a pallid smile – 'had been disposed of by then. In any case, how on earth could I have got hold of Paraquat? It's something you'd notice, I'd have thought – a packet of weedkiller beside your teacup! By the way,' he continued, with a better attempt at a smile, 'I gather I'm in your debt, Sophie.'

'No. How could you be?'

'Marcus came round—'

'Marcus!' I tried to make it a casual prompt, but I could sense Gwen stiffening beside me.

'Oh, yes. We go back years. Played cricket against him when I was at school. Have you got him in the writers' team?'

I nodded. 'Did he want anything special?'

'Brought a couple of relaxation tapes and a pile of books. He told me they tried to terminate my contract and you stuck up for me.'

'Before you were taken ill, you earned what they were paying you twice over. Afzal and I thought you might even be thinking of suing them for workplace stress.'

'So I might. Except for this Paraquat business. You know what these experts are like – they'd seize on one kid's theory and blow my case out of the water. Anyway, thanks to you I'm still being paid.'

'And so am I,' I grinned.

'Funny business about Marcus, though,' he said. 'Getting a nice little earner like that and then chucking it. He said he wanted more time to write, though I'd have thought the money – even if it was only for a week . . . But then, with his background he can probably afford it.'

'Background?' Ampleforth – well, that suggested money, of course. But I'd like to hear more.

'Oh, his grandfather made a mint years back and invested it well.'

'Have you any idea when you'll be coming back?'

He raised rabbit eyes, and then his face collapsed. He pressed one hand to his stomach, and with the other reached for a familiar antacid. If the very thought of work did that to him, he'd surely get compensation. But his wife was a solicitor, for goodness' sake. She should know. I waited for his spasm to subside before producing the Bookfest paperwork.

Without even seeming to focus on the chequebook he scribbled his signature on the cheques; I completed them.

'Do you want me to sign a supply for you?'

I shook my head. 'I'd rather get the board to have my signature authorised. In the meantime, I know it means having to bother you when you're not well . . .'

'I am getting better, honestly. So long as I can have peace and quiet. I've even dug out the novel I started to draft years ago. See.' He pointed to a swirling screen-saver. 'But even the thought of going back to that mayhem—'

'It's not so bad now it's under way. I've pulled in a few favours so I've got people to help.'

'Good. There are some useful people on the board, you know. Acheson's been very good, by the way. Sent me a box of booze, actually. Not that I'm allowed to touch alcohol at the moment. Not until this heals.' He patted his stomach.

Booze? Acheson was supposed to be sending flowers on behalf of us all. And booze and bad tums didn't mix. What was he up to?

'How are you spending your time apart from writing?' Gwen asked.

'Oh, I potter in the garden. That's nice. Especially in this lovely weather. Elly's imposed a news blackout so I don't get stressed by floods or civil strife or whatever.'

Gwen pressed my foot, very hard. She needn't have bothered. I'd kept quiet about Marietta's death so far in the conversation, and I wasn't about to blab about it now. Mind you, by the time Chris had held the news conference scheduled for about now, the whole world would know about it. In fact, my own stomach griped at the mere thought of running the gauntlet of the media who'd no doubt encircle the library and try to penetrate the office itself. To talk to the obvious person: the acting Bookfest director.

I turned to Brian. 'Could I bum one of those tablets of yours?'

We were sitting in my car, folding invoices and cheques and compliments slips into the envelopes I'd brought. I was just about to send the one faxed through before we'd set out.

'I thought faxes would have the number of the transmitting machine,' I said sharply. 'You know, like e-mails.'

'Yes. They do, don't they?'

'Not this one,' I said. 'Look.'

'So it doesn't.' She looked at me sideways. 'Why are you interested?'

'Because something drew Marietta to the office. It couldn't have been an e-mail or a phone call or a letter. After the stalking business all her letters and phone calls were monitored. And the e-mail would still be in her computer, complete with sender's e-mail address, and he'd have either to get into the house to delete it or use someone else's e-mail address. And that wouldn't work because people tend to know who's using their computers.'

'You're suggesting someone *faxed* her an invitation to her death?'

'Not impossible. Provided you faxed an appropriate letter heading and the fax machine didn't automatically state its origin. Say I wanted her to come to the office at an ungodly hour. I could put a letter through on Bookfest headed paper and say I'd meet her at the office.'

'But how would you get rid of the fax copy? It'd be in her bin or wherever. And believe me, there won't be a bin in Marietta's house that SOCO haven't been through.'

I spread my hands. 'Pass.' But I didn't apologise for having a silly idea. The more I thought of it, the better it seemed.

'Where now?' Gwen asked.

'Find somewhere for some lunch.' I flicked a glance at my watch. 'We could go to the cricket ground. Food and drink there.' And, with luck, a glimpse of Mike, I added, under my breath.

Gwen looked at me sideways. 'And a glimpse of Mike,' she said, ironically.

Not a mere glimpse: we saw him take a spectacular catch, to the rapturous applause of all forty-one of us in the ground. But we couldn't stay. Chris phoned to ask me where the hell I was and what I thought I was doing. And, moreover, how the hell I proposed to get back into the library now it was under siege. He stopped. 'You're about to tell me where the back door is, aren't you?'

'I suppose I am. It's the one used for deliveries. It's also the post room for the branch libraries. If we want to mail stuff for free – our publicity material for instance – we take it down there and pop it in giant pigeonholes.'

He'd register that, of course, but didn't take me up on it. 'How is Fairbrother anyway?'

I told him about the Paraquat.

'There's no report from the hospital,' he said. 'So the registrar or whatever must have got it wrong.'

'Hang on,' I said. 'He'd spewed on the way to Piddock Road, at Piddock Road, and on the way home from Piddock Road. And several times in the night. There wouldn't be any vomit they could get analysed, would there?'

'Hmm. In any case, you'd notice if someone shoved a spoonful of poison in your tea. And it would taste funny.'

My stomach kicked. What if it hadn't been administered in a cup of tea? What if it had come in something with a much stronger taste? Whisky, for instance. But it was such a nebulous idea I wouldn't say anything. Not yet. Not till I'd got another piece of information.

'Would you do something for me, Chris? Dave and co. are talking to Marcus and Acheson today, aren't they? Could they possibly "forget" to ask something and get them both to fax some information to you?'

'What are you up to, Sophie?'

'Possibly making a complete ass of myself. But you'll be getting a fax from the Bookfest office as soon as I've run up those backstairs. Maybe I'll tell you in that what I'm doing.'

One of the nice things about staying in a good hotel was the facilities available to its guests. In this case the swimming pool. I always surprise myself in the water. And it's nice to surprise Mike, who is so infinitely superior to me in every other sport, with the possible exception of crown green bowls. Mike's swimming is limited to an ineffectual and splashy breast-stroke. I ploughed fiercely up and down the pool, trying not to think about the Bookfest – Andy was just about to start his gig with the Arthurians, whose audience would at least be swelled by the solid presence of Griff and Ian, at least one of whom would be interested in what was being said. I showed off with a neat racing turn and surfaced to look around me.

Gwen, sitting beside the pool, nursing a remarkably vivid non-alcoholic cocktail, had been joined by a familiar rangy figure: it was time to emerge post-haste from the pool and swathe myself in as many layers as possible. Dave Clarke might have achieved the respectable heights of being a DCI but I didn't wish to renew our acquaintance dressed in nothing but a bikini. As for Mike, he could lounge around in nothing but his swimmies as long as he wanted; there weren't many men of my acquaintance whose anatomies could bear comparison with his.

'Hi, sweetheart,' Dave greeted me as I muffled myself in the giant bathrobe the Mondiale had provided. 'Still making waves, I see.'

I nodded, coincidentally shaking droplets on him. At least that should deter him from demanding a chlorinated kiss. Gwen, completely expressionless, passed me a towel, which I wound into a turban

'What's all this stuff about faxes?'

'I told Chris in the one I sent him: some faxes are programmed to print their origin automatically. Others don't seem to be.'

'The Bookfest one certainly doesn't.' He grinned. 'So you're about to lose it. For forensic tests. We'll get it back to you ASAP, of course.'

I curtsied my thanks. 'What are you testing it for?'

'What a lot of people don't know, Sophie, is that the message remains inside the gubbins, somehow or other. Don't ask me how.'

'So if a fax was involved,' I said, 'there'd be evidence on the machine of whoever sent it. Excellent. And what,' I said, using the tail of the towel to dab an errant trickle, 'about the machine it comes in on? Would it be retained in that memory too?'

'Funny you should ask that,' he said. 'Marietta's is having its entrails examined even as we speak.'

'What about Acheson's and Downing's?'

'They both have headings, I'm afraid. Neither can be switched off, apparently. So the theory is that since they both had access to the Bookfest machine, they might have faxed Marietta from there. Incidentally, you could switch one on if you wanted.'

'But the only one with easy access to the fax was Marcus.'

Dave shook his head. 'Things aren't looking so good for him, are they? He lies to get a job working alongside you. He was a leading light in the drama groups at his school and at university – oh, when we check, Sophie, we check. He's got the opportunity, especially if he pulls out of the Bookfest job.'

'Why does that give him more opportunity? Oh, I suppose his office here was usually awash with people. Motive?' I pursued.

He shrugged. 'Who can get into the heads of nutters who stalk and kill? There's a bit of research but not very much. And what there is doesn't seem to fit our particular bill. It's supposed to be social inadequates, isn't it? Men who couldn't pull a real live bird.' Dave allowed himself a minuscule smirk to show he'd never suffered from that particular problem. 'Or men who can't take it in that a relationship's over. Plus a whole lot of sad women after unattainable men, of course.' A second smirk suggested that he himself, had he been less modest, might have revealed how he'd been pestered.

'What about men obsessed with power?' Mike asked.

We all jumped. I made brief introductions.

'You see,' he continued, 'I've had the chance to do a bit of reading, and it seems to me that's one area that could profitably be explored. Which of your suspects enjoys power for its own sake? Enjoys manipulating people from a distance? I'd say, wouldn't you, there's one of them in the frame, and it certainly isn't Marcus.'

Chapter Twenty-nine

It could have been quite a jolly party in our suite at the Mondiale. Chairing the Arthurian discussion had given Andy a tiny dose of the adulation he'd so loved when he was in the music business, and he was still fizzing with it. Ruth, more sober, none the less beamed with delight, her eyes bright, as she recounted how Andy had been asked by one of the academic worthies which university he taught at. Griff was joshing Ian about a point he'd raised from the floor. Gwen, unfortunately, had been replaced by Tom Horner, eyes still narrowed against the non-existent smoke of the murky dive of his imagination. Chris had just dropped in, off duty enough to sink a couple of glasses of Andy's champagne, to which Ian had already given his seal of approval.

'So what's the latest, Gaffer?' I asked. Being jolly was all well and good, but Mike was sliding surreptitious glances at his watch. It was a working day tomorrow, and professional sportsmen couldn't afford post-booze bleariness – not if they were as conscientious as Mike, anyway. I sat down, pulling Mike down beside me. Chris followed suit, but Andy and his entourage excused themselves and left. Ian stayed behind, however, sitting unobtrusively behind Chris's shoulder.

'Not a lot to report,' Chris admitted. So what was he doing

here, apart from making Dave Clarke look uncomfortable?

'Harvinder's following up connections between Peregrine Burton and Martin Acheson,' Dave put in quickly.

'Which are?'

'Considerable, I should say. Acheson may have his own company now, but he started off in a very humble way. A plumber, actually. And he and Burton seem to have made a point of putting work each other's way for years.'

'A plumber? Well, it makes sense given his current line of business,' Chris reflected.

'Then a heating engineer. Oh, credit where credit's due – the man's pulled himself up with his bootstraps.'

So much for my poking around in Companies House!

'But come on, you did that press conference this afternoon,' Chris continued. 'Surely the regional TV news featured it? Haven't you had any information from Joe Public?'

'I hope the incident room's abuzz with calls even as we speak,' Dave said. 'The trouble is, none of the people at the library seems to have heard or seen anyone like Marietta. Not at a time consistent with her death.'

'Which was?' I asked sharply. Why hadn't I asked before?

'Probably sixteen to twenty-four hours before you found her.'

'So someone lured her there early Saturday morning. Well, it makes sense.'

'Quite. But what doesn't make sense is that no one from the library or security staff remembers seeing her come in. And the security cameras in Victoria Square didn't pick up anyone like her, not even someone like her but with different hair, different clothes. She just seems to have materialised. And, poor woman, died.'

Chris had the grace to look shamefaced. This was something

he should have passed on. 'What about the alternative way in? The one through the goods entrance you mentioned, Sophie?'

'I'll show you where it is, Dave. Quite out of the way. I didn't meet a soul when I used it today. Oh, apart from someone sending out all sorts of mail to branch libraries – there's a huge set of pigeonholes there.'

'But on Saturday you'd expect to be front of house, as it were: the admin people wouldn't be at work, would they?' Chris asked.

Dave shook his head. 'So someone who knows the system very well. So we're back to Acheson or Downing. Both of whom have given extremely plausible – if not watertight – accounts of their Saturdays. The only gaps in their alibis are the sort you'd expect anyone to have driving from place to place. Neither has reacted to prolonged questioning with anything than a normal reaction—'

'Whatever that might be,' Chris said drily. 'And the forensic tests have so far shown nothing conclusive?'

'Both men used the office regularly. Neither has any injury that might have been caused by Marietta trying to defend herself. And there's no indication she did put up much of a fight. There are bruise-marks on her wrists and ankles where she was pinioned, but it looks as if her killer used plastic-covered rope. No fibres to contaminate the assailant's clothing,' he added.

'Has anyone checked with Marietta's fiancé her tastes in sex?' Mike asked.

You could have heard a champagne bubble burst.

'Not to mention Acheson and Downing's tastes in sex,' he continued.

'Or her ex-lover's,' I added, quietly.

'Quite. It just seems to me that if a man wants to undress and tie up a woman it helps if she likes being undressed and tied up,' Mike continued. 'Once you've got her like that, presumably it's easy enough to burn her and break her neck.'

'So you're suggesting an assignation? Well, it might make sense. I suppose the PM didn't reveal any sign of sexual activity, Dave?'

'Not recent enough to interest us. But if she wanted to be tied up before she had her shag, that would be consistent.'

'Only if she knew the man involved,' I said. 'It doesn't make sense for a woman afraid for her life to respond to an invitation to have sex with a stranger in those conditions.'

'But she thought the stalking was over,' Dave said. 'And maybe she fancied – whoever it was.'

'Fancying a man and indulging in bondage with him the first time you have sex are two different matters,' I said. 'And even if you did consent, wouldn't you be a bit alarmed if he suddenly produced a length of rope? Wouldn't you expect to have to make a further assignation so you could get whatever you needed?'

'Pays to be poked by a bloke in uniform – he'd have his cuffs all ready,' Dave said.

'I'll remember that,' I said sourly. 'No, it's got to be her secret lover, hasn't it?'

'Which suggests more strongly that her lover must be Acheson or Marcus,' Chris agreed.

'I'll get someone on to that first thing tomorrow,' Dave said. 'And I'll check Downing and Acheson's preferences, while I'm at it. Whoops.'

No one laughed.

'Any news on the Myakovsky front?' I asked, pointedly.

'Well, he's got his minder, of course,' Dave said, as if

playing for time. Poor man, he'd hardly got his feet under his new desk and he was being badgered.

'Has he been called upon to more than look mean?' I pursued.

'Not that we know of. But, yes, the envelope the threats to Myakovsky came in was the same type as on the fruit and flowers that came for you, Sophie. And the paper.'

'Is that a big plus?'

'Would be if they weren't the most popular brand on the market. Labels ditto. There is one thing: the stamps you saved. The forensic boys—'

'And girls?'

'You and your bloody PC, Sophie! OK, the forensic scientists tell me that you can get enough DNA from the back of a licked postage stamp to identify – the licker. So here's looking at you, Sophie.'

I'm not sure quaffing champagne was the wisest thing he could do in front of Chris, but I thought that bit of news merited it.

'Let's hope he uses saliva, then, not a sponge,' Chris said, at his driest. 'And that we can identify a suspect to gob-swab.'

'Why not ask both Downing and Acheson?' Poor Dave shouldn't have sounded like a junior clerk: it was just the way to make Chris treat him like one.

'Why are you waiting?' Chris asked. 'And I'd have thought, in the circumstances, the budget might just run to a quick analysis, rather than the cheaper one taking three months. Wouldn't you?'

'I'm still not happy about you going to Andy's big gig,' Griff said, helping himself to a croissant. Instead of sitting down at the table, he remained standing, dropping crumbs on the floor.

'I can quite understand why you should want to be there, you being cousins and that—'

'Hang on. Hang on.' I closed my eyes. I should have told someone something, shouldn't I?

'Only—'

'Just shut the fuck up!' I exploded. It must come back. It must come back. I pushed from the table and leaned my forehead against the window, eyes, but not brain, focused on the rush-hour chaos of Broad Street. But I was too busy wondering why on earth I'd overreacted so badly I couldn't pin whatever it was down. 'Sorry, Griff,' I said, turning back.

'That's OK, sweetheart.' He spoke easily, but he still looked concerned, disconcerted, even.

Mike said quietly, 'We'll talk about this later, Griff. Whatever Sophie needs to remember obviously has to be snuck up on, as we say round here.'

Griff looked round for somewhere to dispose of the remains of his croissant but thought better of it and stuffed it into his mouth. Flapping a hand, he ambled out. Tom continued to stare impassively at absolutely nothing.

I found I was crying. Mike gathered me up, and muttered inane but wonderful things into my hair. 'You couldn't just stay here all day.' It was hardly a question. 'I know, you'd go mad. How about you come out to Edgbaston again: I could fix it for you to be in the pavilion. You'd be safer there.'

'I'd love that. But I'd better slip into work first. I shall be all right with Gwen there.'

''Course you will,' he said.

I slapped my hand over my mouth. 'Steph! I forgot – he wanted to have a meal with me. I never got back to him.'

'Phone him and bring him too,' Mike said, with visible forbearance.

* * *

'I must have eaten something,' Gwen said. She, Dave and myself were walking briskly through the unofficial entrance into the library. 'Only I feel that queasy. Not like me at all.'

'Why don't you call in sick?' Dave demanded. 'We'll find someone else.'

I added my mite. 'Tom could stand and stare over my head for a bit longer.'

'No. I shall be all right.'

'You're sure?' Dave stopped to peer at her face.

'You can't say it's hard work, sitting doing my knitting while Sophie answers the phone and that.'

It wasn't the knitting that worried me, it was the quickness of her reactions if she needed them. But now wasn't the time to say that, not with her looking parchment pale. Dave frowned, catching my eye. It was up to him, wasn't it?

'I'll come up to the Bookfest office before I go back to Steelhouse Lane,' he said. 'Just to see how you are.' He smiled, the dazzling sort of smile that made every woman he'd ever smiled at feel special. I wouldn't have thought Gwen was his sort, or he hers, but she responded with a blush from the throat. 'Meanwhile, though it's rather late in the day, I'd better get the lads to have a look round in here.' He looked at the full pigeonholes. 'God, I'm going to be popular, aren't I?'

I tapped in the code, stopped the alarm and reached for the kettle.

'Lock yourself in while I fill it,' she said. 'Not just shut it. Lock it.'

I didn't argue.

Right, then. Time to start the morning's work. I took a deep breath. Everything would be straightforward, wouldn't it? Please! OK, mail first.

A pile of routine invoices grew in my in-tray. All right so far.

There was a knock on the office door. 'Only me!' Gwen sang. I let her in. 'I'll make us a nice cup of tea, shall I?'

'Great.'

Nothing from the Myakovsky madman. Nothing for me. Nothing to worry about on the answerphone. No unpleasant e-mails. I checked the wall chart: yes, Una and Tas would be out all day, collecting and returning writers, so many milk bottles emptied by their library audiences. Presumably Marcus would be allowed to do his stand-in gig for Stonkin Mama before his gob-swabbing. And no doubt Acheson would be busy bossing and his chilly secretary would be keeping folk at arm's length.

A nice, normal day. Except I jumped like a highly trained flea when the phone rang. Claire, near to tears, by the sound of it.

'They didn't want to tell me,' she said. 'But they had to. He's started sending me gifts. Including a photo of me and my bloke. Only he'd cut his face away. And – and where his genitals would be.'

A defaced photo. Could that be related to the defaced Hanging Man that had so upset Tas and Una? And could that mean that whoever had threatened Myakovsky was our stalker?

When I told Gwen about the photo she went paler than ever.

'Look,' I said, 'you heard what Dave said. He'll find someone else. When he comes up, tell him you're taking his advice and going home.'

'I'll think about it,' she said, retiring to her usual chair with her knitting.

Time to invite Steph to Edgbaston. I called his mobile; strange how even the most hard-up kids managed to carry one. I had to leave a message for him to call me back. And then I had nothing to do but stare at the wall. Logically I should have called Acheson to discuss authorising my signature to pay the cheques for all those invoices. But I didn't want to call Acheson. Not with the odds as I suspected they were.

Chapter Thirty

If only I could remember what it was I had to remember. What on earth was it? If only I could do what Mike suggested, sneak up on it. In the meantime, what I could do, while we waited for Dave, was get a piece of paper and think on to that. Threats. Stalkings. The Burton-Acheson connection. Marietta's bondage. What was it I had to remember?

I sprinkled the page with question marks and stared.

Compared with Marietta, the stalker hadn't given me too hard a time. The bits of intimacy he'd subjected me to had been intrusive, but not life-threatening. No nasty business with fast cars on crossings. But Claire had received the horribly defaced photo. So why had I got off comparatively lightly? It wasn't that he didn't know a lot about me, at least. Leaving that card in Andy's car proved that. And then that suggestion that Andy and I were very close for cousins.

But some anonymous stalker hadn't said that. Acheson had said that. Acheson had managed to pick up on something between Andy and me. How on earth, when not even my family knew? But how on earth did any stalker manage to dig up life's tiny, vital intimacies?

Grabbing another sheet of paper I slapped Acheson's name in the middle. Then I scrawled everything I could think of, relevant or not. Obsession with books – all those matching collections. Collections of gubbins and widgets and photos of employees. A secretary I'd thought was hostile but who might have been apprehensive. Of what? I added. She didn't fit the pattern of blue-eyed blondes. But maybe she knew or suspected something. Had she known his wife, if he'd ever had one? Back to Acheson himself: guiding force of Bookfest. Booze for Brian. His weed-free garden. Could he possibly have poisoned Brian simply to get to see more of me? He knew – from experience! – about Brian's dodgy stomach. He left his office to organise drinks for us. Opportunity . . . Motive . . . Where was the lay-by where I'd stopped? I drew a little map for myself. The weather had been fine, and it was probably no one's job to wash pavements. Some poor SOCO might be able to retrieve enough vomit to run tests. He'd certainly sent him alcohol which would have done that poor stomach no good at all had he been tempted. Acheson's friendship with Burton. Now that was an unlikely combination! Interest in me in short skirts. Trying to take over my evenings with work. His big car. The interest when I'd said threats would wear one down like a stone.

A gob-swab might prove Acheson to be the stalker – could I prove him to be Marietta's killer? What about those defaced pictures . . .

The phone rang. I was so preoccupied Gwen coughed apologetically and leant across to pass it to me.

'Yes?'

'Only me,' Andy said mildly. 'I wasn't very happy with what Griff said to you this morning. Can I pop round and we can talk about it?'

'Fine,' I said. 'Bring some fresh milk and I'll make you a cuppa. And show you something.'

'Be round in ten minutes,' he said.

Gwen said, 'Would you mind if I opened that window? It's so stuffy . . .'

'You won't get much that hasn't been used twice already,' I said, getting up and doing it for her. 'Look, Gwen, call Dave now.'

'Maybe when I've finished this row,' she said, sitting back with her eyes closed.

So why should Acheson give the other women a harder time? Marietta had called the police, Claire was in the police – was that a connection? Or was it simply that he had more power over me as my employer? Surely, surely he hadn't really poisoned Brian to slip me into the job? If he had, what on earth might he have done without the presence of the women and Marcus in the office?

I was stuck here but out at Steelhouse Lane was a highly trained team. OK, they'd probably be asking themselves these questions at this very minute, but it wouldn't hurt to add my mite.

'What's Dave's fax number?' I asked Gwen.

'Same as his phone, I think.' She bent to fish her diary from her bag. 'Here you are. Oh . . .'

I shoved the paper in and pressed start. The machine began to chunter.

'Sophie – I've got to—' Gwen was on her feet, holding her mouth. Before I could do anything, she was out of the office: I heard the outer door slam.

On my feet – should I go after her? Simply lock the door behind her? I was distracted by the phone. Years of conditioning made me reach for it. And be polite to a confused and voluble punter at the other end.

Ah! Someone was punching the security keys. I turned to

welcome Gwen back and looked straight into the eyes of Acheson. Neither they nor the rest of his face was reassuring. No, he wasn't on Bookfest business, was he?

What was it they always said? Remind a potential assailant you're a person. Potential assailant? Potential killer, more like. All the more reason to keep him talking, till the safe return of Gwen and her gun.

As if reading my thoughts, he stepped back and slipped the door lock, overriding the entry code. Oh yes, Acheson meant business. Well, I could mean it too. At very least I could hit him with a ballpoint. Better still – I could use one of Gwen's needles. Sorry about the dropped stitches, Gwen. And I could scream for help. I might even be able to escape through the window on to that maintenance walkway running the circumference of the Forum. I was young, fit – I could outrun him. If only I wasn't so bloody scared of heights.

I grabbed the paper from the fax and slipped the knitting needle up my sleeve as he turned back into the office. Remember – remind him you're a human being.

'The Bookfest's going very well, isn't it, Martin? A real triumph for you.'

Almost in spite of himself, he preened. 'You've worked very hard,' he conceded.

'The whole team has. Everyone's come up trumps. Myakovsky's gigs are complete sell-outs. All of them. A real coup for you, getting someone of his calibre.'

Acheson looked at the door. However much he liked hearing his praises sung, oh yes, he'd come for something else, hadn't he!

'And those threats – they were a brilliant idea, too. They'd have been wonderful for publicity – if the press had ever got hold of them.'

Acheson's smile was thin, but he said nothing.

'Pity he couldn't have stayed with the Burtons as you wanted.'

'I never wanted him to stay there.'

'So why did you push the idea?'

He turned away. In irritation? In frustration that he didn't have time to explain?

Now might I do it pat. Except I'd never attacked anyone in cold blood, not even in what I was sure would simply be a pre-emptive strike.

'You never wanted him to stay there,' I repeated slowly. 'So you had to continue with the threats you'd originally meant only for publicity: you got the idea from that Stonkin Mama business, of course. I must say, you've got a fine line in accents – very convincing. Pity,' I lied, 'the voice analysis gave you away.' Well, not so much a lie. More a speculation yet to be proved.

I was pushing my luck. But he hadn't denied anything. In fact, he was looking at me again.

'*Why* didn't you want Myakovsky to stay at the Burtons? What do you have against them? Him, anyway. It'd be something you found when you did some work on the house – plumbing or central heating, wouldn't it? Yes, all those rooms to be turned into posh bathrooms. You'd have had time for a good scout round.'

Shrugging, he turned from me as if it didn't matter that I'd guessed. 'I see you've been busy,' he said, touching the jottings on the corner of my desk. 'Well, I don't think anyone else would be interested in that, do you?' He folded the papers together and slipped them in an inside pocket.

'My minder certainly is,' I said. 'She'll be back any minute.'

'Minder? Not that dumpy-looking little woman? My God,

I'd have thought they could have done better than that, Sophie. I thought she was another of your wretched protégées. Anyway, I don't see her here at the moment. Why don't you sit down so that we can talk?' He laid a lighter and pack of cigarettes on my desk. No, they weren't to smoke, were they? I'd have smelt it for sure on his clothes, on his breath. They were to brand me with a figure 2.

Just at the moment, talking seemed a better option. 'I thought you liked me, Martin.'

'Oh, I did. I do. But I'm not going to share you with anyone else. Look at Marietta – preferring that faceless wonder. When she'd had me. When she still wanted me. And you wanted me. I could tell.'

I shook my head. 'I've been with Mike for ages,' I said. 'I never was available.'

He pointed accusingly to my bare ring finger. 'You misled me.'

'And Claire lives with her man too. Come on, Martin – isn't that what you really want to do – prise a woman away from her existing man? Isn't getting someone else's woman your real game? Or do you just like collecting people in general? All the performers and punters at the Bookfest have been part of your collection, haven't they?'

'Seventy-eight performers, audiences approaching fifteen thousand in total. That's some achievement, Sophie.' This was the first real reaction I'd got from him.

'Not all of them blondes,' I reminded him. 'Why blondes, Martin? Was your wife a blonde? Blue eyes, nice figure, bright?'

Hell, that was a nerve I'd better have left unpoked. What on earth had happened? Had she had the temerity to leave him? Or even jilt him? Was that why he'd burnt the wedding dress?

There was a rattle outside: Gwen was punching the security lock. 'Sophie? It's OK, you can unlock the door! It's only me!'

Acheson wheeled to the door and back again, pointing to me as if I were a dog told to stay. I stayed but I yelled. And pushed the window open wider.

All that did was let in more of the echoing hubbub of the Forum.

'I thought I told you to sit down,' Acheson said. 'Oh, you've got a nice new chair, Sophie. I wonder why you should need that.'

'You overreached yourself,' I said, 'sending me the flowers at the Mondiale. Gave yourself away. In fact, wouldn't it be better for all concerned it you were the one to sit down? I'll let Gwen in and she can tell you your rights.'

'Oh dear. The old PACE caution. I've seen it on television so many times, I've no desire to hear it for myself. No, Sophie, we'll leave this room together – you've become a hostage, my dear.' He produced a knife, the sort I used to slice my vegetables. A knife versus a knitting needle?

'I shan't hurt you, my dear. Not if you co-operate. Which I'm sure you will. After all, I went to a very great deal of trouble to get you on this job. And to make sure you kept it.'

Gwen was thundering on the door.

'Like Marietta co-operated?' I asked. Stupid. Remind him you're a person, not a challenge.

A male voice joined Gwen's outside the door. My God! Steph! Why had he chosen today of all days to pick up his phone messages? He mustn't get involved! But there were thuds: he and Gwen were trying to shoulder down the door.

Acheson's expression changed. 'But I didn't want to harm her pretty face.' God, this sane, highly organised man was certifiable! 'I'm afraid, my dear, I'm going to have to hurt you. And your pretty face.'

The outer door was holding. The window was my only chance. But to get on to the chair to reach it meant turning my back on him. Dare I risk it?

No option. I got on to the chair and, as I put one leg through the window, kicked the chair back at him. He yelled. I rolled, fell through. I had a moment to scrabble to my feet and take stock. Until someone opened a door to release us we'd just go round and round. At least I'd do it loudly.

Someone else did something even more loudly. There was an enormous bang, echoing round the gallery and into the depths of the Forum below. Whatever it was – Gwen shooting through the lock? – didn't deter Acheson. He was already through the window, and after me. No time to scream now. I just had to wheel and dodge through the debris, desperate not to fall.

At least he'd be just as desperate. Fall with a knife in your hand like that, and goodness knew what harm you'd do yourself.

Round and round we'd go, then, round and round till one of us slipped.

Hell! A coil of Christmas lights! I had to slow down, lest I get lassoed and trussed. If I did, so did he. Another scream. Someone would help, surely!

What the hell? Steph was running towards me. No, he mustn't risk it!

'Get out of the way – he's got a knife!' I yelled. 'Let the police—'

What could he do against an armed man? I turned: better for me to face Acheson than my son! By now there was another figure. He was chasing Acheson, visibly gaining on him. But Acheson had a knife.

'Let me get at him, Soph!' Steph yelled from behind me.

'Stay where you are!' I pushed him back.

The knitting needle. I let it slide into my hand. Got a grip on it. Yes, I'd kill for Steph.

There was another bang. Acheson stopped in his tracks. He leapt sideways into the Forum wall. At least his head did. I didn't want to see what happened to his body. My God, all that blood!

The other man stopped too. Then stepped over what he had to and ran on towards me. But he was looking not at me, but over my head. At Steph.

'Jesus Christ, Sophie,' Andy said, looking at a younger version of the face he saw in the mirror every day, a face so like mine we might have been brother and sister. 'Why didn't you tell me?'

Chapter Thirty-one

Gwen had been escorted away by another firearms officer and the whole area cordoned off. There was so much blood around I couldn't imagine anyone wanting to go in the Forum ever again. For all her greenish pallor, Gwen had been remarkably cool about what she'd done. 'It's what I was trained for,' she said simply. 'Have you any idea how close he'd got to you?'

'Too close.'

'And you'd been distracted – I could see that. What I was afraid of was that you'd turn at the wrong minute – or that you'd trust to that needle.'

'Sorry about your knitting,' I began, meaning to thank her and say all sorts of pleasant things. But she clutched her mouth again, and rushed off.

Her boss shrugged philosophically. 'It gets us all sorts of ways,' he said. 'But she'll get over it. Debriefing, counselling – call it what you will. Ways of dealing with stress are built into the system.' He followed her.

I wasn't so sure it was sickness induced by shock. Not unless it was catching. Perhaps I should occupy my own stomach doing something useful. But just at the moment I couldn't think what. In any case the Bookfest office was crammed to the gunwales with police officers.

'It's become a scene of crime,' a uniformed constable said briefly. 'That and thc balcony thing. After all, someone's died out there. We have to investigate. Make sure everything's as it should be.'

'For Gwen's sake?'

He shook his head. 'Not just Gwen's. For everyone's. Yours. Mine. Joe Public's.'

Soon we were back at Steelhouse Lane nick, sitting in the impersonal meeting room Chris had used before.

I picked at my paper-thin suit. Perhaps it wasn't warm enough. Perhaps that was why I was dithering with cold. I swallowed hard.

Chris looked at me with a little crease of anxiety between his eyebrows.

Dave grinned. 'Nice little fax you sent,' he said, sitting beside me. 'Pity I can't read all your writing. Bad as a GP's.'

'Which bits did you manage to decipher?' I asked.

'Well, there's some poor sod scraping sick off the Birmingham-Wolverhampton New Road even as we speak.'

I nodded. I had to make myself speak. 'There's weird stuff in his sexual past. Think about the wedding dress. I tried to talk to him about it – before, before—'

Like Horner before him, Dave burst into song. '*You always kill the one you love!*'

Chris stared.

'Yes, we've come up with something else,' Dave continued. 'Thanks to you and Mike, though the team were on to another aspect of it already. They went round all the pubs, restaurants and hotels they could think of with photos of Marietta and Acheson. They got witnesses prepared to testify that they'd been seen together at – yes – four different locations. Hotels, rather than restaurants. The ubiquitous Mr and Mrs Smith. Now, when we spoke to her fiancé, he looked quite blank. *His* computer was as clean as a whistle. It was Marietta's that was interesting. And her loft – that was interesting too. Just a little suitcase containing her gear. Very interesting gear.'

'But what a risk! When someone was stalking her!'

'Which came first – Acheson her lover or Acheson the stalker? Oh, and one other thing – it was a fax, Sophie, that organised their assignation. The geeks have just got it off your office machine. Well done.'

'Why my office? Why my chair?'

'Why not? Nice bit of black leather!' Dave observed.

'But killing her could have ruined the Bookfest – which everyone agrees is his brainchild.'

'Or,' Ian put in, reminding me of his theory about Stonkin Mama's death threats, 'brought it extra publicity. More people running around over events he was manipulating.'

'But getting rid of me—'

'He might have wanted to step in and do it himself. Or – who can tell? He's certainly not going to be able to answer any questions.'

'I wonder if he'd got so obsessed with his collection of blonde women' – Chris smiled at me and then across at where Claire had been sitting – 'that he lost sight of the Bookfest. Refocused his obsession, as it were.'

'Are there other blondes in his life? Or past life? Like a bride jilting him? And have any other blondes been attacked?' I asked

Chris nodded to a woman, who left the room. Then he returned to what might almost have been a prepared speech. 'Obsessive he certainly was—'

There was a knock at the door. Chris almost tutted with exasperation. A uniformed constable brought in a note which he laid, after a certain amount of hesitation, in front of Dave.

'His library was spectacularly tidy,' I said. 'Obsessively. And his garden.'

'And so was his garden shed,' Dave said, patting the note. 'Complete with garden and – which may have a bearing on that arson business,' he grinned at Harvinder and Chris – 'DIY tools.'

'Such as lengths of Rawlplug?' I asked. If only my stomach would behave!

'Such as lengths of Rawlplug. We'll be able to check the saw marks against our bit of Rawlplug. And there was a supply of paraffin in a nice rusty old can.'

'So the forensic scientists can check for contamination?'

'Absolutely. And not just paraffin. He'd got supplies of Paraquat and other delights. Thanks, mate.' Dave nodded belatedly to the constable, who exited, holding the door open for someone as he left.

It was Claire who came in. 'Gwen's gone home, Gaffer.' It was hard to tell whether she addressed Chris or Dave. 'I'll fix her debriefing when she's better. Something she ate, she reckons.'

'Reckon she could be right. 'Scuse me, Gaffer.' There was no doubt whom Ian considered the boss. But his exit was swift.

My mind ran across last night's supper menu. And landed on something we all had in common. The chicken. No, this had to be just my usual stress tum. Didn't it?

To take my mind off it, I asked, 'So what have you found about that Myakovsky business? First the threats, then the performance with the Burtons and where he should stay.'

Chris looked at Dave, who referred to his notes. 'We'd love to be able to point to some strange military or Masonic or any connection. But we can't, not yet. Sure they have business connections. But nothing sinister. A couple of people we've spoken to have said how much Acheson always deferred to Burton. Junior officer to senior. But Acheson never even did National Service, let alone joined the regular army. Burton himself regards him as,' he cleared his throat, ' "a jumped-up little oik." '

'Old money,' Claire put in sepulchrally.

'Oik he may be. But I'd swear he found something nasty when he was working on a job for Burton. Something even an oik found objectionable. Could Burton have had any dealings with Myakovsky?' I pressed. 'Was Burton ever in the USSR, or in the States?'

'He was all over the bloody world, but we can't pin anything down. Yet.'

Claire leant forward. 'Burton's wife: she didn't give a toss about books or reading, but she was in on this Bookfest. Desperately wanted Myakovsky there.'

'But didn't bother to come to the receptions where he was present,' I said.

'Maybe they were lovers,' Dave put in.

'Who were lovers?'

'Mrs B and Myakovsky.'

'Or even Burton and Myakovsky,' Claire and I said simultaneously. 'And if Burton gives nothing away,' I added, 'talk to Myakovsky after a glass or two: he'll spill any beans you want spilt.' I swallowed hard. This wasn't my usual tum. It must have been the chicken we ate for supper last night. Mike – had Mike had chicken too? And he was out in the field, in this heat? It was so hot in here the room was beginning to swim. 'Have we,' I asked, making one last effort, 'have we—'

I just made it to the loo.

Eventually I made myself return to the fray, trying to convince myself that I was made of sterner stuff than the others, and that I should be able to bring my powers of reason to sort out the mess. But I was wrong. Even Chris's smelling salts were impotent. It was no consolation at all to return to my own home, and share a bed with Mike, who'd left Edgbaston as ill as I was. We lay semi-conscious, ignoring phone and front door alike. From time to time I'd observe that I wanted to die; then I remembered what forms death could take and shut up.

The Mondiale had packed our stuff for us and returned it, with a very agitated note telling us that they hoped we would accept our accommodation with their compliments. They didn't need to add, 'And please don't report us to the environmental health department.' We availed ourselves of their kind offer, knowing full well that the inspectors were probably even now taking swabs from every available kitchen surface. They'd wanted what they darkly referred to as 'specimens' from us.

'So it's all over, bar the shouting,' Mike said, late that evening, tentatively sipping mineral water. If it stayed down it would be the first to do so today.

'Not quite,' I said. 'There's a couple of things. The business of Andy and Steph for starters.'

'I should imagine they've got that worked out by now,' he said.

'I don't know. Andy – he'll just think that Steph's my illegitimate son. After all, he was so out of it when he raped me . . . And he's never once alluded to our having sex. But Steph knows I've always been cagey about his dad; he'll be the one to make the connections. The thing is, what will he have said to Andy?' They'd had plenty of time for full and frank exchanges. 'Oh, there are a lot of questions to ask. A lot of answers to forgive.'

He nodded, and took another sip. 'If you've forgiven Andy for what he did to you in the first place, I should imagine they can both forgive you for not introducing them earlier.'

'Forgiveness isn't a matter of logic, is it? And Steph's very young. Oh, Mike . . .'

After a while, he asked, 'And what's the other thing on your mind?'

I managed a smile. 'Whether I shall be well enough to play in the match on Sunday.'

The prognosis was good. We were both up and about, if doddery, on Wednesday, and I was insisting I'd be back at my desk first thing on Thursday. I was sure Marcus and the women would have held everything together in my absence, but had to see for myself. Even though it had been decided that Mike wasn't match fit, and we could have had a couple of days on our own. Non-conformist work ethic? Addiction?

We were just having the lightest of lunches – no wine, just water, and some home-made soup – when Andy appeared. Mike prepared to make himself scarce, but Andy motioned him back on to the chair. Noticing the soup still simmering on the hob, he ladled some into a bowl and sat down between us at the kitchen table.

'I take it you knew, Mike?'

Mike didn't try to prevaricate. 'It – became apparent. Sophie wouldn't have told me otherwise.'

'Steph and I are very much feeling our way, still,' I said. 'It took him nine months to mention me to his parents. We've only met once, in fact.'

'I'm not talking about them. I'm talking about you and Steph. I'm— Surely you could have told me? Damn it – we're more than cousins. We're friends. And you never trusted me.' Pushing the soup away untasted, he thrust an angry forefinger inches from my nose. 'You should have told me!'

'Andy—' Mike was on his feet.

'Mike, love, this is between Andy and me. He's got things to say. So have I. Just leave us for five minutes.'

'Ruth's outside in the car,' Andy said.

Mike blinked. 'I'll go and talk to her, then.' He kissed me on the hair and left, shutting the door gently behind him.

'You've got some explaining to do,' Andy started.

'And you've got some listening.' I lowered my voice. 'Stephan isn't just my son – he's—'

'Whose?'

My God, hadn't he guessed? 'There's no easy way to say this. You remember your drugs period?'

'Not likely to forget it.' Nor was anyone else. Andy had been an assiduous anti-drugs campaigner for years.

'Well, one evening you were out of your brain. Completely. And – Andy, you raped me.'

'What?'

I was afraid he was going to keel over. I grabbed his wrist, made him sit down.

'Raped me. You were completely out of your skull on something. I happened to be there when you wanted sex. You raped me.'

'I couldn't have . . .'

'You could and did. My dear, how else do you think it could have happened? Immaculate conception? I was one of those lucky girls who gets pregnant the first time she has sex.'

'A virgin . . . You – you were—'

'Oh, what does virginity matter?' I didn't want him to get side-tracked.

'You should have told me!' He was almost in tears.

'During which brief interval of lucidity? No, you were on the road with your group, by then. Available groupies by the score, I should think. And I was alone up in Leeds and dealt with it the only way I could.'

'The family . . .?'

'They'd have come down on you like a ton of bricks and made us get married! No way.'

'So . . .'

'Till last summer no one, repeat no one, knew about you and what you did to me. For Steph's sake, I had him adopted—'

'Steph's sake! What about yours? It would have been mighty inconvenient for you to have a baby around, Ms Careerwoman.' Trust Andy to twist the blame. He'd never had to face up to responsibility for anything, had he? Well, my fault, I suppose – I'd always been there to shield him.

But I couldn't any more. 'Oh yes? I was a student! I couldn't have reared him without help from you! And were you in a position to give it? I think not.'

He lowered his eyes. 'Out of it most of the time, wasn't I?'

'You certainly were the night you raped me.'

'I wish you wouldn't keep saying that.'

I allowed myself a slight snort. 'What other word would you prefer? It certainly wasn't a romantic seduction after a candle-lit dinner. And you really don't remember anything of it?'

He shook his head. 'Christ, what a mess I was.' He stared at the table. 'But you should have told me before this.'

'I tried as soon as Steph came back into my life. There wasn't any point before.'

'You should have let me be the judge of that!'

I nodded. Maybe I should. 'I wanted to tell you in private so you could digest it before you told Ruth. It isn't the sort of thing you can e-mail, you know. But I tried practically every time we've been alone since you came up. Each time . . .' I shrugged.

He stared. 'That was what you were trying to say the night Chris turned up?'

'Right.'

'And at the office?'

'Yes.'

'But what about Steph? He deserves to know.'

'And will now I've told you. He may even have worked it out – you look so alike. He doesn't know the circumstances of his conception. Maybe it's best he doesn't. What do you think?'

'I can't think.' He pushed away from the table and fossicked in the fridge. He slopped some of the sauvignon blanc he found there into a tumbler. It wasn't till after he'd downed almost a full glass he waved the bottle at me. I shook my head.

'Jesus,' he said, sinking back on to the chair, 'he's almost a clone, isn't he?'

'Yes. Seems to be making a mess of his life too.'

'Would he accept any help?'

'He'd go one of two ways – decide the sun shines out of your ears, or hate and resent everything you've done and are doing. And he'd almost certainly want to touch you for a few quid. That's his speciality. Though whether you should hand over dosh is another matter. I haven't resolved it for myself yet, so I can hardly advise you.' I poured myself some water. 'Did he say anything – about me?'

'Not a lot. Not an emotionally articulate young man, is he?'

'Were you?'

Andy gulped some more wine and looked shamefaced. 'I'm not now, am I? I suppose what I should be saying is thank you for not destroying my son, and how can I ever repay you?'

I wanted to say noble things about not needing repayment and just wanting forgiveness. Instead I walked out into the garden so he wouldn't see me in tears. And what was I crying for? I wasn't sure myself, but I knew it was only when Mike came and wrapped his arms round me and rocked me that I started to feel better.

Chris must have noticed my puffy eyes and the highly charged atmosphere when he dropped by half an hour later. I'd never known Ruth at a loss for words before, or Andy, for that matter. It seemed that they intended to stay here again. Why didn't they simply return to the Mondiale or some other hotel? No, they hadn't succumbed to the salmonella or whatever – not because they'd followed Andy's occasional hair-shirt diet but because they'd tucked into lobster, for heaven's sake. So there they were, both getting tight, sitting side by side on my sofa, when Chris walked in.

'News about Myakovsky and Burton at last,' he said, flopping down into what had been Mike's armchair.

Mike pulled up a dining chair, sitting astride it and leaning his arms on the back. Then he dismounted, and produced a glass and the bottle into which Andy and Ruth had made such inroads. Shrugging, he went off and fetched another, plus the corkscrew. He poured and sat down, as before. And then he got up and brought two more glasses. 'For our stomachs' sakes,' he said, pouring for us.

Why not?

Chris frowned enquiringly at me, but said nothing. He raised his glass.

There was a ragged, not at all cheerful, chorus of 'Cheers'.

'So we had a long talk with both Myakovsky and Burton,' Chris said. 'And while we were doing that Claire talked to Mrs Burton again. And, oddly enough, she seems to be the key.'

He waited for a murmur that didn't come.

'It seems it's to do with money and power and social standing. She was Burton's secretary. Classic thing, they have an affair lasting years, and when his wife pops her clogs, he marries her. But she's insecure in the midst of all that wealth, so she decides she has to make her mark her own way. She's already become a councillor – in a party he doesn't approve of, let alone support. So now she decides she wants to go down the literary hostess road. Burton supports her, puts a little pressure on Acheson since they're business associates and bingo.'

We sat in silence.

At last, Mike removed an arm from the back of his chair, the better to scratch his chin. 'If anyone else had told me that,

Chris, I'd have said it was a load of cobblers.'

Chris's face lit up in a smile of pure delight. 'Funny you should say that,' he said. 'That's exactly what I think!'

Chapter Thirty-two

'So it was money and power all along,' Andy said, the following Sunday afternoon, sitting down beside me in the pavilion, and worrying a hangnail. I hadn't seen him for a few days – he and Ruth had had things to sort out, not to mention him and Steph.

He looked very good in his cricket whites.

'With a house like that, you'd expect it to be,' I agreed. 'More particularly, according to Chris and Dave, a great desire to hold on to both. It had to be something to do with Burton's past, didn't it? Coupled with Myakovsky's unparalleled ability to make enemies of people by discovering and revealing unpleasant things about them. His KGB background I suppose. Look at the people he'd already spilt very public beans about: Communists, Mafioso, Mossad, CIA – and next in line might be our own dear Peregrine Burton, currency and arms dealer extraordinaire. Not necessarily because he wanted to shop him, but because he seems constitutionally incapable of keeping any information to himself.'

As I'd predicted, he'd been happy to spill can-loads of beans. Burton had brokered arms deals even while he was still in the army, but had gone on to do it big time. Forget UN arms embargoes, don't mention common morality – our Mr Burton would be happy to oblige.

'Arms! The bastard. So why wasn't he court-martialled and hanged or something?'

'He did leave the army under something of a cloud. But somehow things got hushed up. Friends in high places?'

'Old money, old pals,' Andy said.

'Quite.'

'So when Myakovsky was mooted as a guest speaker, Burton saw it as a wonderful opportunity to silence him – one way or another. I'm reasonably sure – and according to Chris, Brian Fairbrother says something similar – that Acheson at first simply saw Myakovsky as a Big Name. In fact, Brian is sure that he himself made the suggestion, not Acheson.'

Andy started on another nail.

'Now – this is where Dave Clarke's Fraud background came in handy! Acheson's accounts show that his business was in a big mess – strong pound, underinvestment, too much time swanning around pursuing Literature. And blondes. No wonder his secretary was so frosty whenever I tried to speak to him; she must have known he ought to be devoting all his energies to his firm. Burton helped him out. At a price, clearly. But when Burton started pushing the idea that Myakovsky should stay with him, Acheson must have got suspicious. He'd seen something when he was working on the Burtons' house. I'm sure of that. He was far too deeply in debt to Burton to argue face to face. But the one thing he didn't want to happen was one of the world's great writers getting snuffed out at his festival. He really loved books. Perhaps,' I added sadly, 'because they provided him with perfect miniature worlds. Everything controlled and enclosed within two covers.'

'So why kill a writer? Why bump off poor Marietta?'

'Because she refused to be controlled? Because she still intended to marry her fiancé? Because having ultimate power over her was too big a temptation to resist? Again Dave came up with bright ideas. He checked personnel files at Acheson's factory going back to day one. About a year after the wedding that wasn't.' I had been right about him being jilted. Poor man, everything had been going hunky and indeed dory. He'd organised the wedding down to the last detail – and then his bride had simply not turned up. No message. No nothing. Then several unsolved sex attacks in the area.

'All those nice photos, all that neatly documented information. Just what the detective ordered. And he's checking every single one of his women employees.'

'Don't tell me – the gentleman preferred blondes!'

'Had quite a high turnover of them, apparently. So Dave wants to find out exactly why each one left. And what happened to each one during and after her employment.' The irony was it was Dave who was having to do it! 'Dave's looking for – at very least – sexual harassment.'

'So why didn't the women take him to industrial tribunal or whatever?'

'In the Black Country, Andy, we women have always had a reputation for endurance – sorry, I meant nail-makers and—'

He reached for my hand. 'OK. Even if you didn't, I deserve it.' He coughed, unconvincingly. 'Tell me . . . there's that bit in Jane Austen . . . about love. About women loving longest when all hope was gone.'

It would do no one any good if I admitted I'd wasted some thirty-five years of my life loving Andy. 'I love Mike,' I said firmly and truthfully. 'But the potential Mrs Acheson doesn't seemed to have loved him.' Better to stick to what Chris would have called our moutons. 'She got round to sending a message to the church. Eventually. Poor bastard.'

Andy straightened. 'So what about all those phone calls and the funny voices?'

'I think Acheson functioned on two different planes. Half of him was obsessed by his pursuit of blonde women. The other half was shit scared that if Myakovsky did stay with the Burtons, then one of his great literary idols would be very seriously at risk. So he put his skill at mimicry to another use — to do his best to dissuade Myakovsky from coming. But all the time Brian was doing his damnedest to get him to come!'

'Was that why he poisoned him? If he was poisoned?'

'They're still waiting for the forensic science lab to confirm it. But it would be a good motive. Or it could have been to do with his pursuit of me. Less Brian, more Sophie. What we do know is that the saliva under the stamps on those anonymous letters produced enough DNA to prove he licked them.'

'Well done, Sophie and her recycling ways.' There was a long pause. At last, Andy looked sideways at me. 'How are you feeling?' I took it he was referring to my current anxieties rather than past ones.

'How would you expect me to feel? How about you?'

He looked around him. Edgbaston cricket ground was by no means full, but a combination of sun and celebrities had brought out a decent crowd. 'Shit scared. I always am before I go out to bat. Even though they didn't give us a big total to get.'

'You bowled well.'

'Had a good teacher, didn't I?' He patted my hand in affectionate acknowledgement. 'All those years ago. What would have happened if I'd given up music and played for Warwickshire?'

What indeed? What if he'd settled down to a respectable

life, would I now be his wife, Steph our legitimate son?

'You did well,' he said, after a while.

I chose to take it that once again he referred to this afternoon. No, I hadn't done badly. Mike and his mates had had to take my bowling seriously, even if the wicket I'd taken was a fluke. I was proud of my catch down on the boundary, though I could have wished it hadn't dismissed Mike.

'You couldn't have persuaded Steph to come and watch?'

He shook his head. 'He's not feeling so good. The injections and stuff have caught up with him. I've told him he can't come out till his exams are over, but he'll be on the first plane after that.'

'Does he realise Mwandara's not going to be a bowl of cherries? That he'll be dealing with sick people in primitive conditions?'

'Says so, at least. It'll do him good to work his bollocks off for a change, anyway. Oh God, they've never given him out! Not leg before – it was miles down the off-side.'

However creative the umpiring, the consequence was inevitable. I picked up my bat and helmet, and ran down the pavilion steps, heading towards the middle. The light was brighter out here, the space bigger than when you're just fielding. I heard what my father had said, all those years ago on the back lawn, in the days when he was respectable and caring. I heard what Mike had repeated. 'Keep your eye on the ball and use your feet.'

I did both, until at fifty-three I ran out of partners when we were still a few runs short of the Bears' total. Andy had managed a respectable forty-seven, Marcus – apparently bearing no grudges against me or the police – thirty. Some of the other writers, too, had clearly benefited from an hour of net practice under a coach's eye. Except, perhaps Myakovsky, who'd insisted on playing on the grounds he was now an expert on baseball. And why not? We'd slotted him in at number eleven.

I don't remember any of the strokes I made, though there was a good smattering of fours and one six – over the shortest boundary. What I do remember is Myakovsky's first and only stroke. It was a tremendous hay-making swipe. He promptly dropped his bat, took off for cover point, circled the bowler and fetched up by the square leg umpire – hot, triumphant and run out.

The Big Brum Bookfest was over.